DEATH
OF A
SCHEMER

DEATH OF A SCHEMER

The Frank May Chronicles

Lawrence Friedman

A QP Mystery

QP BOOKS
New Orleans, Louisiana

DEATH OF A SCHEMER
The Frank May Chronicles

A QP Mystery, published in 2015 by QP Books.

QUID PRO, LLC
5860 Citrus Blvd., Suite D-101
New Orleans, Louisiana 70123
www.qpbooks.com

ISBN 978-1-61027-306-0 (paperback)
ISBN 978-1-61027-307-7 (eBook)

Cover design © 2015 by Michele Veade.

Publisher's Cataloging-in-Publication

Friedman, Lawrence.
  Death of a Schemer / Lawrence Friedman.
    p. cm.
  Series: *The Frank May Chronicles* (#9)
  ISBN 978-1-61027-306-0 (pbk.)

1. Lawyers—California—Fiction. 2. San Mateo (Cal.)—Fiction. 3. May, Frank (Fictitious character)—Fiction. I. Friedman, Lawrence. II. Title. III. Series.

PS357.F789 2015

           813.'2'7251—dc22
               20154191932
                   CIP

for Leah, Jane, Amy, Sarah,
David, Lucy, and Irene

DEATH
OF A
SCHEMER

1

Let me begin by introducing myself. My name is Frank May. I'm an American, and a typical member (I guess) of the bourgeois middle class. I'm in my 40s. I'm of medium height and weight. I'm not handsome but not ugly, and I have fairly regular features. No obvious moles or scars. I am, however, beginning to lose my hair. What's left of it, too, is starting to turn gray. I've considered dyeing my hair, but I've never quite had the nerve to do it. My wife, Celia, is also turning gray; she, too, refuses to dye her hair. On her, I think, the gray is quite attractive.

We have two teenaged daughters. I love them dearly. Sometimes they can be a colossal pain. But that's standard, I believe.

I'm a lawyer by trade. I think I'm a fairly good lawyer, if I do say so myself. I think I'm reliable, careful—a decent craftsman, as it were. I also have (I think) a good sense of humor; I'm wry—if that's the right word—and a bit on the skeptical side. Maybe that's necessary in my profession. You see all kinds of people in my line of work.

I'm also a law-abiding, conventional, and basically peace-loving sort of guy. I don't do martial arts, and I don't like violence, blood, and anything that smacks of violence, unless it's in the movies or a novel. Even there, I don't like anything extreme. I don't own a gun. I've never owned a gun. I don't live in Texas or any of those places where everybody swaggers around with a gun. I live in northern California. It's the land of bean sprouts and ratatouille. I'm not susceptible to road rage. I get irritated, like everybody else, at the antics of my fellow human beings, but I keep the lid on, so to speak. In general, I like a simple and orderly life. At least, that's what I aspire to. Yet somehow, without meaning to, I seem to get involved in sordid cases of murder, one after another. It's my karma, somehow. My fate. It's as if—as if something is *chasing* me. I mean, not *literally* me. Something is chasing my clients.

I'm a solo practitioner, and I have a general practice of the usual type: wills, real estate work, a divorce now and then, minor corporate work for people who own small businesses. Many lawyers are connected with giant law firms, mega-firms with hundreds of lawyers, thick rugs on the floor, chrome and leather chairs, and branches in places like Riyadh and Beijing. They have clients on the Fortune 500 list. I'm on my own. I have no partners. My practice is small but decent. I have (thank God) an acceptable stable of clients. Most of them even pay their bills on time. And, of course, I'm always on the lookout for new clients. But here's what's strange. On a number of occasions, I've lost a client in a most unusual way: the client just happens to get himself murdered. Or a client is accused of murder, or is somehow involved in a murder case. This happened, for instance, with two clients named Barney and Blanche. They were married. She was killed, and he was blamed because he was the obvious subject. And I got involved. But that's a different story.

This problem of mine has come up so often that I'm beginning to wonder: is it me? Is it something about me? The average person goes through an entire life without getting involved in even *one* murder. I don't seem able to go a full year without a homicide bedeviling my footsteps. Do I attract victims and predators the way a light attracts moths? I have no answer to this question.

Anyway, this particular story, the one I'm about to tell, concerns the latest of these episodes. It centers pretty much on a client, a youngish man named Andrew Wright. He met an untimely death. Somebody hit him over the head with something hard, maybe a baseball bat or the equivalent, knocked him out cold, and then smothered him to death with a pillow.

Oddly enough, another client died in precisely this way. Weird. But that too is another story.

I had no particular love for Andrew Wright and certainly no desire to become enmeshed in finding out who killed him. But whether I wanted to or not, I *did* become enmeshed.

I realize I'm getting ahead of myself. I have to begin much earlier, with the general background. I'll start with the first time I met Andrew.

As I told you, I'm in the private practice of law. I'm also a married man, as I said, with a wife, two children, and a house in the south part of Palo Alto. The wife, daughters, and house do not figure very much in this story. My office is in San Mateo, California. That's south of San Francisco, for those of you unlucky enough to know nothing about northern California. Much of my work is about death and dying—but the ordinary kind of death and dying, the kind of death and dying that is the common fate of all humankind, if I can wax poetic for a moment. I write wills, draft trusts, and deal with probate, estates, legacies, heirs, and that sort of thing. It's not the only thing I do, but it's the thing I like the most.

It's a nice line of work. It brings me in contact with people. I prefer people to corporations. Corporations have a lot more money, but people are more engaging. They have more character. They're also a lot more aggravating than corporations, or can be, but that's the trade-off.

Of course, if a Fortune 500 company came along, and wanted to make me general counsel, complete with stock options, a private jet, a personal trainer, and a private secretary, I think I could persuade myself to take the position. It isn't likely to happen.

* * *

It was a bright summer day when I first met Andrew. In California, you don't need to say "bright summer day." Summer day would be good enough. All summer days in California are bright. Usually there's not a cloud in the sky. In fact, it doesn't rain at all in the summer. Not a single drop. If you plan a picnic for the Fourth of July, you don't need Plan B. It simply isn't going to rain. I can promise you that.

Some people from the East say that they miss the rain. I'm not one of them. Constant sunshine is just fine for me.

Andrew had called me on the phone. "Hi," he said, "are you Frank May?"

"That's me."

"My name is Andrew Wright. You don't know me. I was wondering if I can have an appointment. I need a lawyer."

The voice struck me as a young man's voice, maybe because of the more or less brash way he talked. Of course, you can't always tell age over the phone, but the brashness was there alright. This would become perfectly plain later on. "Well, I'm a lawyer," I said. "I don't deny it. Exactly what's your problem?"

Sometimes I get calls from people who are friends of friends, or friends of friends of friends, who are picked up for drunk driving or once in a while for something more serious. I turn all these people down. I don't do that kind of work. There are lawyers who specialize in criminal law. Most criminal lawyers do nothing but criminal law. Usually, too, the rest of us stay as far away from criminal work as we possibly can. That includes me. I never touch the stuff.

"Business deal," he said. "I need to incorporate. Can I come see you?"

"Naturally," I said. "Can I ask where you got my name? Did somebody recommend me?"

"Yes," he said, "Guy I know. Name's Tommy."

"Tommy? Tommy who?"

"Just Tommy. I don't know his last name," he said. "Young guy. Maybe late 20s. Blond hair, blue eyes. Nice guy. I met him in a bar."

I knew exactly who he meant. Who could forget Tommy? Tommy had been a figure in one of the weirdest episodes of my career. Tommy, young as he was, had run off to Las Vegas and married a rich woman who was over 80 years old at the time, believe it or not. Then she died under mysterious circumstances. It was quite a situation. I've written it up, and I can tell you all about it. But some other time.

When all that was happening, I got to know Tommy quite well. I liked him. He was sweet but a bit dim-witted. His marriage ... well, it wasn't as crazy as it seems on the surface. There's a story behind it. For Tommy, the story had a happy ending. He inherited a great deal of money. I handled the old lady's estate. It wasn't that much work, and the fee was very nice.

"Right," I said. "Tommy. Sure. I know him. Haven't seen him in a while. How's he doing?"

"OK, I guess. He's not really a friend. I just met him, like I told you, in this bar. Local bar in Palo Alto. Real friendly guy, Tommy. We started talking. He was with some chick, maybe his girlfriend. I told him I was looking for a lawyer, you know, for my business thing. He said, I know just the guy. Gave me your name. And here I am."

A new client, of course, is always welcome. Where would I be without a constant flow of new clients? But the circumstances were not exactly promising. Meeting Tommy in a bar, having a drink, and getting Tommy's recommendation—that didn't bode very well. Tommy had money, but not much business sense. When he got his inheritance, I felt he would run through it very quickly, either because somebody would cheat him out of it, or he'd invest it in some absolutely nutty scheme. So I talked him into a trust fund, which I drafted, and now his money is controlled by a bank, which doles out the income every few months. It's not ironclad, but for now it'll do.

The point is, though, that I need well-to-do, solid clients. People with money, brains, and some genuine legal problems. I rely on word-of-mouth, but preferably not word that spreads from mouth to mouth in a bar in Palo Alto. My clients—the good ones—don't hang out in bars. I doubted very much that Andrew would turn out to be a solid citizen and a respectable client. That was my guess. I was a hundred percent correct.

Andrew showed up the next day for his appointment, 15 minutes late, which I found somewhat annoying, but it was actually for my benefit. I was working on a complicated will, struggling over some of the clauses, and I needed the time. But still, I like people to be punctual.

I looked him over carefully. He was fairly young—maybe 30, which, now that I'm 45, I consider quite young. He was medium height, medium build. His hair was a nondescript brownish color. It was somewhat curly, and a bit longer than I personally would have worn. He had a slightly hooked nose and greenish eyes. I think you could call him good-looking, or at least moderately good-looking. He carried himself like someone who was totally convinced he was good-looking. He was wearing sandals, no socks, very neat and new-looking jeans, and a blue and white checked shirt, open at the neck. I always look to see if a person is wearing a wedding ring. He wasn't.

I said hello, and added something inane about the weather. He said, "Yeah, it's nice. Around here it's always nice."

"We like it that way," I said.

"I hate cold weather," he said. "Ice and snow. Who needs it? Do you go skiing?"

"Not really. Look. You said something on the phone about a business deal. By the way, just call me Frank."

"Sure thing, Frank."

"What business are you in, Andrew?"

"Monkey business. Seriously, I'm not in business at all. Not yet. I've got some ideas, you know, about starting a business. That's why I want to incorporate."

Another disappointing answer. I wrote him off in my mind as a client right then and there. I won't say I'm a perfect judge of character—I'm not—but I couldn't imagine Andrew as a businessman, even after five minutes of knowing him. This was going nowhere, I decided.

Things are never that simple.

He went on: "There's stuff I want to do, deals, you know? I think I have a chance to make real money, serious money."

"Don't we all," I said.

"Hey, you're right," he said. "I mean, not absolutely everybody. You take the Dalai Lama, for instance, but you know, he does OK, without even trying. Writes books and stuff, and people pay to hear him talk. And those guys on TV—the televangelists. They're in it strictly for the money, if you ask me, but they say they're not, you know? They roll their eyes around and they talk about Jesus, and the suckers send in the cash."

I had no real response to this blazing insight.

"Around here," he said, "money is everything, right? I mean, people here, they're swimming in money. Silicon Valley, stock options, even some of the secretaries, they're worth millions, and they don't even have to screw the boss. I said to myself, why not me? This guy Tommy, for example, he's got money, and as a result, he's really popular, if you know what I mean. Women were buzzing around him like bees on honey. What has he got that I haven't got? Not brains, I'll tell you that. He struck me as borderline stupid. So what's the attraction? It's the money, right?"

"You've got a point," I said, for want of anything else.

"This Tommy, now you tell me: where'd the money come from?"

"He's a client," I said. "Was a client. I don't talk about clients' affairs."

"OK, OK, I understand. I wouldn't want you blabbing about my stuff, either. Anyway, around here, as I said, you can almost smell the money. Houses, they cost millions. But people buy them. When you do deals, anyway, you need a lawyer. You're crazy if you don't have a lawyer. There's sharks out there. They'll eat you alive."

I stopped him. "Could you be more specific? I don't mean about sharks. About the deal you have in mind."

"Well," he said, "I don't know you, yet, how much to confide in you. We have to get to know each other, see if we trust each other."

"I charge by the hour," I said.

"Hey, isn't the first hour free? I read that somewhere."

"Don't believe everything you read," I said. I tried to sound cool and professional. I had no intention of encouraging this guy. "Look, I have to charge for my time. It's the only thing I have to sell. Time and professional knowledge. I can't give these things away. I hope you understand."

Actually, I hoped he didn't understand. I wanted him to get up and leave and never come back. But no such luck.

"OK, OK, I get it. You're right, you're right. But maybe we can have dinner some time, talk things over. Right now, I'm not exactly rolling in money. I don't think I could pay, but maybe later on...."

"I don't usually do dinner," I said, "Not with clients. I try to, uh, keep my distance."

Not that this was literally true. For a good client, I do breakfast, lunch, dinner, weddings, funerals, bar mitzvahs, confirmations, anything. I wanted Andrew to take the hint. Any ordinary person would. But Andrew was no ordinary person, as I found out. He was persistent. His mind bubbled with ideas, none of them conventional, and he had a way of getting what he wanted.

He said, "Well, you can always make an exception. Frank, isn't that right? I don't bite. I don't have body odor. We'll go out some evening. We'll eat. We'll talk things over. It won't kill you."

"Really, Andrew."

"Aw, come on, Frank! Don't be stubborn. When's a good time? Pick any day. We'll sit down, you can listen to me, my line of stuff, hear what I have to say. Then you can decide if you want to be my lawyer, help me out, or call the whole thing off."

"I don't know."

"What have you got to lose, Frank? And it goes both ways. I can decide if you're the right lawyer for me. Anyway, I'm good at sizing people up."

I found the whole idea repellent. Of course, I do have demanding clients, sometimes quite obnoxious ones, even repulsive ones. And there are lots of people who think nothing of taking up my time and paying me nothing. It happens all too often. An elderly couple comes to see me. They talk. I talk. They say something. I say something. I smile. I tell them things they should know. I give some preliminary advice. They nod their heads. They go, and I never see them again. Or, if they come back, they want everything done as cheaply as possible, even though they have tons of money. Or they want instant service. Or they want to talk to me for half an hour on the telephone, asking me all sorts of questions, but God forbid I should bill them for this time. "Frank, it was just a phone call," they insist.

If they have enough money and potential, I give clients what they want, even when it's totally unreasonable. After they're dead and they've turned into an estate, they have lost the capacity to pester me and make my life miserable. Of course, at that point there's an heir—a widow or widower, or some big oaf of a son—to take over the job of making my life totally miserable.

But this was a privilege reserved for people with money. Since Andrew, by his own admission, had none, I wrote him off completely, and I declined his kind invitation. But Andrew wouldn't take no for an answer. He would say, "how about Wednesday?" and if I said I was busy, he would say, "how about Thursday?" I had two choices: give in and accept his invitation, or just tell him I just don't want to do it.

I gave in.

This was one of Andrew's traits. He was thick-skinned, impervious. He wore me down. In the end, I thought, a dinner won't kill me. I picked a night when Celia was going to be out at her book group. Celia was a teacher, and her group was made up of women from her school. They would choose a recent novel and discuss it. Actually, they would spend half the session arguing about which book to read next. Sometimes Celia wanted me to read the book, too. I rarely liked what I read. Most of them seemed to be written by women, and the protagonists were women. But really miserably unhappy women. And why? Because, as you found out after about 150 pages, something truly awful had happened to them in their childhood.

The book they were discussing that night was loathsome. Even Celia, who was quite tolerant, hated it. It was about a woman who whined and complained for hundreds of pages, all because of a chain of events that started when her stepbrother raped her at the age of nine. This made it impossible for her to have a normal, decent relationship, even with the alcoholic poet she fell in love with. Oh, and he had AIDS and never bothered to tell her.

At least in this book the woman was raped by her step-brother. Usually it was her father. Or her blood brother.

Whatever. Celia loves the group, whether or not she loves the novel. The women have a good time getting together. They have cake and coffee and cookies, and they all eat happily, except for the ones on diets, who nibble on grapes. Then they talk about the book for a while, and then about other things. I suppose they share a lot of gossip, or is that a sexist thing to think?

This was the second book group she belonged to. The previous one had disbanded. That, too, is the subject of another story that, believe it or not, involved a murder.

In any event, that evening was the ideal time to eat out. It was either that or leftovers. My daughters were home for dinner as rarely as possible, so that was no issue either. Since they reached puberty, they found it impossible to imagine a real conversation with a parent, since parents were, by definition, members of a different species. Were we even primates?

But that's neither here nor there. A week later, I found myself at a nice Italian restaurant in Menlo Park, waiting for Andrew. The place wasn't crowded at all. Andrew, who arrived 20 minutes late, didn't like the first table the waiter showed us, and insisted on a booth. "I like booths," he said. The waiter said all the booths were reserved. He was a young guy, with an Italian accent. He had spiky hair, and a gold earring in his left ear.

"Right," he said, "reserved for me."

"No, sir, they're reserved for other parties," said the waiter.

I found this embarrassing. Andrew did not. He insisted. And, in the end, he got his booth.

"You can't let people step on you," he said.

"I guess."

"This is a great place," he said. "You should order cannelloni. They make great cannelloni. Skip the soup. They say it's minestrone, but it tastes like dishwater. I told them about it, but they don't listen."

I ordered prosciutto and melon, and a chicken breast in tomato sauce. Andrew asked, "Want some wine?" I thought not. But Andrew wanted wine. He called over the waiter. "What's a good wine? I want a glass of red wine. Something with zip.

Something that puts hair on your chest."

I was asking myself, of course, why I had ever agreed to this dinner. I was hoping the food would redeem the evening.

Andrew conducted a long wine conversation with the waiter, argued about types, and finally settled on a glass of wine from some vineyard I never heard of. Not that I've heard of many vineyards. When the waiter brought it, Andrew took a sip, swished it around in the glass, studied it, sniffed at it, then nodded his head at the waiter. It passed the test. He drank some of the wine, and then said, "OK, Frank. Now tell me about yourself. Where were you born, where did you go to school, why did you decide to become a lawyer, what's your weak points, what's your strong points?"

"What's this?" I asked him, "A job interview?"

"In a way it is, right?"

"I don't like talking about myself," I said.

"Oh, come on. Are these things state secrets, Frank?"

It seemed easier to humor him than to debate him, so I plunged in. "OK. So I was born in Detroit. I spent exactly five weeks there. Then my parents moved to Los Angeles. I went to law school in San Francisco, at Hastings. It's part of the UC system. I'm married and I have two children, both girls. That's about all I care to tell you, Andrew. My weak points, my strong points, what my inner life is like—some of this is none of your business, and the rest of it, I just don't care to go into."

This came out a bit more sharply than I had intended. If I thought Andrew would be put off, or offended, I was wrong. It took a lot more than that to offend him.

"OK, OK. Whatever," he said. "I guess a lawyer is supposed to be discreet. Maybe that's a good thing. You wouldn't want a blabbermouth lawyer. I need somebody who can keep his mouth shut. So you passed the first test."

"This is a test?" I said sarcastically.

He went right on. "OK, so now I'll tell you about myself. I'm footloose, you know? I'm a rolling stone. I've got nobody. No family. In a way, everybody's got a family, a mother, a father. After all, the stork didn't bring me. But my folks, I don't know who they were.

"I was adopted. I'm one of those adopted kids. I guess my mother was dead. Anyway, she wasn't on the scene. Who knows if I had a real father, maybe somebody just screwed her, and she was a teenager or something? I thought about trying to trace them once, my real parents, but then I didn't. I mean, what for? They were bound to be losers.

"Anyway, I had foster parents, at first, maybe for a year or two. I don't remember. I was just a baby. Maybe a couple of foster parents. Then this family, the Wrights, they adopted me. They lived in Los Angeles. They were nearly 50. I don't think it was a legal adoption, not kosher, if you know what I'm referring to. I mean, the agencies, they don't let old people adopt, do they? Well, whatever. Anyway, they're dead. She died first. Breast cancer. I was ten years old. She was sick for years. She wasn't much of a mother, because she was sick all the time, starting when I was still in diapers, but I think she tried at least. I mean, tried to be a mother. Him, I never got along with. We fought like cats and dogs. He was always surly, depressed. His business wasn't going anywhere. He was lonely, his wife died, not that he ever gave two pins for her, and then he had this rambunctious teenage moron on his hands. He didn't know what to make of me. He never should have raised a kid. A lot of people think they want children, but they really don't, if you know what I mean. They're no good at it. They should stick to cats and dogs.

"My father and I were always yelling at each other. He called me every name under the sun, because I was always in trouble, you know? Said I was killing him. Well, something killed him, but it wasn't me. A heart attack, actually. I was glad when he died. I was 18. It was a relief. People, neighbors, they said, Andrew, poor guy, you're all alone in the world. They were so sensitive, you know what I mean? They were all over me. They brought me casseroles, that kind of thing. Poor guy, he's got nobody left, they said. All alone in the world. They kept on saying this, you know? All alone in that house. But, hey, I was excited. I felt it was an adventure. Just me, all by myself, nobody to answer to, no old creep growling at me, criticizing me, telling me I was scum. First thing I did, I brought my girlfriend to the house, and hey, we had some wild sex in the living room. Twice. I didn't even pull down the window shades. And we drank his liquor. Wow. The old man would have had a fit."

Was I doomed to hear every detail of his life, including his sex life? God forbid. "So you haven't got any family at all?" I was barely interested.

"There was an aunt, an uncle. We never saw them. Maybe they're dead by now. There was also a granny. Mother's mother. She wasn't even at my dad's funeral. She had Alzheimer's. She finally died, a few years ago, when she was 92. Sure, there are some cousins somewhere, but who cares? I never had anything to do with them. I wouldn't recognize them if they were right in front of my nose.

"When dad died, I had just finished high school. I actually went to college for a while. The old goat left me all his money. Well, not exactly. He didn't have a will, and I was the only close relative, so I got it all. Plus the house. Anyway, the money wasn't a whole lot, but it gave me a chance to try some things out. So I tried college. I went to community college. I had lousy grades in high school, so that was the best I could do. Then I transferred to Los Angeles State. That didn't work out. I got sick of it. I'm smart, real smart, but I couldn't take the grind. I thought the professors were jerks, you know? So full of themselves.

"I always had this idea that I'm cut out for bigger things. I said to myself, you've got brains, Andrew, what you need now is imagination. You need an idea. I mean, I had to figure out what I could do. I had to decide what was my strength. Some things, well, I just wouldn't be able to do it—like, invent a computer, or software, or whatever. You need to know math or engineering to do that. Frankly, I don't know shit. I got tired of living in this boring neighborhood with all those nosy neighbors, so I got a broker, and we sold the house. It had a big mortgage, but there was something left over. Real estate keeps going up and up in California. There was enough for me to live on for a while. I got a few thousand bucks from the old grandma, too, when she died. But that was later on. Anyway, I hitchhiked places. I picked up girls. I went to Europe. I went to Yellowstone. I bummed around. Then I got tired of that stuff. I said, 'Andrew, think. Think. Think of something.' Then it came to me.

"I was in Los Angeles. I was working various jobs, this and that. Well, some of the time anyway. I was with this girl at the time. I don't have much to tell you about her—we split up later—and she's history. Anyway, she worked for a broker, made good money. She paid the rent, so it was a good deal for me. Anyway. You know that big earthquake in the suburbs of Los Angeles? It was 2004 I think. Bunch of people got killed. Some building collapsed. It really shook people up, broke dishes, that sort of thing. Scared the shit out of people. Well, it happened around 11:00 at night, or shortly after. I read somewhere, that's when most people have sex. Married people. They watch TV. They've got these programs they like to watch. Maybe he has a beer. They get undressed. They watch the ten o'clock news in bed, and then they switch off the TV, turn off the lights, and next thing you know, they're doing it. Screwing."

I squirmed uncomfortably. Where was this going?

The arrival of the appetizers interrupted his flow, but only briefly. I started eating. He went on. "OK, I'm not married, and I'm not like most of those suburban people, but anyway, I was living with this girlfriend, and she was hot for the ten o'clock news, God knows why, and I was hot for her body. Anyway, as soon as she turned off the set, we starting having sex, and right in the middle—wow! Here comes the earthquake. There was this shaking and quaking, and noise. It's like a truck is rumbling by. The whole house was swaying back and forth. She was plenty scared, believe me.

"Well, it didn't last that long, maybe ten seconds, but it had a real impact, believe me. She turned on the TV again, and naturally she wouldn't dream of going back and doing the sex thing. She was too nervous she said, and then she started calling her mother and sister and, like, oh mother are you OK? And so on. So I'm lying in bed, naked and all hot and bothered, and I started thinking. Like, we couldn't be the only couple having sex in Los Angeles when the earthquake came. I mean, it's LA, you know? Zillions of people. It's a wide open city.

Plenty of sex. Lots of Mexican people—they have all those babies. Hollywood people—they screw constantly, and so on.

"So I put an ad in the local newspapers, including those weekly things. They're free. They're in all the Los Angeles suburbs, and the Valley, and so on. I even advertised in San Bernardino and San Diego. I said in the ad I'm writing a book. I'm looking for people who were having sex in the middle of the earthquake. I want to know what it was like, what happened. My idea was I'd get all these stories, and I'd put it together, and peddle it to some publisher. I had a great name for this book. I'd call it *The Earth Moved.*"

It was a great name, I had to agree. And I had to admit I was intrigued. Andrew had a certain amount of imagination. That much was clear. I said, "So? Did you get responses? Did people answer your ad?"

"Believe you me!" he answered quickly, "I got tons of responses. I mean, people are crazy nowadays. They'll tell you anything. It's like the people on the Jerry Springer show. No self-restraint. Nothing embarrasses them. Well, some people keep themselves private, you know, but thank God not everybody. I went out with a tape recorder. I went to people's homes. Some of the stories, you wouldn't believe the things they told me. Incredible. Guy and his girlfriend, the house starts shaking. She runs out into the street, stark naked, screaming. She's lost it totally. You know what I mean? Sheer panic. And he goes running after her with a towel wrapped around him, only the towel falls off. Ever try running with a towel tied around you? Meanwhile, there's another guy, living in the same house. Two-story house. He's on the second floor. He's got a video camera, would you believe it, and he's taking pictures of the whole scene. Awesome. It's night, but there's a full moon and lots of streetlights. You can see the whole thing. I've got the tape. He let me have it. By the way, it turns out the woman, the one running around in the street, is married, but not to the guy she was screwing.

"That's just one story. I've got others. They're dynamite, some of them. It takes all kinds—you know what I mean? Anyway, I've got all this material, and when I'm done, you know, writing it up, I'm going to get an agent, get it published. Do you know any agents?"

"Not personally," I answered. "The only agents I know are real estate agents."

We paused again, because my chicken breast with tomato sauce and Andrew's cannelloni had arrived. Telling the story seemed to invigorate him, and he attacked his food with great gusto. After he had swallowed a few mouthfuls, he plunged on.

"This book is going to be terrific," he said, "it'll make real money. Big money. It's a great story, you know? I'll get interviews. I'll be on *The Daily Show*. People love that stuff. Sex, with a comic angle, it's a real winner. Kinky stuff, too. Like, people who are into bondage. How's that for something? You're handcuffed to the bed, and somebody is doing some sex thing to you, and suddenly the whole house is shaking, and you're in handcuffs, right? Oh, I've got that story. I've got every kind. Lesbians. Gays. You name it. And other stuff, human interest.... One of the guys, for instance, guy who answered my ad, young man, good looking. He had some kind of condition, fatal condition—I mean eventually it was going to be fatal. He was doomed. He knew it. No cure, that sort of thing. You wouldn't know it to look at him, but he's got only months to live, maybe a year or two at most. Well, he's having sex with this chick. The house starts shaking. He thinks, this is it, this is an attack. I'm going to die right here and now. And I've got other stories, too. I've got files and files. I've got tapes and videos. It's going to be fantastic, a real winner, don't you think?"

Wearily, I said yes.

"There's more. I've got a real blockbuster," Andrew continued. "This could make headlines. Let's say here's a guy, he's having sex with a chick, somebody he met in a bar, and then the earthquake comes. Bam! The ceiling collapses. She's pinned down. She thinks she's going to die. They're trapped, the two of them, right? He's OK. He manages to free himself, but she's pinned down. He can't get her out by himself, so he says, I'll get help. She's shouting and screaming, I'm going to die, I'm going to die, it's a punishment, I deserved it, God forgive me, that sort of thing. He tries to calm her down, but he can't, and she's wailing how she's committed a crime, big-time, murder in fact, and she got away with it...."

"Murder? She says she committed a murder?"

"That's what I said."

"And you've got the story? She told you about it?"

"Not her. Him. He promised her he wouldn't tell, but guess what? He broke his promise."

"But ... that's kind of wrong, isn't it?"

"Where are you from?" Andrew seemed surprised. "Don't be naïve. Sure, when they got her out, she made him swear not to tell, but when he saw my ad, well, he told me anyway. I promised him some of the royalties. Anyway, the woman's crazy. She's a psychopath. What does it matter? Actually, the guy who told me, the guy who was balling her, he's dead. He was totaled in a car accident a month after he told me this story. Well, not exactly an accident. He was dead drunk at the time. So he doesn't get any of the royalties. A break for me, no?"

"I guess."

The waiter came by and asked about coffee and dessert. Andrew declined, and, reluctantly, so did I. At least the dessert. I did ask for decaffeinated coffee. Andrew said, "So you see why I need a lawyer. You know, to incorporate, and all that. Book deals, stuff like that."

"It's not my specialty, Andrew."

"Hey, if you're smart, you can learn. Don't you want to make money? And listen: I've got another idea. If that one was dynamite, this one is the frigging atom bomb, Frank. It is going to make millions. Millions. It's an idea for a TV show. It's going to be the greatest one ever. I don't say that lightly, Frank."

I have to admit this statement piqued my curiosity. In my personal opinion, it wouldn't take much to make the greatest TV show, considering the garbage you see on the tube. Celia and I have cable. We get God knows how many channels, but most of the time, there's nothing worth watching. Well, there's the weather channel. It's nice to know some monstrous storm is about to engulf our area. At least the people on that channel don't seem brain dead.

I have to say, too, that I can't stand commercials. They drive me crazy.

I do like nature programs. Saw one recently about the cheetah. Fastest animal on earth, according to the program. There were terrific shots of a cheetah, catching a gazelle and then munching on the poor creature's body. My kids, who dropped in briefly, caught a bit of this scene and pronounced it gross.

Andrew went right on. "It'll be the greatest, Frank. The absolute greatest. But I'm going to need legal help, Frank. That's where you come in."

He leaned forward, and I saw a kind of glint in his eye. "OK, here's my idea. You've got eight people living in a house, right? And there's these cameras all over, got it? Cameras in every room. OK. So far, nothing new. That's already on TV. Boring. But this is different. This is really different. Here's the deal: one of the people in the house is planning to kill somebody else in the house. Now the audience, they're in on it. Well, they're in on part of it. They're watching, and they know somebody is going to get killed, only they don't know who and they don't know who's going to do the killing. So they watch and watch. And then they see it live on TV. An actual, real-life murder. Frank, can you imagine? It'll make headlines. Think of the publicity."

I said, "Andrew, are you out of your mind? What TV company is going to let you do that? And how can you even think of doing such a thing? You're telling me that personally you have this show, you know somebody's going to get killed, and you just let it happen?"

"I'm telling you exactly that," he said with a grin.

"It's out of the question. Think about it. A live murder? On TV? I mean, you can't be serious, Andrew."

"I'm serious. I have to admit, I haven't worked out all the details."

"Right. The details."

He caught the sarcasm in my voice. "You don't think I can pull this off? I think I can. Oh, sure, there's a few kinks."

"Kinks? Andrew, it's totally insane. You'll never do it. And you shouldn't do it."

"Oh, I'm going to do it, Frank. Some things I'm still working on. For instance, when you see the murder, do you see who the murderer is, or is it kind of like in shadows? You know what I mean? So you can't see who it is."

"Andrew, this isn't going to happen. Don't even think about it. It's a bad idea. Nobody's going to let this happen."

"You think? Listen, these networks, they'll do anything for money. I mean, look at what they have now. I mean, they're putting on real garbage, but it sells. People want garbage. You've got freak shows, people practically killing each other, spilling their guts on TV, letting the whole world know their dirty little secrets, picking somebody to marry on TV, or somebody to screw. I'm telling you, anything goes."

"They don't screw on camera, Andrew. Not on the networks."

"OK, not on camera. Not on the networks. But that's coming as sure as I'm sitting here. You can see sex already, on some of these satellite things. Anyway, we're not talking sex. I'm talking murder. You'll see. I'm going to pull this off. I mean it."

"Look," I said, "I don't want to sound moralistic, God forbid, but don't you think it's just plain wrong, even if you could manage it?"

"Give me credit for some brains, Frank."

"I'll give you a lot of credit. Especially if you give up the idea. Believe me, it's going nowhere."

"No? I already have the house. I've already got the set-up. Even that part. It's quite a story, Frank. Want to hear about it?"

I didn't really, but I figured I had to humor him, and I had asked for a cup of decaffeinated coffee, and it hadn't yet arrived. I had had about enough of Andrew Wright. I was tempted to forget the coffee, say I had to go, then pick up the bill, pay it, and walk out the door. But I stayed. And there was no stopping Andrew Wright.

"I'm living in the house right now," he said. "The murder house. It's perfect."

At that point, I figured I might as well have dessert. I needed it. I called the waiter and ordered tiramisu. A rich dessert might just possibly salvage the evening.

"This house," he went on. "You just wouldn't believe it. It's got rooms inside the rooms, if you know what I mean. Ten bathrooms, I swear it. Well, seven. You could rotate taking a shower, different bathroom, every day of the week. And the size of them, I mean, you could have a naked shower party. Hey! Not a bad idea. I don't think the old lady would like it, though."

"The old lady?"

"Owns the place. I'm coming to that. Anyway, here's this house. Humongous lot, too. Right in Palo Alto, but it must have an acre of ground. I mean, Jesus, it's worth a zillion dollars. Maybe two zillion."

"You live there?"

"I do. I actually do."

"Whose house is it, Andrew? Your family's?"

Somehow I knew it wasn't, but there was always a chance. And if it were his house, or if it belonged to his family, that would be finally something about Andrew that evoked my interest. I daydream about clients who live in houses worth a zillion dollars. Maybe two zillion, as he put it. There were such people, but of course they took their rich, fat business to the big San Francisco firms, or the big Palo Alto firms, like Wilson, Soncini. They never came to me. Still, after all, there are people who win the lottery, aren't there? It's always possible to dream.

"Not my family," he said. "I told you I don't have a family. Where would I get the money for a house like that? No way."

My daydream vanished.

"Here's the story," Andrew said. "I'm walking in Palo Alto, downtown, I'm between situations, as they say, and I'm just hanging around. I came up here, lived in San Francisco for awhile. I was with this woman I met there. Then she threw me out. Caught me with another woman. I mean, it wasn't like we were married or anything. Sometimes, women, I just don't understand them. Anyway, I got my own place for a while, but the rent was too steep. I had to find something else. Well, I knew this guy, met him on one of my trips—he had a condo in Palo Alto—and I more or less moved in with him. Just temporary, I told him. He was in computers, something like that. He traveled a lot, so it wasn't a big deal for him, but I knew I couldn't stay. Meanwhile, I'm thinking, what's my next move? Where do I go from here?

"Anyway, I'm in Palo Alto, not much to do. I'm on University Avenue, which is sort of the main street, shops, restaurants, banks, pretty upscale. I'm lusting for a double espresso, you know? It's late afternoon, little bit chilly, not too bad. I'm walking along. I see this old lady. She's standing on a corner, looking dazed, lost, out to lunch, if you know what I mean. Then she sits down on the curb right there. I went over and said, you know, like a good guy, which I am, sometimes anyway, and I say, 'Anything the matter, ma'am, can I help you?' It turns out, she's a little confused. More than a little, I'd say. I said, 'Well, can I take you home?' And she says, 'Oh dear, I can't remember where I live.'

"She's clutching this small black purse. So I opened it up, looking for something, a wallet, a driver's license, some kind of identification. Sure enough, she's got a driver's license. Expired ten years ago, but she's still carrying it around. It's got an address on it. I figured maybe she still lives there. So I asked her, 'Is this your address? Santa Rosa Court?' She says, 'I think so. I'm not sure.'

"So I took her arm. I said, 'It's only a couple of blocks. I'll take you home.' She says, 'Oh, you're such a dear.' That's what she said. 'Such a dear.' Anyway, I took her home. The house—! Frank, it was a frigging mansion! Beautiful old furniture, staircase, you know, fabulous layout, but what a mess. I mean, she was living in one room, and the house was so filthy, it was disgusting. A big yard, all weeds. The neighbors must have been hopping mad. Junk piled everywhere, ten-year old newspapers, cobwebs.... Anyway, to make a long story short, I found out, she was a widow, no kids. Husband was a really rich guy, real estate or something. Left her everything. Well, when the husband died, she lived there in the house with a nephew. A real creep as far as I could tell. Not a bad guy, but a total loser. Never married. Never could hold a job. Nervous guy. Maybe a bit on the mental illness side, but not stupid. Had a drinking problem, I think. Still, he took care of her, did the shopping, paid the bills, kept things going. But then he upped and died several years ago, I'm not sure exactly, and she was alone. And she started losing it, or maybe she had already started, and I guess she just let everything slide. I mean, she had this desk, and there were dividend checks, social security checks, years old. She just couldn't cope. You know what I mean?

"So I took over. I moved in. Was I trying to be a boy scout? Yes and no. Believe it or not, I actually liked the old lady. Angelica Finster, that was her name. She reminded me of my grandmother, the way she was before she got Alzheimer's. And while she had Alzheimer's. This old lady, she was like that. I don't know if it was Alzheimer's or what, but she wasn't playing with a full deck, if you know what I mean. She had good days and bad days. But she was harmless, no trouble at all. I thought, this is my lucky break. I've got karma or whatever. I saw an opportunity. I could do her a lot of good, and she could do me a lot of good. Anyway, I got the checks deposited. I took her to the doctor. OK, I got free room and board, but I earned it. I got the place in shape. I hired a cleaning service. They spent days getting rid of all the accumulated muck. I had painters. I had carpenters. Made the place livable. I threw out some of the furniture. It was Salvation Army stuff after all those years. I bought new stuff, not too expensive, but OK. Stuff from Sears, from Ikea. I got everything in order. And I kept it that way. The cleaning service, they still come once a week. Mexican guys. The place sparkles, you know? I opened bank accounts. I got power of attorney. She'll sign anything when I ask her to. But I'm not stealing from her, not really, believe it or not. I just take a bit, not much, kind of a salary. Just some spending money. Well, sometimes a little more. Anyway, I earn it. I deserve it. Meanwhile, I started renting out rooms. I mean, why waste all that space? Brings in money, too. It's probably illegal, you know, zoning or whatever, but nobody's complained yet, so what the hell?

"Anyway, that's the story. The old lady, she's happy. She loves the company. She just loves having people around. You know, I think it's good for her. Peps her up. Gets the juices going. I mean, she's still kind of confused, some days worse than others, forgets things sometimes, can't tell if it's Tuesday or Wednesday, but, hey, she was heading downhill fast when I met her. Now, I won't say she's sharp, but it could be worse. And we've got the place filled. Eight people living there. It's a perfect set-up. I picked the people, and I made sure we had the right mix. I've been working on this, you know. Just a few details. That's all I need. I'll be ready to go."

I was stunned. His self-confidence was breathtaking. "You've got eight people? Living in the house?"

"That's what I said."

"And it's OK with them? Installing the cameras?"

"Well, not exactly. Not yet. We haven't talked about this. Hey, do they have to know about the cameras?"

"Andrew, of course they do. You know that."

"OK, OK. Well, they'll agree. I'll tell them about the money. For money, people will do anything. That part won't be hard."

I had no idea, of course, who the eight people were, but if I had to guess, I would bet he was heading for a lot more trouble than he thought. How would he convince eight normal people to let cameras in, all over the house?

But maybe I was wrong. After all, he said he picked the people. He could have collected an outstanding bunch of weird exhibitionists. I wouldn't put it past him.

Even so, his idea would never, never work. It was utterly preposterous. To arrange a murder and televise it? Even a fake murder, but only the producers know it's a fake.... No way. I looked at Andrew closely. He was a supreme optimist, and supremely egocentric. Cocky as all get out.

Celia would say about somebody like Andrew, that all that ego just papers over some inner insecurity. When Celia was working on her education degree, she also took a lot of courses in social work. She thinks she's a good judge of character, and mostly she is. But here, I think, she might be wrong. Not that I knew Andrew all that well, but I detected not the slightest whiff of inner insecurity. If there was any inner insecurity, it was buried so far down in the inners that it might as well not be there.

We finished our dessert, and the waiter brought the bill. I could tell from Andrew's body language that he had no intention of picking up the check. *He* had invited *me*, but still he made no move to pay or even to contribute.

Oh well, I thought. Chalk it up to experience. I picked the check up from the plastic tray, looked to make sure it was roughly alright, and slid my credit card onto the tray. Andrew did nothing. After the server returned with the receipt, Andrew said, "Hey, Frank, thank you. That was nice of you."

"Don't mention it."

We got up to go. He said he'd be in touch. I said to myself, no, we won't be.

I drove home, thinking about the conversation with Andrew and the terrible impression he had made on me. I never wanted to see him again.

When I went into the house, I found Celia sitting in the living room, reading a book. "How was it?" she asked.

"Weird."

"Oh? In what way?"

"I'll tell you later," I said. "A real jerk."

"New client?"

"No," I said. "I wouldn't touch him with a ten-foot pole."

I sat down on the sofa and picked up a magazine. I was still processing the evening. Andrew's idea had failure written all over. The man might be pushy and self-assured, but he would soon find out that TV moguls are not so gullible, and the TV world not so easily crashed. All his dreams about incorporating and making a killing (no pun intended) would burst like a pricked balloon. I resolved to wash my hands of the whole affair and never see him again.

In fact, I never did. But not the way I imagined it. Rather, it was because he ended up dead. Extremely and mysteriously dead.

2

Lawyers tend to meet some unusual people. Andrew Wright was only one of many, although I have to admit I had never heard quite so crazy a scheme.

A month or so went by. Basically, I forgot all about him. I was busy with other things.

Clients, for example: a small businessman who wanted to incorporate his tanning salon, old ladies who wanted to change their wills (again and again), old friends who were selling their house, the tangled affairs of a client who died two months after he married his fourth wife, and a neighbor whose dog had gotten loose and bitten a child. Much of the work was routine. Much of it hardly qualified as the practice of law, but it brought in revenue, and for that I am always grateful.

I had other worries, too. My younger daughter wasn't doing as well in school as she should, and her grades in algebra were appalling ("but Daddy, it's so booooring"). And I was worried about my older daughter, too. At 16, she seemed to have a boyfriend—something I wasn't quite ready for, though she apparently was. His name was Ryan. He looked like something the cat dragged in, with his baggy pants, and he wore a single earring. His hair seemed to be every known color and to stick out in all directions. What she saw in him totally escaped me. He came over to the house from time to time, slouching and talking in monosyllables.

More often, she went to his place. Is it possible, oh God, that they were having sex? I visualized the house, parents away, a rec room in the basement with a sofa; or the two of them going to his room, and shutting the door. The mere thought of my daughter sleeping with this Ryan was enough to destroy my fatherly peace of mind.

But were they really doing that? No way to know for sure, short of catching them in the act. I could, of course, ask her what was going on. There was no chance she would give me an honest answer. Or any answer at all, except the usual sullen grunts. I could ask Celia to help me out. She had more rapport with the girls. Not a lot of rapport, but some.

Celia, however, had decided to redo the tile in one of our bathrooms.

"Celia," I said, "there's nothing wrong with the tile."

"Frank," she answered, "just look at them. They're old and disgusting. It's time to replace them, and I hate the color. I always have."

"What's wrong with the color? They're light blue. What's wrong with that?"

"They're light green, Frank. Are you blind?"

She wins all these arguments. That's no surprise. I'm helpless. So we embarked on a course of visiting tile stores and contractors. I know something about contractors, from my law practice. I always have at least one client who is anxious to sue his contractor. For good reason. Most contractors seem to be one small step above the level of organized crime. Except that they're disorganized crime.

I can think of no easier way to ruin a perfectly good weekend than to spend it talking to contractors and visiting warehouses full of hundreds of samples of tile. Celia said: "It has to be done." And she insisted that I had to come along. "Frank, I need your input." Of course, I had no input to speak of. At least 90% of the tiles we looked at seemed exactly the same to me. But none of this is germane to our story.

It was the Monday after a dreadful Sunday spent looking at bathroom tile. It was around 11, as I recollect. I was working on some documents. Out of the blue, I had a phone call from Andrew Wright.

"Frank," he said, "it's Andrew Wright."

"Oh, sure, hi Andrew, how's it going?"

"Great, Frank. Just great. Frank, everything's falling into place. I'm very excited."

"Falling into place?"

"You know. My projects. I've been working on *The Earth Moved*, and it's really coming along. I'm just about ready to start showing it around, talking to agents, and I guess we'll need to have contracts, right? Royalties, and stuff, no?"

"Well...."

"But never mind that, right now. I want to talk about the other thing. You remember, Frank. My scheme. The reality show. I've been working on that, too. There were some kinks, you know? But now, I've got most of the details worked out. I've got a plan, Frank. It's going to be fantastic. I mean, fantastic. I need to talk to you, about it."

"Talk to me? Andrew, I told you—"

He didn't let me finish the sentence. "I need a lawyer, Frank, and that's you. We've got to make arrangements, you know, incorporating, tax stuff. I need to be able to market this thing to the big companies, the networks, maybe cable. There's real opportunities here. But everybody says, you have to be careful. You've got to have a lawyer, somebody who knows all the tricks. Those guys out there are sharks. They'll eat you up, if you aren't careful. They'll steal your stuff, cut off your balls if you let them get away with it. That's why I need you, Frank."

I didn't quite know what to say.

"You've got the cameras in?" I asked lamely. "The people in the house agreed?"

"Well, they basically agreed. I'll tell you about it. The cameras, they're not in yet. But we're on track. This is going to be big, Frank."

I was speechless.

"Frank, are you there?"

"I'm here, Andrew. You know what I think of your plan."

"Sure, sure. But you don't have to love me or love my plan, Frank. All you have to do is say you'll help me out."

"Andrew, can I be honest? I don't want to help you out. I really don't. And I'll give you some advice: forget about it. Drop it. The whole thing. That's my advice. Free advice."

"Frank, Frank, I know you have to say that. That's what lawyers do, right? You ask them something, something that's not quite kosher, and they always tell you not to do it. Then you do it anyway. I mean, they can't stop you. And then you go back to them, and they help you out. That's their job. That's what I want you to do, Frank."

"Andrew, I'm not that kind of lawyer."

"You're a lawyer, aren't you? Member of the bar and all that."

"Yes, but..."

"And you're my lawyer, Frank. That's all that matters."

"Andrew," I said, "I'm really not your lawyer. And, as I told you, over and over again, I wouldn't touch this with a ten-foot pole."

"I haven't got a ten-foot pole. Listen, Frank, can you come over?"

"Come over?"

"Yes. Come over. To the house. I want to show you something. And ask your advice."

"Andrew, I already gave you advice. Free advice. Over the phone. You didn't seem to hear it. The advice is to drop the whole idea. I hate to break the news to you, but there are laws against killing people."

"You think I don't know that, Frank? Give me credit for some brain cells, OK? It's going to be alright, believe me. I'm going to tell you all my secrets. I'm going to explain to you exactly how it's going to happen. Anyway, when can you come see me?"

"Not today. I'm busy, Andrew. And I really don't think—"

"Frank, you can't say no. I'm a client."

"Andrew, you're not a client. And you're not going to be a client."

"Frank," he said. "I'm going to ignore that last remark. You can't get rid of me that way. Hey, I'm like a leech. I stick to people, you know? I don't take no for an answer. I never do. And there could be big money here. Don't tell me you're not interested in big money. You have to live, right? Anyway, can you come over tonight?"

"Tonight? No, not really."

"Wait. I have a better idea. I'm feeling hyper. Let's have dinner. My treat. Anyplace you like. But it has to be late. 8:00, 8:15, something like that."

"I really shouldn't."

"You shouldn't, or you don't want to? Frank, Frank, be smart. I tell you, this is worth millions. And you'll get a share."

"Andrew," I said, "I don't want a share. I don't want anything to do with your plans. I'm a respectable lawyer. I'm ethical. I'm on bar committees. What do you think I am? A lawyer for the mob? This is way out of my league. I'm serious, Andrew."

He just laughed. "A free dinner, Frank. What could be the harm? You're not signing a contract, right? Anyway, I want you to come by the place where I live. I'll show it to you. 'Fess up. You're dying of curiosity. You want to see what it's like. It's quite a place, believe me."

I had to admit he had a point. I did want to see the house. I was curious. He had hit on my Achilles heel.

He went on: "I'll give you the address. You got a pencil? Write it down."

I reached for a pad of paper. He repeated the address. It was on Santa Rosa Court, in Palo Alto. "You know how to get there?" he asked.

"Sure. No problem," I said.

"There's a side entrance," he added, "you go around the house, on the left, there's a little path. You'll see the door. Just knock on the door or ring the bell. I'm in a room, nice room. Actually it used to be a maid's room. It's not the biggest room, but I like it, because it has its own entrance. It makes it more private, you know what I mean? We can talk for a little bit, then I'll give you the grand tour, then we'll have dinner."

Why did I say yes? Was I crazy? Probably. I was curious, though, as I said. Also, as luck would have it, I really did need some place to go. Celia was having her book group over again. They have an ironclad rule: no husbands. Only children are allowed to be around on book-group night. But in fact, my daughters were each going to a friend's house. Or so they said. The older girl was going over to Ryan's house. They did anything they could to avoid their dreaded parents. At least my children did. Did Ryan have parents? Maybe his parents were swingers. Who knows? I made a mental note to find out.

But in short, I was at loose ends. I could have gone off, by myself, to my favorite sushi bar. I should have done that. Yet an evil voice inside of me said, what's the harm, I'll have dinner with this guy, I'll see the house, and that will be all. No further obligations. And so, against my better judgment, I heard myself saying "OK."

"Good boy," he said. "I knew you'd see the light. I'll make the reservations. Don't bother yourself."

It was midsummer. I worked late, since I had quite a back-log of work. I finished up a draft of a living trust for one of my better clients, a man who owned two Armenian restaurants. Then I got in my car and drove south to Palo Alto.

The sun was beginning to set. The sky was reddish-orange. It was beautiful. The air was crisp and cool, as it always is in the evening. It was a wonderful day. No wonder millions of people want to live in California.

Angelica Finster's house was not far from downtown Palo Alto. Palo Alto is not completely upscale—not everybody is a millionaire—but it's upscale enough, especially in Angelica's neighborhood. After all, if people like the presidents of Apple and Facebook live there, then it can hardly be a slum.

Downtown is a thick warren of expresso joints, sushi bars, and Italian restaurants. A few banks and specialty shops, an expensive hardware store, an art gallery, and that was about it. University Avenue is the main street of downtown. The streets leading away from University Avenue get leafier and pricier as you go, until the tide turns and they get less leafy and less pricey about a mile from downtown.

I recognized the house on Santa Rosa Court. Santa Rosa was a street of large houses, expansive lots, and a general feeling of quiet affluence. You never saw anybody much on the street. There was a light breeze, and the towering trees that lined the street were swaying gently.

When I got to the Finster house, I found it quite familiar. I had driven by it many times, and it always caught my eye. It would catch most people's eye. It was a big, rambling house, about two and a half stories tall. It was sheathed in dark wood, and the lot seemed to be enormous—enormous, that is, by urban standards. An iron grillwork fence surrounded the property. The grounds looked a bit unkempt, but not disgracefully so. There were clumps of agapanthus in the front, near the grillwork fence, but they seemed to droop a little. Also in the front of the house, there were two tall, very skinny palm trees. They looked somewhat naked and forlorn.

There was a path around the side of the house, and I followed it, as per my instructions, to a plain door, which I took to be the door to Andrew's room. I rang the bell.

There was no answer. I rang again. It was around 8:15 or so. There was still a bit of daylight, though disappearing fast.

In the back, as I noted, there were fairly extensive grounds. But on the side where Andrew's door was located, only about ten feet or so separated the Finster house from what must have been the property line. A few yards beyond that was the hulking shape of a large, rambling, two-story house. A window was open on the second floor. An old man with white hair was sitting in the room with his chair close to the window. He seemed to be staring at me. Nosy old bastard, I thought. I imagined that he sat there all day, looking out to see what he could see. Not that he would ever see much of anything, let alone anything that might stir his ancient bones.

I found myself feeling somehow irritated, as if the man's staring somehow violated me. Don't be an ageist, I told myself. Someday I'll be old and gray myself. He could be a very lonely man. Maybe he was losing his short-term memory. Maybe he's lost in a fog of dementia. In fact, he was far from demented— sharp, in fact. This was something I would later regret.

I rang a third time. There was still no answer. Did I have the time wrong? Had I misunderstood something about our arrangement? I went back down the path, and turned toward the front door. Maybe he was elsewhere in the house. Maybe he assumed I would go to the front door. No, I reminded myself, he had said go around the side.

I rang the doorbell.

Fairly quickly, I heard someone at the door. A young woman opened it, and looked at me rather suspiciously. She was, I would say, in her early 30s. She had dark hair, very curly, possibly dyed, although I'm not sure what gave me that impression. She was not beautiful, but striking somehow, with sharp, well-defined features, and strong eyes. She was wearing a plain white T-shirt—a little bit too tight, I would say, but it certainly got my attention. Her neatly pressed blue jeans seemed pasted to her hips. She had on sandals. She seemed to be wearing no make-up.

She said, "yes?" I wouldn't describe her voice as friendly.

"I'm looking for Andrew. Andrew Wright."

"He's got his own entrance," she said.

"I know that. I rang the bell. He didn't answer, and I thought, maybe he's somewhere else in the house."

"I didn't see him. He's not in the living room. That's where I was. Was he expecting you?"

"He was. We had an arrangement. For dinner. He invited me."

"Well, maybe he changed his mind. How well do you know Andrew?"

"Not all that well."

"Well, if you did...." She didn't finish the sentence. She just stood there. Obviously, she wanted me to go.

I said: "Could you look for him?"

"It's a big house."

"I mean, in his room."

She looked dubious. Then she said. "Alright, I suppose. I'll knock on his door. But if you rang the bell, and he didn't answer, then what's the use? Either he's not there, or he doesn't want to see you."

"Please," I said.

She scowled and went away. She never bothered to ask me in. I stood outside the door, waiting.

A few minutes later, she was back. "He doesn't answer. I guess he's out."

"That's funny. We had an appointment."

"You told me that," she said. "Well, he stood you up. You'll get over it. He's not the most reliable person, in case you didn't know."

"Can I leave a message?"

"I suppose," she said. There was a look on her face of utter indifference.

"My name's Frank May. I'm a lawyer."

Her whole expression changed. She dropped the look of bored exasperation. "Oh, so you're Frank May. Andrew mentioned you."

"And you?"

"I'm Sheila. Sheila Donnelly."

The name meant nothing to me. Andrew had never mentioned her. I mumbled something vague, pleased to meet you or something along those lines. She said, "Andrew talked about you a lot." That bothered me, but I didn't say anything. She went on. "I know something about Andrew's, uh, business ideas. And, well, sometime—not now though—I'd like to talk to you. Maybe in your office."

"Sure."

"Anyway, you can leave Andrew a note. Just give it to me. I'll slip it under his door."

I groped in my pocket for a piece of paper. She asked, "You need something to write on?"

"I do."

"Wait here. I'll get you something." She came back a minute or so later with a small square of white notepaper. I held it up against the door, and scribbled on it, more or less legibly: "Andrew: You weren't here. I waited for you until 8:30 or so. Sorry for the mix-up. Frank." I folded it carefully, wrote on the outside, "Andrew Wright," and gave it back to Sheila. She took it from me. I turned and left. She closed the door behind me.

And that, I thought, was that. By now it was dark, and the streetlights were glimmering in a soft fog. I got in my car, and threaded my way through the streets of Palo Alto until I reached El Camino Real. Once, many years ago, El Camino was a dusty road along which missionaries trudged, hoping to reach the next mission church and save a few more souls for the greater glory of God. What would they think of this jungle of strip malls, fast-food parlors, and cheap motels?

Not all of El Camino is tacky. It all depends on which stretch of road you're driving on. I don't know where the missionaries planned to get their next meal, but on El Camino today, it's no problem, unless you're pining for a gourmet restaurant. I spurned Taco Bell and Jack-in-the-Box and settled for a Japanese buffet restaurant (all you can eat for $10.95).

As I ate, I thought about Andrew Wright and his mysterious behavior. It was a puzzle, but I had no intention of solving it. I was a bit disappointed about not seeing the house, but on the whole, somewhat relieved. I thought I was rid of Andrew Wright. I had seen the last of him.

That turned out to be true. I had seen the last of Andrew Wright. And so had everybody else. Around the time I came by, but probably a bit earlier—nobody knows for sure—Andrew had come to an untimely end. Somebody hit him on the head with a hard object. Maybe a baseball bat, maybe something else. I guess the people in the crime labs know what it was that collided with Andrew's head, but they weren't saying, and the newspapers were merely speculating. Anyway, whatever it was, it knocked him unconscious. Then whoever hit him dragged his body to the bed, and smothered him to death. It gave me the creeps to think that he was lying there dead, while I was ringing or even worse, that somebody inside was putting the finishing touches to Andrew Wright while I stood there leaning on the bell.

I found out about Andrew the next day from the newspaper. I happened to have an appointment with my dentist. My appointment was for 1:00, but he was running late. I sat in the waiting room, looking for a suitable magazine. There was the usual trash: *Golf Digest*, a woman's magazine (Eight Ways to Arouse Your Lover's Passion), *People* magazine, and a stale copy of *The New Yorker* from months before. I had already read it anyway. Well, not exactly. I had seen all the cartoons.

Bored and a bit desperate, I picked up a copy of the *Palo Alto Daily News*. This is one of those free newspapers that spring up in suburban areas like mushrooms, making a living from classified ads, I suppose. The murder of Andrew Wright was not something *The New York Times* or *The Wall Street Journal* would care two pins about, perhaps not even the *San Jose Mercury News* or the *San Francisco Chronicle*. But it was front page headline stuff in the *Palo Alto Daily News*, indeed, the stuff of a screaming headline: "Man Murdered in Palo Alto Mansion." It identified the victim as unemployed Andrew Wright, age 32. It described him as renting a room in a home owned by Angelica Finster, aged 85, a widow. The house was "a large and historic local mansion." There was a photograph of the house. "Mr. Wright had a room on the ground floor, with its own private entrance." His housemates (said the story) had discovered him dead in his room.

None of the housemates, apparently, had been eager to talk to the *Daily*; none of them were quoted. There were the usual banal remarks by neighbors (who had seen and heard nothing, and had nothing of interest to say). According to one, Wright "seemed quiet and well-mannered. I don't think anybody in the neighborhood knew him very well." Another neighbor complained about "things going on in the house" and that "too many people seemed to be living there." A third neighbor said Mrs. Finster was "a fine old lady, very friendly," but admitted she had not seen or spoken to her in months and maybe years. There was a sidebar about the history of the house, which was built in the 1920s. It had been owned by the Wigginworths, a prominent local family until it was sold in 1973 to real-estate developer Morris Finster, now deceased.

There was little in the story about the crime itself. There was speculation that Wright had been knocked unconscious, and then smothered. The police were "investigating the crime. Police officials refused to comment on the investigation itself. However, it was learned that no arrests have yet been made. No motive has been suggested for the crime."

I read the story in a state of profound shock. I forgot all

about the dentist or my upper and lower teeth. Andrew dead! Last night! The very night I had gone to see him. I had been stood up by a dead man. I sat there stunned, unable to think of anything else. The dental technician had to call my name twice before I even heard her. I couldn't get the story out of my mind, even while she poked and scraped and fiddled with my teeth, and made her usual idle conversation. I grunted a yes or no to her blather, but I was in no mood for talk. I kept seeing in my mind the closed door, a small room, and Andrew lying dead somewhere inside. I saw myself ringing the doorbell, while a shadowy figure inside put the finishing touches to Andrew Wright.

The dental technician, who had told me her name was Martha, was young, blonde, and professional. She took x-rays of my mouth then cleaned my teeth. Afterwards, the dentist, Dr. Lutz, a jovial fat man in his 40s, came in to see me for about 40 seconds. He said I had no cavities, and he had nothing but praise for the state of my gums. Apparently, I could be proud of my gums, as if they were some sort of marvelous personal achievement. Then he left me for the next patient.

I got up from the dentist's chair. Martha, who was still hovering about, asked, "Do you floss regularly?" I said, "Not really." She waggled her finger, and gave me a short lecture about flossing. Actually, I never, never floss, but I don't dare admit it in dental circles, or anywhere else. I don't want to floss. Flossing is one of those modern crazes, like breast-feeding and no-cal diet soda, all of them, in my view, seriously overrated. And the only thing I wanted to do, at the moment, was get out of the dental office. I made some sort of promise to mend my ways and floss. She handed me a free toothbrush and a small container of no-wax dental floss. I left the office like a sleep-walker. I hoped Martha and Dr. Lutz hadn't noticed how upset I was—or if they did, I hope they ascribed it to the usual phobia people have about dentists.

I sat in my car, as if paralyzed, thinking. An awful thought suddenly entered my mind. I had been so engrossed in the thought of Andrew and his corpse that I had forgotten the terrible possibility that somehow I could be dragged into this sordid mess. I remembered the neighbor, the old man with white hair, that old busybody sitting in the house next door. He had seen me ringing the doorbell. Would he tell the police? Of course, they wouldn't suspect me of killing Andrew. After all, I hadn't gotten into the house. But they'd be around with questions, questions, questions, and more question.

I told myself I had nothing to worry about. From that quarter anyway. I don't think the old man had seen my face, and he'd have no idea who I was. But there was a greater danger: Sheila. She would remember me, my name, my face. Oh lord. I had asked after Andrew, and I had left him a note. She slipped it under the door. That note! The police must have it at this very minute. They would have it in the crime lab. They would give it the full forensic treatment. They'd analyze the paper and find my fingerprints.

I felt sick to my stomach. I was in this thing up to my neck. Any day, or maybe any hour, they'd be knocking on my door. "Mr. May, this is Officer So-and-So. I'd like to ask you a few questions."

The last thing I wanted was another murder case.

But maybe it won't happen, I said to myself. Maybe this will all blow over. Most of the time, the police arrest somebody very quickly. A burglar. An ex-girlfriend, wild with jealousy. Something like that. The case would be closed. The police would lose all interest in unimportant, peripheral details, like a note under the door, or a man who rang the doorbell. The whole case would disappear, and life would go on as always.

Or maybe not. With regard to things of this sort, my natural pessimism makes itself felt. Maybe no burglar would materialize, no ex-girlfriend, no old enemy settling scores—and therefore no quick arrest. The whole process could be long and complicated, with no easy solution in sight. This, I thought, was more likely.

How right I was.

3

Somehow I got through the rest of the day. I managed to deal with clients, paperwork, and emails. I came home feeling exhausted and distressed. Celia had gotten home early and made a beef stew for dinner. Normally I ate with great zest, but tonight I just picked at the food. Celia saw immediately that something was wrong. Wives develop a kind of radar. I can't really hide anything from her. She said nothing, though, in front of the girls. The dinner was not much of a success. One of the girls declared the stew to be "totally gross," and the other, worried by the appearance of a renegade pimple, announced she had decided to turn vegetarian. After dinner, they vanished into their rooms in their usual sullen way. Celia sighed. I got up and did the dishes.

Then Celia and I went into the living room. I picked up the newspaper. "What is it, Frank?" she asked. "I know something is bothering you."

"You're right. Something is."

I told her the whole story, from start to finish. She listened and was properly sympathetic. "But why do these things always happen to you, Frank?" I had no idea, I told her. Bad karma. Fortunately, nobody knew my secret. My clients would avoid me like a leper, if they ever came to think I was jinxed—that hiring me was the equivalent of a death sentence or a tour of duty in some place like Afghanistan.

It was good to talk to Celia. It was good to get things off my chest. She said soothing things, and gave me advice—psychological advice, advice how to handle the problem. Above all, she told me not to worry myself to death. But that was easier said than done. I tossed and turned all night. I had nightmares. I felt worn-out and depressed in the morning, when I dragged myself out of bed, bleary-eyed, to face the day. I kept expecting the police to come after me. Every time the phone rang, at home or at work, I nearly jumped out of my skin. Still, two days passed, and there was no word from the police. Was it possible that they never found the note? Was it possible they hadn't talked to Sheila?

I looked at the *Palo Alto Daily News* every day. There was little about the case, very little follow-up. Hardly any news, good or bad. Of course, it was too big a story to ignore altogether, but clearly the *Daily* had nothing to report, except the fact that there was nothing to report, and that the police seemed to be making little progress. Meanwhile, serious problems had developed with regard to local storm sewers; and some citizens were screaming about the high salary paid to the city manager, "and for what? Tell me one thing this man has accomplished." I noticed that the storm sewers and city managers pushed Andrew Wright off the front page.

On the third day, I got a phone call. "Mr. May? Sheila Donnelly. You remember.... I was there, I opened the door, the night Andrew died?"

How could I forget? "Of course, Ms. Donnelly."

"Call me Sheila."

I was dying to ask her about the note under the door, about the progress of the investigation, and what she knew about it. The police must have grilled her—and everybody else who was living in Angelica's house. But I didn't dare ask these questions. Instead I said, "Sure, Sheila. And call me Frank. What can I do for you?"

"Frank, I need to talk to you. You were Andrew's lawyer."

"Well, sort of."

"What does sort of mean?"

I swallowed hard. "I mean, yes, he came to see me, but we never, uh, had any kind of final agreement. It was all very tentative, so I'm not sure you could call me his lawyer."

"Whatever. You can spare me the technicalities. Now that

he's dead, he's no use to you. I know you were his lawyer. I don't know why you're denying it."

Her tone was as sharp as a needle. I didn't need this. I have enough grief from clients who pay me good money. I don't need to be berated by a non-client. But I said nothing. I was tempted, though, to hang up the phone.

"Listen," she said, "I need a lawyer. I haven't got much money, but ... I'm willing to pay what I can."

"OK, but why me?" I had no desire to have Sheila as a client, and especially as a client without money.

"I don't know any lawyers. I've spent my life avoiding lawyers. I'm talking to you because Andrew trusted you. He thought you were honest."

"There are a lot of honest lawyers."

"There are? It's news to me."

"You'd be surprised," I said. "Anyway, can I ask: why do you need a lawyer, Sheila? What's the problem?"

She said: "Well, the police, as you can imagine, they're asking all sorts of questions. They're swarming all over the place. I want to know what my rights are, do I have to answer things, that kind of issue."

"Do you have anything to hide?"

"Let's say I don't."

"What does that mean?" I asked. "Do you or don't you?"

"I don't want to talk about this. Not on the phone. Somebody could be listening. Anyway, they're suspicious of everybody. Everybody in the house."

"Why is that?"

"Well, isn't it obvious, Frank? *Somebody* killed him."

"Somebody in the house?"

"Maybe. Do you know how he died?"

"Sort of. I read it in the paper."

"Somebody bashed him in the head, knocked him unconscious, then smothered him with a pillow. I mean, he didn't do that himself, did he? We keep telling the police it must have been a prowler. Somebody who came in, wanted to steal something. But they don't believe us."

"Why not?"

"Well, it's not like this happened in the middle of the night. And nobody broke in, they said. At least, there's no signs of a break-in. No broken windows, no forced doors. Of course, he could have let somebody in.... That's probably what happened. But I don't think prowlers ring the bell ... it's all very mysterious."

I thought of the old man with white hair. Was he always sitting there, looking out the window, watching the passing parade? I imagined that was probably the case. In any event, he had seen *me*. That much was perfectly obvious. He was just the type to tell his story to the police. A little excitement in a dull and pointless life. On the other hand, maybe he had Alzheimer's disease. Maybe he had no short-term memory. I don't wish this dreadful disease on most people, but in this case, I made an exception. If I had any luck, this man was hopelessly confused, and had no memory of me at all.

But then there was the note.... What had happened to the note? Did the police have it? "The note under the door..." I said, with a kind of quaver in my voice. "You remember, I asked you to ... give it to him, slip it under the door. I suppose, well, the police.... They must have the note."

"Don't worry about the note. The police don't have it. They never saw it. I picked it up and tore it to pieces."

I was amazed. "You tore it up?"

"I just said so, Frank."

"Why did you do that? I mean, thank you, but...."

"Listen," she said, "What was the point of leaving it there? Andrew was dead. You had nothing to do with it, obviously. Why make trouble for you?"

"That's awfully nice of you...."

I heard a kind of scornful laugh. "Frank," she said, "you don't know me. Nice has nothing to do with it. I was looking out for number one, if you know what I mean. I felt, maybe I need a favor. Maybe I need a lawyer. Maybe you might feel like helping me out.... Look, I don't want to talk about this on the phone. I'd like to come see you."

Of course I agreed. I was a little disturbed by what she

said. Some sort of favor? Ten to one it was something shady or illegal. And there was more than a little whiff of blackmail about Sheila's good deed. Help me, or I might tell the police about the note. But the mere fact that she had torn it up—that gave me a tremendous lift. Now I could sleep at night.

We made an appointment for the next day. I gave her the address and directions. She showed up promptly. She was neatly dressed in a skirt and blouse, and it looked to my untrained eye as if she had had her hair done for the occasion. I assume she spent very little time in lawyers' offices, so she may have felt she had to dress accordingly. I had no court appointment that day, and no other client interviews. I was actually wearing blue jeans. Whenever I need to feel liberated, I wear blue jeans. I take off my tie—I hate neckties—and I put on a pair of worn, baggy blue jeans. My daughters laugh at me. They think I'm just trying to be "cool," which, in their eyes of course, is simply not possible.

Sheila and I shook hands, and I motioned her to a seat. I said: "You know, I'm not a criminal lawyer. If you think you need somebody who does that kind of work, I can make a recommendation."

She said, "That's not my problem. I don't need Perry Mason, believe me. I might, if the police decided to arrest me, but why would they? The idea that I would kill Andrew? It's ridiculous. In fact we had a relationship. Of sorts."

"A relationship."

"I don't have to draw you a picture. You're a grown-up, no? We had a relationship."

Nowadays, we all know what people mean by a relationship. They mean sex. Similarly, if they say they're "dating," or "seeing" somebody. More sex. It's a brave new world out there, a world of relationships. Somehow it had passed me by. First I was too young for that sort of thing, and then I was too old. I suppose my children even wonder how their mother and I managed to make babies. But let's not get into that.

A relationship with Andrew.... But I couldn't help wondering. She didn't appear to be particularly grief-stricken. Her "relationship," the man she presumably loved, was resting in the morgue in a steel drawer covered with a sheet, extremely dead. Yet she seemed as cool as a cucumber.

"We talked a lot," she said. "Andrew and I. He mentioned you to me. That's why I thought I should come to you."

"Did you know much about, uh, his plans? About his scheme?"

"What scheme?"

I wondered if this was a delicate subject. I gulped and said, "He had a kind of wild idea...."

She laughed. "Oh, you mean, sex and earthquakes. The earth moved. That project. Yeah, I knew all about it."

"No, not that. Something else.... I'm not sure it's something he wanted me to talk about with other people."

"Oh, you mean putting the cameras all over the house. Yes, we talked about that."

"And ... something else?"

"What do you mean, something else? What else was there? Wasn't that enough? I can tell you, it created quite a stir. You know, the house, it's like a commune. Well, not exactly. If it was a commune, believe me, I'd be out of there in a flash. But we do share a kitchen, and so on. Andrew's little idea, the cameras, you can imagine.... There was a lot of discussion, a lot of controversy. We were talking about it, actually, a bunch of us, that very night at dinner. The night he died."

"That night. Could you tell me what happened? You know, Sheila, really, all I know about this whole business is what I read in the newspapers; and they always get things wrong."

She said, "It started out as nothing special. Lots of times, we eat together. Whoever's there. That night, everybody was there, for dinner. That maybe happens once a week. We had pizza. We have a system. You put down if you expect to be there for dinner. After all, there's only one kitchen; people take turns cooking. They don't have to, though. It's pretty haphazard.... Most of us are rotten cooks. One guy, Chuck, is a vegetarian. That's a pain in the ass by itself. Anyway, half the time, the person in charge just shows up with Chinese fast food, in little take-out boxes, with fortune cookies. Whatever. Anyway, that night, we kind of decided, let's have pizza. Nobody felt like cooking. We had it delivered. The usual wrangling, who wants pepperoni, who wants this, should we get a salad. Anyway, Andrew, he sat down with us, had a beer. He said, I'm not having dinner. I'm going out, but later on. We all heard him say that. He didn't say where he was going or why. Maybe somebody asked him, where are you going? If somebody did, I don't remember the answer. Anyway, now I know. He had an appointment with you."

I froze again. "Do the police know this? About the appointment with me?"

She said, "I don't think so. I don't think anybody remembered if he said where he was going. I certainly didn't say anything to the police, and I'm telling you now, I won't."

I felt a bit relieved. I said, "Go on."

"You know, maybe I was the last person to see Andrew.... Except for whoever killed him, I mean. Anyway, there was dinner—pizza, green salad. I remember, I wasn't particularly hungry. Billy—you don't know about Billy yet—I guess you don't know much about the people in the house. Anyway, Billy said he wasn't feeling good. I think he had one mouthful, then he got up and left. I don't remember the exact time. I think he went to his room. Then Fletcher and Lydia left. And Chuck, I think. And maybe Kurt too. The old lady, Angelica. She went to her room. Carmen too. Those are the people, the ones who live in the house. They all finished eating, and they went their way. Oh, I think Kurt did the dishes, then he left.

"After a while, must have been 7:00 or so, it was just the two of us at the table. I was having a cup of coffee. Andrew said, come to my room. I said ... no. He laughed and said, hey, why so reluctant, Sheila? He was always after me, for sex. In fact, he wanted me to move in with him. He kept saying, I've got a nice room, we can rent yours out. I said, oh, so you want another tenant, more rent, is that it? But he just laughed. He said, I'm not that bad. Hey, come on Sheila. But I said, no, I'm not going to your room. I'm not in the mood. He said, hey, it won't kill you. I want to show you something. So we went. Well, we talked for a while, and then we had sex. I guess that's what he wanted to show me, his beautiful body, or what he used to refer to as his beautiful body, not that I hadn't seen it all before.... Then I went back to my own room."

"What did you talk about?

"This and that. We didn't exactly have a lengthy conversation. He had sex on his mind from the start. That was clear. Anyway, the whole business didn't take long. Andrew, like most men, he thought he was a real stud, a regular tiger in the bedroom, but believe me, he wasn't. Never mind the details. Then I left. He was still in the room. Maybe he took a shower, I don't know. He had his own bathroom. I didn't see him after that."

"When was this? When you left him?"

"Maybe 8:00. Maybe 7:45."

"Did he lock his door?"

"Outside or inside?"

"Inside. The door to his room."

"No," she said, "It's a house. None of the doors have locks."

"Not even Andrew's?"

"Not his either."

"Did you hear anything? And did you see anybody?"

"No. I stayed upstairs. I took a shower, and, well, I felt pretty tired, so I thought I'd just loaf around, look at my email, read a book. I had been reading a novel, and I remembered I left it in the dining room, or maybe the living room. So I went downstairs. Then I heard the doorbell.... It was you. I opened the door, and I talked to you. After that, I went back to my room, and that's about it. No, I didn't see anybody else. That doesn't mean they weren't there. In fact, Kurt says he saw *me*...."

"Did you hear anything?

"Not a sound. Anyway, you have to know something about the layout of the house. Most of the bedrooms are on the second and third floors. Andrew's room was the only one on the ground floor. It was more private than the rest of the rooms. He wanted it that way. He had his own entrance, you know that."

"And the other people? The people in the house? Were they around?"

"Well, I'm not sure. Billy was sick. He left a note in the kitchen. Went to the emergency room. He didn't come back until after midnight. Anyway, that's what he said. Fletcher and Lydia had gone out. He's a medical student. I don't know when they got back. I think he spent the night in her room. He has his own place, but sometimes he stays here, in Lydia's room. Kurt and Chuck, no idea. Carmen—also, no idea. I mean, we don't check up on each other."

"So ... it could have been—"

"Anybody. Or somebody from outside."

"Doesn't seem likely," I said.

She nodded. I still had no idea why she thought she needed a lawyer. She began to talk again. She said, "Let me tell you something about myself. I'm from the Midwest, suburb of Chicago. I went to school in Chicago, DePaul University. It's in downtown Chicago. I decided to go to the west coast, to LA. Because of weather. I was sick of ice and snow. And I was sick of my family. My mother had gotten religion in her old age, and she was totally intolerable. Always going on about the Bible. Could drive you nuts. Anyway, I had some cousins, in LA, and an aunt, and some friends I made in college.

"I met Andrew because of the earthquake. You know all about it, *The Earth Moved*, Andrew's project...."

"Right. We talked about it."

"Well, I'm in it," she said. "I'm one of his prize exhibits. I was with a guy. We were having sex, the earthquake started, and I panicked and ran into the street, I mean stark naked. I have a thing about earthquakes, they freak me out totally.... This guy, Jordan, he ran after me. He was afraid I would do something crazy, and I was acting crazy, I have to admit it. I mean, in my life, I tend to put on a show, you know, I let people think I'm tough as nails, but underneath, I'm just as neurotic as the next one. Anyway, he ran after me, Jordan did. He was afraid I'd do something weird, as if running out naked in the street isn't weird enough. He was wrapped in a towel, and then it fell off, which isn't surprising.... Just try running through the streets with nothing on but a towel, and you'll see what I mean."

I could readily imagine. "Andrew told me about this incident," I said. "But no names."

She went on: "Anyway, it was all over in a few minutes, and I stopped freaking out. The shaking stopped, and I realized, this was crazy, what I was doing. Jordan and I were standing there laughing, totally naked, in the middle of the street, and then we went back in, straight to the bedroom. He said, well, there's no structural damage, and I said to him, OK, prove it. By then I was calmed down. We got back in bed and finished up what we started. The earthquake, well, aside from breaking a few dishes, all it seemed to do was make Jordan terrifically horny.

"But I found out later about the videotape. Andrew had it. This moron who lived upstairs of Jordan—he always struck me as the closest thing to a pervert—somehow, he had the idea and the presence of mind to look out the window, get the camera, and film the whole thing. It was night-time, but there was a street light there, blazing away. He could see absolutely everything. Then I guess he saw Andrew's ad in the paper, and he gave the film to Andrew. Or maybe he sold it, whatever."

"This guy Jordan—who was he?"

"Just a friend. A married friend, actually. Not married to me, though."

"And you? You were single, right?"

"As a matter of fact, I was married too. But that didn't last. Even before Jordan, we weren't getting along. Never mind. I'm divorced now."

"And how did you find out, about the tape? I mean, that Andrew had it."

She said: "He came to see me. He said he thought maybe he needed my permission, he didn't want a lawsuit."

"And you gave it to him? The permission? Didn't you find the whole thing, well, embarrassing?"

"Of course I found it embarrassing. I wouldn't want my mother to see the tape. But, for God's sake, this is the modern world. What did you see on the tape? Two naked bodies. Big deal. So, in the end, I told him it was OK. You know, he had a kind of snake-like charm. Andrew wasn't your ordinary guy. He wasn't white-bread. I was getting mighty tired of Jordan. Always whining about his wife, and so on. Andrew fascinated me. So I said, OK, but why don't you block out the faces, so people won't recognize us? He said, sure, sure. He said, I'll do that. But of course he had no intention of doing any such thing. He was lying."

"Lying? You think so?"

"I think he'd blush if he told the truth. You couldn't trust Andrew. But I didn't know that yet. And anyway, I didn't care. Block out the faces, or don't block out the faces: I really didn't feel it made much difference."

"And this guy Jordan? Did he give his permission?"

She said, "How the hell should I know? That was Andrew's business. Anyway, Andrew and I became friendly. Then very friendly. Look: more and more, I saw that he was a skunk, a liar, maybe a sociopath. But I wasn't marrying the guy. I had gotten a divorce, I was on the point of dumping Jordan, and Andrew was just what the doctor ordered. He turned me on. Believe me, I know what I'm doing.... We were just using each other, that's all. Anyway, he moved up here, and I came too. Not with him. Not like that. But I was sick of LA and wanted a change. So I came here, to Silicon Valley. I got a job and I moved into Andrew's house. Well, it's not Andrew's house, but you know what I mean.

"But look, all this is background. It's not why I'm here. I'm just nervous about this whole investigation. The police, they're talking to everybody. And everybody remembers I went to Andrew's room. Kurt saw me come out, but nobody saw Andrew come out. You know, maybe I killed him, and then just walked out, as bold as brass, and just closed the door...."

"But the time of death?"

"Oh, you're reading too many mysteries, Frank. They say he was killed between this and that hour, but they can't say he was dead at 8:00 exactly. And of course, Kurt told them some things which, well, I rather he didn't. He told them that I went in the room and rummaged around. *After* we found the body. Which I did. I admit it. But so what? He was already dead. Anyway, I've been answering so many questions my head spins.

They're driving me crazy. Yesterday, I told them I was so upset, I couldn't answer questions, I was under a doctor's care...."

"Is this true?"

"Not exactly. I got a prescription from Fletcher, something for my nerves. He's Lydia's boyfriend, and he's a resident—so that counts as a doctor, doesn't it? Not that I took the medicine. I can't stand people who take pills all the time. Look: I don't care if it's a lie. I needed time, to think and to see you. I need your advice...."

"My advice? On what?"

She said: "Well, first of all, all these questions. Do I really have to put up with them? You know, questions, questions, where were you blah blah, and why did you do such and such? Maybe they think I killed Andrew. They kept asking me, why did you go in the room? You knew that Andrew Wright was dead, you knew the police had been called, and you went into the room. Why was that? I told them I had been in Andrew's room before, earlier in the evening, and I left something behind. In there before, they asked. For what purpose? I said, none of your business. They said, oh, but it is our business.... I said, well if you must know, we had sexual intercourse. That shut them up for a while. That's something they respect. But then they said, well, what was it you left behind, if we might ask. I said, a bracelet, a gold bracelet. Of course, they didn't believe me. Maybe I should have said I left my bra behind."

"And?"

"Well, then there were a million more questions. The sex thing, that really got their attention. They wanted to know all about it. What was my relationship with the deceased, blah blah. I could see myself becoming more and more suspicious in their eyes. Crime of passion, or jealousy or something. That's when I said, I can't answer any more questions, I'm too upset. You have no right and this has been a terrible shock, can't you understand that? We were so close, Andrew and I, can you imagine how I feel, and so on. Then I squeezed some tears out of my eyes, and I said, the doctor told me to avoid stress, I'm too involved emotionally, and that line of crap. So they had to give me a little breathing space."

"Did they believe you? About the shock, the doctor's advice, and all that?"

"Of course not. They never believe anybody. That's their business. They deal with liars and slimeballs every day. They think everybody's in that category. Anyway, I *was* lying, but that's not the point. They weren't about to arrest me, you know, read me my rights or that kind of thing. They did believe that I had a thing going on with Andrew, so naturally I'd be upset. Anyway, your lover gets smothered, it's enough to throw anybody off their stride. Even without the sex angle, dead bodies upset people, unless you're in the dead body business, like those police guys I suppose. So they're letting me alone for now."

I still didn't see where I came in. "Sheila," I said, "OK, I hear you. But what do you want me to do? I don't get it."

"I want you to represent me. Be my lawyer."

"Represent you?"

"Look, I've seen it on TV. The police question people. They have a lawyer sitting next to them, whispering God-knows-what in their ear. Or maybe it's just a security blanket. I want a lawyer the next time they question me. Somebody who knows my rights."

"Sheila," I said, "I'll say it again: I'm not a criminal lawyer. I don't do that kind of work. You need an expert. If you need somebody at all."

"Alright," she said. "I hear you. But there's something else. And here I *know* you can help me. It concerns you personally."

"Me personally?" I said, with a slight hint of anxiety in my voice.

"Here's the story," she said. "I went back into the room, you know that. And I wasn't looking for any bracelet. I went through his desk, file cabinets, in a hurry. I wanted to get rid of the tape, the notes, if I could find it, you know, the material for his book *The Earth Moved*, that thing. I didn't find the stuff. Of course, I didn't have much time. And, look, I'm tough, I've been through a lot, but for God's sake, there *was* a dead body in the room. Andrew was lying there stone cold dead, and he looked all funny. Here's this man, a couple of hours before we were making love, and now he's a corpse. It gave me the creeps, you can imagine. I couldn't wait to get out of there. The stuff was gone, I tell you. Unless he hid it someplace. But I did find something else. He's got a computer in his room, and a printer. He had obviously printed something out, but the sheet of paper was still sitting in the printer. I guess whoever killed him overlooked it, or wasn't interested, or whatever. I picked it up, and took it with me."

"And?"

"I want you to explain it to me. I've got it here, with me."

"I still don't see...."

She opened her bag, and took out a plain white sheet of paper, which she handed to me. I started reading. At the top, it said, Topics to be Covered in Conversation with Attorney Frank May. Then, underneath, there were a few lines of text: "Discuss incorporation, and the tax aspects. Arrangements with net-works. Should there be open bidding? Hiring of agent? Possible provisions with regard to sudden death of X. How much has to be disclosed? Chances of some kind of liability. Licensing arrangements and foreign rights?"

I felt sick to my stomach.

She said, "OK, Mr. Lawyer, what's this all about? I know he was going to see you, and I thought he was going to talk to you about his project—you know, the earthquake thing, his book. But this doesn't make sense to me. What's this busi-ness about the 'sudden death of X'? Who is this X, and what is this all about?"

"Did you show this to the police?"

"Of course not. Do you think I'm crazy? The less they know the better."

"Sheila, I'm not sure that's the right attitude. For one thing, you could get in trouble. This is evidence. You shouldn't have taken it." But of course I was actually glad she had taken it. This woman was protecting me—not for my sake, I suppose. Still, I liked the result. First, she tore up the note, and then she took this piece of paper and kept this too from the police. And it had my actual name on it yet!

"Don't be a baby," she said. "Just tell me, what does it mean?"

I thought it over for a minute or two. Should I say something about Andrew's crazy idea? The silence was oppressive. I felt her eyes boring into me. She was saying to herself, what is he hiding?

I decided to tell her. I don't know why. Maybe it was foolish. Maybe it was even a breach of confidence, although, since Andrew was dead, his confidences hardly mattered. So, despite my doubts, I told her everything. About Andrew's plan. The murder—fake or not, I still wasn't sure—in the house, a murder that would be televised. I told her, too, that I had advised Andrew that it would never work, that it was a bad idea, and my advice to him was to forget about it. "And I thought he had," I said. "Forgotten it, I mean. Then he called me up, and said he was going ahead, that he had worked out the details, and so on. He wanted me to come over and talk to him about it."

"And you did?"

"I tried to. I couldn't imagine what he had in mind, and I wanted no part of it. But I was curious, I have to admit. So I went there. That's when I saw you. Remember? He didn't answer the door. He was probably already dead."

Sheila didn't strike me as a person who was easily thrown for a loop. But she seemed utterly amazed at my story. "You can't be serious. Killing somebody on TV?"

"That's what he said."

"God. He was even crazier than I thought."

"And you ... knew nothing about this?"

"Absolutely nothing."

"And the other people in the house?"

"As far as I know, they didn't. Nobody mentioned it at least."

But somebody knew about it, I thought to myself. Somebody killed Andrew, maybe to stop him from going through with the plan. Or maybe because of the tapes and the rest of the material on *The Earth Moved*. Maybe somebody didn't want any of this to come to light. Andrew said there was some amazing stuff in his files. Maybe there was something so amazing a person might kill to get rid of it.

"I can't believe this," Sheila said. "The bastard. We were all supposed to be guinea pigs in his little reality show. What a bastard."

I said nothing. What was there to say? She went on: "And he was actually going to go through with it? He actually had some sort of plan, some way to carry it out?"

"That's what he said."

"And you have no idea what it was?"

"No, I don't. I guess he would have told me, but he never got the chance."

That was yet another thought. Could it be that his appointment with me was some sort of trigger? That I had to be kept from hearing his plan?

Her face was white as a sheet. Suddenly she said: "I've got to go." She got up abruptly and left my office. I thought it was odd behavior. Maybe she needed time and space, she needed to think, to digest what I'd told her. Who can blame her? I felt the same way myself.

4

I did need time to think. But I also had to earn a living. I spent the rest of the day in honest labor, working on legal matters.

I had an appointment with one of my oldest clients, Lily Morley—oldest in both senses of the word. She was a nice white-haired lady on the wrong side of 80, who wanted to "do something" for her granddaughter Tiffany.

"Do you think I should set up a trust?" she asked me. "My neighbor, Mrs. Switzer, said she did that for *her* granddaughter."

I thought it was a good idea, considering the circumstances. Lily's daughter had been a single mother, who died in an auto accident. I can't remember who took Tiffany in. I had met her only once, a few years back, when she brought her grandma to see me. Tiffany had scraggly hair, which she dyed some weird color, and a nose ring. When she opened her mouth, she had one of those disgusting things through her tongue. Tiffany was now 22. She had dropped out of college, and made pottery or candles or something along those lines. She lived with some sort of boyfriend. I had never met him. He too probably had something stuck through his tongue, and who knows, maybe his penis as well. I assume the two of them were stoned half the time. Or could it be that these were nothing but stereotypes and prejudices? Tiffany wasn't all bad. Perhaps not bad at all. She was nice to her grandmother, very thoughtful, and even respectful.

"Lily," I said, "I think a trust is a good idea. She's a good girl, but I wouldn't let her get her hands on the principal."

She nodded her head. "Oh, Frank, I'm afraid you're right. Mr. Morley left her some money," she said, "in his will. And she spent it all in a year. Every penny of it. Went to India or Nepal or some place like that, and I was worried sick. I don't think there were telephones over there. Maybe it was Bhutan. I can't remember. She met some awful boy who took some of the money. I love her, but she has no money sense at all."

I kept thinking of Tiffany, with her nose rings. I pictured her smoking pot or whatever in Katmandu. Was this how my own daughters would turn out, God forbid? The thought was unsettling. I dismissed it. In general, working on other people's affairs was therapeutic. It took my mind off my troubles, specifically, off worries about what would become of my daughters.

It took my mind off the case of Andrew Wright as well. That was worse than the thought of a future full of nose rings. I was still terrified at the idea that I might get sucked into that tawdry affair. I distrusted Sheila's motives, but so far she had protected me. I had some worries about the old man next door, but how could he possibly identify me?

A day or so went by, without a phone call from police authorities or a knock on the door. Then Sheila called. She wanted to see me again, "as soon as possible." I had no particular desire to see her, but I had to say yes. I fixed a time in the afternoon, right after lunch, and she hesitated a minute, saying something about her job, but then she agreed.

She came in promptly, sat down in my office, and without any preliminaries, she launched into the business at hand. "Well, we had a kind of council of war, at the house."

"Council of war?"

"Frank, it's just an expression. We had a house meeting. Everybody but the old lady. She wasn't at her best, and there was no point in having her around. We put her in her room, with the television on, full blast. She'll watch anything, the weather channel, evangelists. It's all the same to her. She's a bit deaf anyway. But the rest of us came to the meeting. I'm the one that called for it. I told everybody it was terrifically important. They knew it had something to do with Andrew, of course."

"And?"

"Well, I told them what Andrew had in mind. I told them exactly the things you told me. This crazy idea, the cameras, a murder, and televising it for the whole world to see."

I was horrified. As far as I was concerned, the less people who knew about Andrew's plans the better. My face must have told her the story. She said: "You're shocked?"

"Frankly, Sheila—yes. Why on earth did you do that?"

"Because I wanted to know who else knew about it. You know, *somebody* did."

"Why did you say that?"

"Figure it out for yourself, Frank. Andrew told you he had worked things out, right? Now, we know he was a terrific liar. A bullshit artist, first class. But he wouldn't have called you, right? Unless he had gotten, well, a little farther along with these wild and crazy plans. He must have figured out how to do this, and he must have recruited somebody, no? A victim, maybe the murderer."

"Unless the 'victim' wouldn't *know* he was the victim, until it was too late. That's the usual thing with victims, isn't it? And maybe Andrew was going to be the killer himself," I said.

"Andrew? No way. I can't imagine it," she said, "he wouldn't take that risk. I mean, he wasn't the type. No, I figure, it was somebody else."

"But who would do such a thing? Hello, I'd like you to kill somebody. Why would somebody agree?"

"Frank, how should I know? Anyway, I can think of some reasons. The usual ones. Especially money. Take a hitman: I mean, they kill other people for the money. I suppose Andrew could dangle money in front of somebody."

"But Sheila, you know the people in your house. I don't. Is there an obvious killer there? For money or whatever?"

She shrugged her shoulders. "Everybody has a price," she said.

"Right," I said, "and think of all the nice things you can buy on death row."

"Maybe he was blackmailing somebody," she said. "I wouldn't put it past him."

I said, "I suppose. Anyway, did you get results? Did you find anything out?"

She said, "Nothing. Everybody pretended to be shocked. We knew about the camera deal, you know, the cameras in the house. But not this business ... about the murder. They asked me a million questions, but I didn't have any answers. They were all totally freaked out. They've all been on edge, ever since Andrew died, you can understand that. And then, on top of that, here comes this scheme. They can put two and two together."

"And get what?"

"They get the idea that somebody in the house was going to be playing the role of a killer—more than a role, somebody was going to *be* a killer. Besides, somebody in the house probably *was* a killer. They just couldn't believe it, blah blah, and they were into denial, oh, this can't be right, and all that shit. But in the end, they had to believe me. Had to. Because I was telling the truth. And because of the source of my information."

"The source? Sheila, you didn't!"

"I did, Frank. You're the source, aren't you? I told them that."

"Oh, God."

"They all want to come see you, Frank."

I had a sinking feeling in the pit of my stomach. "Sheila, what have you done to me? And why do they want to see me?"

She said, "I'll tell you. You know what a blowhard Andrew was. They didn't know about the murder business, but, as I said, they knew about the cameras. I'll get back to that. Anyway, they knew Andrew had these big ideas, and he kept saying: don't worry about technicalities, I've got a smart lawyer, he'll fix everything."

All I could do was say "oh, God" again.

"They thought that you were drawing up papers, contracts, you know, all that stuff, about the cameras and the TV deal. I have to tell you, the last big house meeting we had was about those cameras. Andrew told us his idea, you know, about the cameras all over the house; and he opened it up for discussion."

"And what did people say?"

"Some people were dead set against it. That's no big surprise. I mean, when we rented our rooms, we didn't imagine we were going to be in some kind of reality TV show. The upshot was, there was a vote...."

"And?"

"I was surprised. The cameras won. Meanwhile, during the argument, Andrew kept making his pitch. He said all sorts of things. He had a gift of gab.... But the one thing he kept harping on was *you*...."

"Me?"

"Yes, you. He kept saying, I've got this lawyer, his name's Frank May. He's a real hot-shot. He does all of these deals, big deals, big clients, famous people, you know, TV and Hollywood. He represents them. There's real money here. You can't throw away real money. All that bullshit. Did people believe it? I think so. Look: I knew what a phony he was, but frankly, he was so smooth about it, even *I* started thinking, maybe he's right."

I was speechless. The sheer audacity of the late Andrew Wright absolutely overwhelmed me. And I was scared. The last thing I wanted was involvement in this mess. But it was coming at me, like a roaring locomotive with steam pouring out of it, and I felt as if I was tied down on the railroad tracks, or paralyzed, unable to move or get out of the way.

I said, feebly, "And that's why ... they want to see me?"

"They want to know about these plans, these crazy plans: the cameras, the murder. They think you know something."

"Sheila, I don't know a thing."

"Well, can you tell them that? Come over to the house. Talk to us. That wouldn't kill you, Frank. Otherwise, they'll all be knocking at your door."

In a way, I hated the idea, but maybe it was for the best. Maybe I could get rid of them that way. I could tell them point-blank that Andrew was a liar, that I knew nothing, really, that he told me about his plans, yes, but I refused to have anything to do with them, that I had nothing to tell them at all, nothing of any use. And by the way, I wasn't an entertainment lawyer. I didn't do big deals. I didn't have Tom Cruise for a client. I knew as much about Hollywood as they did. Basta. And goodbye. Out of their lives forever.

She said, "Well, Frank, is it a deal?"

"It's a deal," I answered.

"Great. When will you come? The sooner the better."

"You tell me."

She replied: "Thursday? About 8:00?"

"OK. Meanwhile, Sheila, can you tell me something about the people? The ones in the house. I think you said, there were eight of you. Or maybe it's seven now that Andrew, uh, is dead...."

"You'll meet them all," said Sheila. "First of all, there's the old lady. She doesn't really count. I don't know if she'll be there. She's pretty loopy, most of the time. She's in and out, if you know what I mean. She can't get it through her head that's Andrew's dead. She keeps saying, where's Andrew? I haven't seen Andrew. Chuck—I'll tell you about Chuck in a minute—he said, 'Look, grandma, he's dead. You know he's dead. You're the one who found him dead.'"

"She did?"

"She did. I mean, she wanders through the house, sometimes. She has good days and bad days. On the bad days, she goes around and around in some sort of a daze. Sometimes she even wanders out into the street, but we always fetch her back. Or she roams around the house. Sometimes she makes a mistake, goes in the wrong door. Can be awfully embarrassing at times. She came in once when Lydia was hooking up with her boyfriend, Fletcher. I think she said excuse me and walked out. She has funny sleep habits. It's dementia, it ruins your sleep. I read that somewhere. Anyway, she went in to Andrew's room, about 11:00 that night. I was in my room, I was already asleep. Usually I stay up later, but I was really zoned out that day...."

"Oh, yes: Lydia and Fletcher went to the movies. They said they asked Carmen along, but she said she had a headache.... So I guess she stayed home. Billy got sick and went somewhere, the emergency room I think, something like that. I think I told you. He's in poor health. I don't know the details. Maybe he's a hypochondriac. He came back late at night. Chuck was around—at least he was around when Angelica found the body. I think he was watching TV. I have no idea what Kurt was up to. Well, by midnight, everybody was home—by that time the police were there, too, as you can imagine. The place was crawling with them. Forensic experts, detectives, God knows what else. People looking for fingerprints, photographers, who knows?

"But that was later. It was about 11:00, I said, and Angelica had wandered into Andrew's room. She came out and said to Chuck, I think Andrew's dead. He looks just like my nephew did, when I found him. Found who? My nephew she said. He was in that same room. Then she started going on and on about her nephew. Chuck, he got up, went to the room himself—there was Andrew, and he *was* dead.... He closed the door, took Angelica back to her room, very gently, and then he came upstairs, woke me up and told me: we've got a problem here, Sheila. I said what's up, and he said Andrew's dead. He's in his room and he's dead. Of course, I was shocked, and then Chuck said, there's something fishy about it, too. He's lying on his bed, and there's a huge bruise on the back of his head, and I've got an awful feeling this wasn't an accident...."

"That must have been a shock."

"What do you think?"

I said, "I suppose you called the police right away."

"No, we didn't. Chuck wanted to, but I said, don't call them. Not yet. He said, why? I said, I want to go in there.... Can you wait ten minutes? He said: don't go in there, Sheila, it's not something you want to see. But I told him, I'm not squeamish."

"So you went...."

"Well, I did. Chuck wasn't happy. He said, you know, you're not supposed to touch things. Suppose somebody killed Andrew, and it's a job for the police. I said, well, why do you think so? I mean, maybe he fell, and got that bruise, and it was concussion or something. He said, I think he was smothered. There was a pillow over his head.... You can't do that to yourself.

"I went in anyway. Before the police got there. I told you that. That's when I picked up the note you wrote, and put it in my pocket. I don't think Chuck even noticed the note. It was right there on the floor, but he had other things on his mind—a dead body, for one thing. Anyway, I went in because I wanted to find the material, the stuff about the earthquake. I knew exactly where he kept it. He had a file cabinet, three drawers. The stuff was in the top drawer."

"And?"

"It wasn't there. Either he had moved it, which I doubt, or destroyed it himself, which is impossible. Why should he? Or somebody took it."

"Who? You don't mean ... whoever killed Andrew?"

"Well, who else?"

I said: "So you think there was something there, something in that stuff, that this somebody wanted and ... maybe it's why they killed him."

She shrugged her shoulder. "I'm not playing guessing games, Frank. I have no idea."

I couldn't help wondering, what did *Sheila* want? Why did she go into Andrew's room? What was she looking for, and why? She said she was looking for the material he had gathered for his earthquake book. Was she telling the truth? And if so, why worry about that book? What was so crucial about the material? True, there was a video that showed her standing naked in the middle of the street. Was she embarrassed? It didn't seem quite in character. Was it important enough for her to break the rules and disrupt a crime scene? Everybody knows from TV that this is forbidden. Yet she went into a room with a corpse lying on the bed, and rummaged through the files.

I couldn't help asking her: why?

"I'd rather not say, if you don't mind."

"Actually," I said, "I do mind."

"Well, Frank, I'm afraid you'll just have to curb your curiosity."

"But you're making me suspicious, Sheila."

"Suspicious? Of what? Of killing Andrew? Honestly,

Frank."

"No, not that…. But you're saying you looked for the stuff, and it wasn't there. But maybe it *was* there, and you just took it."

"Suit yourself. I'm telling you I didn't."

This was going nowhere. She changed the subject. "Let's get back to the point, Frank. When are you coming out to the house?"

"I'm not sure I want to."

"Oh come on. Anyway," she added, "Somebody told me you're good at this kind of thing. Solving mysteries."

"Well, somebody told you wrong. I'm not a detective, not even an amateur. And I especially want nothing to do with this particular affair."

"But you've got to come out to the house, meet people, talk to them. Before we all move on. You said you would. They're all on edge. Can you blame them? A murder in the house, and the police, the yellow tape, reporters from the stupid local paper, and so on. It's like some kind of bad cop show on TV. I wouldn't be surprised if all of us didn't start packing our bags and getting the hell out of there, as soon as we can. That's why I want you to come *soon* and talk to us."

"What? All together?"

"No, one at a time."

"I really don't want to." I know I had agreed to come on Thursday; but now I was sorry I had said so. "Maybe I shouldn't come, after all."

But she insisted, and she had a trump card, too, which she was only too willing to play: the note under the door. So, reluctant as I was, in the end I agreed to stick to my promise: Thursday night at 8:00. It was against my better judgment, as the phrase goes. But half or more of what we do in life is against our better judgment. Our better judgment is a bore and a nag. Everything that's exciting and novel is against our better judgment. Besides, I was curious about the house itself. The night Andrew died, I never actually got inside.

"We'll all be there, Frank," she said.

"Let me get the cast of characters straight," I said. "There's Angelica, and there was Andrew. And you, Sheila. And you mentioned some other names. Lydia, you said; and Chuck and Kurt. And somebody named Fletcher, the med student?"

"Fletcher doesn't live there. He's Lydia's boyfriend. He just comes over. Sometimes he spends the night. There's also Billy, he's a real geek.... And a woman named Carmen. That's the bunch."

"And ... you were all there that night?

"We were all there at dinner, I told you that. Maybe people went out later. I don't know, I don't keep track of their comings and goings."

I made a note of the names and tried to remember them: Sheila, Angelica, Lydia, and Carmen; Billy, Kurt, and Chuck; perhaps also Fletcher. Mentally, I prepared to meet them in person.

5

Like a good husband, I brought Celia up to date. She listened carefully. This was right after dinner, when the dishes had been cleared away and stashed in the dishwasher, and the girls had disappeared into their rooms.

Celia said, "Do you want my advice?"

I didn't really, because I knew what it would be. Don't go to the house. Absolutely don't go. Don't touch the thing with a ten-foot pole.

It's like what I said about our better judgment. Celia is the very personification of a better judgment. That's one of the reasons I love her. She is terrifically sensible. But I don't always listen to her. That's the honest truth. And this was definitely going to be one of those situations.

Besides, there was Sheila, and her power over me—all because of that note I wrote, which turned out to have been a terrible mistake.

But I do have a lively curiosity. You might call me nosy, but I think that's unfair. I don't like to tell other people about myself; but I love to hear *their* stories. Maybe that's what led me to the practice of law. A lot of my classmates are making tons of money, merging corporations, or filing SEC forms or developing huge shopping centers, and whatever else they do. They also work 100 hours a week. I don't envy them. I like my kind of practice. I like talking to people, hearing about their lives, why they don't want to leave a dime to their snotty daughter, why they think their hair salon is going bankrupt, why they don't trust their wife or husband with the management of money or an estate. I like all the gory details about family histories and relationships, and the aches and pains and thrills and chills of running a small business in partnership with your cousin who gambles too much, or that the chef in your restaurant is a drunk who doesn't show up half the time. I love to hear every word of it.

As a lawyer, I have an excuse for asking all sorts of impertinent questions. I would even inquire about peoples' sex lives, if I could think of a reason to ask. Actually, I do get a whiff of the salacious in some of the more tangled family matters—and most definitely in some of the divorce cases I've handled.

So Celia gave me good advice, and she knew and I knew that I had no intention of taking it. I was going to run the risk of getting totally enmeshed in a sordid but interesting affair.

I had come to the conclusion that the world was probably better off without Andrew Wright, all things considered. But his sheer audacity fascinated me. And the whole setup—the house, the old lady, the cast of characters, and, yes, the murder itself—drew me like a moth to the flame. So I left the office a shade earlier than usual and, after dinner at home, got in my car and drove to Palo Alto, notebook in hand, with a curiosity that gnawed at me—made me insatiably hungry, a kind of metaphorical tapeworm in my belly.

I rang the doorbell. Sheila opened it. I peeked into a large living room. She led me in and I had a chance to take a closer look. Actually, the house was something of a disappointment, as I should have known. It was certainly grand. The living room was immense, and a beautiful staircase of carved wood led to the second floor. But aside from a few pieces that were obviously left over from better times, the furniture was late Salvation Army or bottom-of-the-line Sears. The place was clean but nondescript. There were few pictures on the wall: one or two dreary landscapes and a large oil painting of a dog.

I never got to see the upstairs. There were three floors, I was told, with many bedrooms and bathrooms. On the main floor was this huge living room, a dining room, a kitchen—both of them nothing special—and a couple of rooms that were originally studies or libraries or whatnot. One of them of course was the maid's room that the late Andrew Wright had lived in, and where he came to an untimely end.

Sheila led me into the living room. There was nobody there. I said, "Where's your housemates?" She said, "They're in their rooms. You'll talk to them one by one. They each have something to say."

I found this odd. Creepy, even. Suddenly I had an attack of cold feet. (Celia's better judgment was right, as usual.) What on earth was I doing here? What kind of questions were they going to ask? And how was I going to answer them?

Sheila said, "You can talk to me first."

"I already have, Sheila."

"Well, we can talk some more." She motioned me toward a somewhat beat-up couch, and I sat down.

She said, "I know you keep saying, you're not a detective, you don't do criminal work, you don't have any knack for this sort of thing; but frankly, none of us believe you. They've heard all kinds of rumors, about other cases, how you solved them...."

"Cases? Solved? No way," I said. "Sometimes I got lucky...."

"Well, maybe you can get lucky again. Maybe you can find out who killed Andrew."

I said: "I can understand that you want that, Sheila, believe me. You and he were close, and it's natural, you know, grief, frustration, anger."

"Oh, skip it, Frank. Don't talk to me as if I'm a gold-star mother or something. On the personal level, I didn't care that much about Andrew. Despite the sex. It's not about Andrew at all. It's the tension in the house. It's like something out of Agatha Christie, you know, *Ten Little Indians*, or whatever. People can't help thinking it could be one of us. They think they're living in the same house as a murderer."

I said, "It could have been an outsider. He had his own entrance. Somebody could have come over, you know, knocked on the door, rang the bell. Andrew answers it, lets them in. Nobody else would see this, right?" Of course, in my mind I could see the old man watching *me* from across the way, so I knew someone *could* have seen the killer—or (gulp) me.

"Sure. It's possible. Or maybe someone did see that. But why would he let somebody in?"

"Well, maybe it was somebody he knew," I said. "Remember, he was expecting me, but later. Anyway, suppose it *was* somebody he knew, somebody who didn't live here. After all, why would somebody who lived here go outside and ring his bell? Anyway, I wouldn't rule anything out. But I'm sure the police are looking into this."

"Oh, they're looking and looking, I suppose," she said. "Looking for a mysterious stranger. But they won't find one."

"Why not?"

"Because for one thing, they just don't have anything to go on. All they have is a statement from the old creep who lives next door. He's a pain in the ass, always has been. He's retired. He's got nothing else to do. He lives with his son and daughter-in-law. They all hate each other, but that's not the issue. He's always complaining, complaining. Mostly about noise."

"What noise?"

"Exactly. There never was any noise. You'd think we were a frat house with kegs of beer, people screwing in the hallways, and a rap group that could make anybody deaf. Anyway, what does he care about noise? He can't hear the noise. He wears a hearing aid, but it doesn't seem to do him any good. He's just an old fart with too much time on his hands. Andrew, actually, was always trying to humor him. He was afraid the guy would complain to the zoning authorities, or the city, or whoever's in charge. Andrew didn't want the city poking their nose in. I mean, it's not exactly legal, running a boarding house in this fancy neighborhood. We're probably the only people for blocks around who don't have stock options or a portfolio."

"Do you happen to know what the old man said? To the police?" I tried to sound neutral, nonchalant.

"He says he saw people. He sits in his window, more or less spying on us. He can see anybody who comes in the side door, anybody who knocks on Andrew's door."

As you can imagine, this was making me nervous.

She went on: "He said he was watching all the time, the whole evening. I mean, do you believe it? No TV, no visits to the bathroom, nothing. He's lying. He could have easily missed somebody. Anyway, he said he saw two people, people who came to see Andrew. The police wrote it all down, naturally. The old guy also told the story to the newspapers. He loved the attention. Probably the publicity gave him his first erection in twenty years."

I made a mental note never to revisit that imagery, ever. But I was more concerned with how I'd been spotted at the door that evening. "He said he saw ... two guys? Not together, though?"

"I'm just going by what I read in the paper. Around 7:00 or so, he saw a man. Couldn't identify him.... The man rang the bell. Andrew let him in, but the man didn't stay long."

"A man? Who was it?"

"Who the hell knows? Maybe he was confused, the old man. Maybe it was somebody from Jehovah's Witnesses."

I doubted that last observation: don't they always travel in pairs? Like the buddy system for a grade school field trip? "Did he give a description?"

"Not really. He said the guy was wearing a blue suit, jacket, tie, you know. That's about all he could say. Old or young? Middle-aged, maybe. Not much to go on. The people from Jehovah's Witnesses always wear suits. It could have been a cable TV salesman, but I doubt it. Or it could have been the murderer."

"Maybe," I said. "But ... was this before you and Andrew, uh, got together?"

She said, "Well, if the old fart is right about what time it was, then I guess so. But who knows how good he is at telling time? I think we had our little fun around 7:30. I don't know, exactly. I wasn't timing things. Anyway, the old man says he saw the guy leave. And then around 8:00, he said, another guy came to the door and rang the bell. Nobody answered. That was you."

"Do the police know ... it was me?"

"Frank," she said. "They don't. They just know they have two mysterious strangers. No idea who they are. I'm the only one who knows about you. And I'm not talking."

I was nervous, of course. But so long as Sheila kept quiet, there was no risk of exposure. After all, what could the old guy see? The top of my head? I wondered who the other visitor was. No way to know. Curiously, between around 7:00 and 8:00, Andrew Wright managed to have sex, entertain a visitor, and get himself murdered. It was a tight squeeze. It would be less tight if the visitor was the person who killed him. But that couldn't be, unless Sheila was lying or if she made love to a corpse.

I was turning all this over in my mind. Sheila interrupted my chain of thought. She got up, and said, "Are you ready Frank? I'll send them in."

6

I sat on the sofa, waiting for the first customer (so to speak). It was an awkward situation. I kept asking myself, why am I doing this? I never came up with a satisfactory answer.

The first to come in was a man who looked to be about my age, or maybe a few years younger—40 or so. He said, "Hello, my name is Chuck. Chuck Novak."

"I'm Frank. Pleased to meet you."

We shook hands. He had a strong grip. He looked extremely athletic. He was blond with very regular features. His hair was cut extremely short, as if he was a member of the Marine Corps. He was wearing a faded gray t-shirt and blue jeans. You could see the muscles rippling underneath his shirt. He was smiling. Chuck, it turned out, smiled a great deal.

"What can I do for you, Chuck?"

"Not much. It's a mess here, a total mess. You can imagine the atmosphere. I call it our own brand of air pollution. Terribly unhealthy. Jesus! A murder! Who would have thought? Not that Andrew is a great loss to the world. He's not, to be perfectly honest. But still, it's wrong to kill *anybody*."

I nodded my head in understated agreement. He went on. "Sheila said we should kind of introduce ourselves, tell you who we are, what makes us tick. I know I look like an athlete, and I am an athlete. But I don't have an athlete's mentality. I don't believe men should be tough guys. Personally, I'm a strong believer in nonviolence. Like Gandhi, or the Dalai Lama. I'm a total pacifist and a vegetarian. People like Andrew, they lead unhealthy lives. All that red meat, I really think that does something to people. It's like they're eating and drinking blood. OK, he didn't smoke, that's one thing I'll say for him. I wouldn't stay in the same house with him if he smoked."

I interrupted this monolog. "Have you been here long? In this house."

He replied, "Couple of months. I work with computers. I guess I'm one of those Silicon Valley computer types. I'm with Quisquad, Inc. Ever heard of them?"

I hadn't. He said, "We've got some really exciting products. And we're working on a new kind of search engine."

I nodded.

"But I'm not a total geek," he said. "Don't get me wrong. My passion, it's swimming. I swim every day, 5:00 a.m. Gets the juices going. I go to the pool at Stanford, or the YMCA. Stanford has an Olympic pool. In my age class, I'm one of the best there is. It's a big part of my life, swimming is."

He did have a certain pale, waterlogged look to him, despite the muscles.

He went on: "So, I'm always in training, if you know what I mean. I'm really careful, what I eat. Salads, mostly. I think the body can synthesize everything from salads. You don't need other stuff. Look at all the animals that just eat grass. OK, I take vitamins, but I'm not sure it's necessary. I avoid carbs like the plague. And—well, I told you, I don't eat meat. I don't believe in killing living things. Well, oysters and clams. You know, different kinds of shellfish. They don't have brains. I don't think an oyster suffers when you eat it; I mean, I'm not some kind of extreme food nut. They're healthy, too. Oysters. I don't mean the oysters are healthy, I mean it's healthy to eat them. Lots of good stuff in oysters."

"Chuck," I said, "Let's get back to Andrew. This plan of his—the TV program. Did you know about it?"

"Which plan? The cameras? Sure...."

"No, the other thing—the murder thing...."

"Sheila told us all about it last night. I didn't know a thing about it before. You could have knocked me over with a feather. Absolutely crazy. Crazy!"

"But you knew about the camera business. You just said

so," I said.

"That's right."

"And you agreed to that, right?"

"Sure I did. People were surprised, but I liked the idea. I had something in common with Andrew, believe it or not. I'm an ambitious guy. I want to get somewhere. I've got ideas. Software ideas, other ideas. I'm trying to get people interested, venture capitalists, the guys with the money. There's one guy I go swimming with, at the Stanford pool. In the morning, before the team comes on, some of us older guys go swimming. Well, you know what I mean by older. To the students, 30 is old, and when you're 40, you're like Methuselah. Anyway, this guy, he's got millions to invest, you know? He's got a company on Sandhill Road. He comes out all the time and goes swimming. He needs it, too. He's getting fat. It's not good for his swimming. He does tennis, too, so I guess he's trying. We've gotten pretty friendly. I said to him, Mervyn, you've got to cut out the animal fat. It's poison. You're abusing your body...."

I wondered if Andrew purposely rented to people like himself—people who just talked and talked and talked.

Chuck went on. "This Mervyn, he seemed interested. Not totally interested, but at least a little bit interested. I mean, he's not about to throw his money at me. These guys, the venture capital guys, they have to be shrewd. They want to make a killing. So he said, if you could raise some cash, get yourself in a position to help out with the financing, we might talk turkey. My people, he said, don't like to take 100% of the risk. I don't like risks myself, he said. I came right back at him: you don't take risks? Just look at the stuff you're putting in your body, all those potato chips and nachos. Compared to that, I said, this is no risk at all. But he just gave me a smile. Anyway, that's where Andrew comes in."

"Andrew?"

"He came to me with this line about the cameras, in the house. He talked about making a killing. I was skeptical at first."

"Doesn't surprise me."

"Right. He wanted to go out to dinner, talk it over. I said

OK. I suggested a vegetarian place, but he insisted on an Italian restaurant. I ordered a salad. Italians make great salad. I had the dressing on the side. Anyway, I said to him, cameras? Come on, who'd be interested? He said, it's big money, believe me. I said, you're crazy. The old lady, she'll be wandering around the house, Billy will be sulking in his room, what's to see? He said, well, you Chuck, you've got a great body, you know that. The chicks will drool over you. Maybe you can jerk off on camera—can you believe it? He actually suggested that. I said, Andrew, I'm not that kind of person. I have a great deal of personal pride. He said, you can walk around in your underwear, show off your abs. There's lots of women who'll pay good money to see you take a shower, Chuck. I said, Andrew, you honestly expect me to get undressed in front of these cameras? He said, yes, Chuck, I do. And not just you. I said, who else? You can't mean Billy, I told him, he's such a scrawny nerd. He said, well, there's Lydia and Fletcher. I said, you mean, people will watch them make out? He said, damn right, and Sheila, too, making out with me."

"And you agreed?"

"Not right away. I argued with him. I told him, the FCC or whatever it's called, they won't allow you to show sex, not on prime time TV. Even on cable, I don't think they let you. Maybe they have porno channels, I don't know. Anyway, he said, I know all those angles, Chuck. The sex will be on the internet. For the TV show, we'll clean it up a little. No sex. Just you in your underwear. You wear jockey shorts. That's pretty sexy. And Lydia. She's worth seeing in *her* underwear. I said to myself, this guy is out of his mind. He's higher than a kite. I honestly thought maybe he's taking drugs. But, you know, you can get high on sugar, junk food. He was eating a pizza, four different kinds of cheese. That's a tremendous load of fat. And ice cream for dessert, with chocolate sauce. Anyway, he laughed and he said, I'm dead serious, Chuck. This is for real."

"And you said yes? I thought ... from what you just told me—"

"I did say yes. In the end. Listen, I didn't think it would work. But Andrew never took no for an answer. He was that kind of a guy. I have to confess, the idea started to appeal to me. In sort of a malicious way. My ex-wife, she's gotten religion. She's one of these born-again types. She goes around talking about family values, chastity and all that bullshit, and something called the rapture, when I'm going to hell and she's going to be saved. Can you imagine? She's completely out of her mind. She eats meat from slaughtered animals, cheeseburgers and whatever. Still, she's spouting about moral values, etc. I thought about her, her name's Mary, I could just see her watching the show. There I am in my underwear, there's Fletcher and Lydia. She'd have a cow."

He laughed and went on. "Andrew was shrewd, I'll give him that. He sensed that, despite all the stuff I was saying to him, I'm not as prudish as I made out. After all, I'm proud of my body. I work hard on it. I used to go to a nude beach. There's one in San Francisco, but there were too many gay guys there. Not that I have anything against gay people. Hey, everybody's entitled to his thing. A lot of them exercise regularly, they watch their diets. Anyway, frankly, getting back to Andrew, it was the money that sucked me in. Andrew said, Chuck, there's $100,000 for you, up front, if you sign up, if you sign on the dotted line so to speak. We're going to do this thing, one way or another; and if anybody in the house won't go for it, we'll get somebody else...."

"He promised you $100,000?"

"In advance. He said that was just the beginning. He said he had the money, he had investors, they were putting up cash. He said he deposited the money, in escrow, with his lawyer. I could draw on it any time."

"His lawyer? Me?"

"Yes, of course it was you, Frank. You're his lawyer, aren't you? Anyway, he gave us your name, but he said not to call, because it was all still confidential. So ... I was wondering ... about the money. Of course, he's dead and all that, probably the contract is no good. But is there any chance—?"

"Chuck, I hate to break the news to you. It's a complete fabrication. The money. I don't have it. There never was any. He never gave me a nickel. I met him exactly twice in my entire life. There's not a word of truth in what he told you. What he said about me, at any rate."

He was silent for a while. Then he finally said, "I should have guessed. He was a phony, through and through. No wonder somebody killed him. Shit. I really wanted that money."

I said, "Chuck, you were there that night. You were the first to see him dead, besides Angelica. It's none of my business, really, but still, I can't help but be interested. He was a client, sort of. Well, a potential client. Do you have any idea who did this? Any idea at all?"

"Yes and no."

"Yes and no? What's the yes part?"

He paused for a second. Then he said, "Frankly, I'd rather not say. Not now, anyway. Maybe later. I've got to check on some things first."

"Things? What things?"

He smiled. "Can't tell you. I really can't. If I'm wrong, well, let's just leave it at that." And with that slight air of mystery, he left the room.

* * *

I sat for a while, by myself. It was getting dark outside. Those sudden California nightfalls, when the temperature drops like a plummet, and the fog rolls in from the ocean. The sky goes from blue to gold to black. It was a moonless night. There were shadows all over the room. I had an uneasy feeling. Why did I ever get mixed up with Andrew Wright? I should have known no good would come of it. Sooner or later, I would have to deal with the police, and there was nothing I wanted less.

I was thinking these awful thoughts when a young couple came into the room. They introduced themselves: "Hi," said the man, "I'm Fletcher, and this is Lydia." I nodded to them.

Fletcher turned on the light and asked, "Why are you sitting in the dark?" It was a fairly feeble, yellowish light, from a table lamp. But it was better than nothing.

They were an attractive couple. Lydia was in her early 20s, I'd say. She was wearing sandals, a tight t-shirt, and tight black pants, which showed off her body. Her hair was dark blonde, and worn loose over her shoulder. Fletcher was wearing chino pants and a blue Polo shirt. He looked to be about the same age. He was wearing sandals that appeared to match Lydia's. He had a nice smile, unruly brown hair, and one gold earring. Otherwise he seemed extremely normal. Of course, with young people, even university students, all sorts of things can be lurking under their clothes—tattoos, maybe, or navel rings, or even, god forbid, rings on their nipples.

Those were two things I've been absolutely adamant about, as far as my daughters were concerned. They could dye their hair purple or orange. That was reversible, after all. Pierced tongues or navels were completely out. Also tattoos. I don't care how fashionable any of this might be, or become. I want no part of them.

My daughters thought of me as something left over from the dark ages.

From the start, I found Fletcher and Lydia to be pleasant, attractive people. They *looked* pleasant and attractive. I decided that neither of them had anything piercing their navels.

Fletcher was the first one to speak. "I'm an intern," he said. "Stanford Hospital. I'm going to specialize in rheumatology. Lydia's been a graduate student in the communications department. She was studying film. But she's stopping right now."

Lydia spoke up: "I've got a job. I'm an administrative assistant in the political science department. I need to earn some money."

Fletcher continued, "When I'm finished, when I've done my residency and all, and I can earn some good money, she'll go back to the communications department. She's an ABD."

"ABD?"

"All but the dissertation," Lydia said. "Student jargon. It means I don't have any more course work. All I have to do is write my thesis. I don't really have a topic yet."

Fletcher said, "You're the lawyer, right? So everything I say is confidential?"

I replied, "Well, maybe. I'm not *your* lawyer. I'm not anybody's lawyer, frankly. I mean, not in this house. I wasn't really

Andrew's lawyer. He did come to see me, yes; and we talked about some stuff. But it didn't go very far. You're not supposed to speak ill of the dead and all that, but he was one ferocious liar. The things he told people—"

Fletcher interrupted: "It doesn't matter. The confidentiality stuff. I'll just tell you exactly what I told the police. I told them, I had this weird conversation with Andrew. He came to me, he said, Fletcher, you're a medical student. *Was*, I said. I'm an intern now, I'm an actual doctor. He said, whatever; that's even better. He said, I want to talk about poison. Said he was interested in poison. So I asked him, why? He said he was writing a mystery. Suppose I wanted to get a poison, something that couldn't be traced, how would I do it? And could I get it for him?"

"What did you say?"

"I said no, of course. I didn't know about such a poison, and if I did, I wouldn't get it for him. He said, how about rat poison? In the books, they're always using rat poison. I said, do we have rats? He said, no, we don't, that's not the point. Then he dropped the subject. This was, oh, maybe a month ago. Then maybe a week ago, I don't remember exactly, he came and said, forget what I said about poison. I'm not interested anymore, just forget it, OK?"

"Well, what do you make of that?"

Fletcher said, "I don't know. Maybe he was thinking of poison, you know, as a way of killing somebody for this crazy program, this murder thing. Then he changed his mind."

"Maybe."

"I'll be honest with you," he said. "I couldn't stand the guy. He was a real creep. He was always coming on to Lydia. I told him, watch it, buddy. He just laughed and said, it's not the middle ages any more, Fletcher. Queen Victoria's dead, in case you haven't heard the news. Lydia can make up her own mind. If she doesn't like it, she can tell me herself. She doesn't need you. Can you imagine? The colossal gall he had. I think he was the kind of guy who would sneak around, look in the keyholes, just to see what Lydia and I were up to."

Lydia said, "Fletcher, be fair. You don't know that. You're

just guessing."

"Maybe. But, well, somebody was lurking around. I thought I heard somebody, you remember, honey, the other day. I went out in the hall, I saw somebody disappearing around the corner of the hall. Somebody nosy, spying on us."

She said, "It could have been Angelica. She wanders around sometimes. They call it sundowning. People with Alzheimer's. You told me that yourself. They get agitated, they start walking up and back. She does that. I feel sorry for her. She's in a fog most of the time."

I said, "I want to go back a bit. You had a general meeting, right? That was when Andrew said he was going to install cameras in the house."

Lydia nodded. "Yes. We had a kind of meeting. Fletcher wasn't there that night. I can't remember exactly when it was. Once in a while, we had meetings, mostly when there was something we had to decide. One time, it was a new hot water heater, and who was going to pay for it. We all knew Andrew was in charge. When we had this meeting, Andrew brought in dinner, Chinese take-out. I wondered, what's going on, why is he treating us to free food?

"We were all there, besides Fletcher. And not Angelica either. But we didn't need her.... She seemed more than usually distracted. She adored Andrew, by the way.

"So we ate our Chinese food, and drank beer and coke, and then Andrew started talking. He said, hey, how would you all like to live here rent-free? From now on. Not a cent. Completely free. And some new furniture, and a bigger TV and all that sort of thing. Of course, we said, sure, but what's the catch?

"He told us his idea about installing the cameras, and having them on day and night. A whole bunch of cameras. One in every room in the house, including the bathrooms. Naturally, I said no. I said I'd never heard such a crazy idea. I was the first one to talk. But then—the reaction from the others, I was amazed. Sheila spoke up and said, oh, it's a kick. It's a great idea. Can you imagine? We'll be famous, I love it. I said, I don't want to be famous, Sheila, count me out. Then came Billy. And he said, yes, it's a good idea. I couldn't believe it. I said, Billy, *you*? You're the biggest nerd on earth, and I mean that as a compliment. You're a quiet guy, minding your own business— and you're willing to let everybody see you walking around in your underwear? He said, why not? What's wrong with my underwear?

"Then there was Kurt: he said, yes, sure, great idea. Another surprise. Chuck said, I have to think about it. I said, think about it? What's to think? It's out of the question, totally out of the question. Anyway, Carmen said no way—she was the only one, besides me, who said flatly, no. Andrew said, I think we have a majority; there's five votes yes, one abstention, and two votes no.... Majority rule, right?

"There was something funny going on. I said, well, I'm definitely in the opposition. I couldn't believe what had gotten into all of them. I mean, it was getting to be a steamroller. Why were all of them agreeing to this disgusting thing? I called Fletcher and I told him I'd better start looking for a new place to live. I told Andrew, let me know what's happening. When those cameras come in, *if* they come in, I'm out of here."

"But you all knew nothing about the other thing? The murder scheme?" I said.

"Not a word," she said. "That was a terrific shock ... when Sheila told us. I always thought Andrew was a bit over the top. But that! I just couldn't believe it."

Fletcher added, "We were going to move anyway, at least we were talking about it. Because of the cameras and because of Andrew, and the way he kept making moves on Lydia. That other thing, that would have been the finishing touch."

Now, of course, they didn't have to move. I suppose this might be construed as some sort of motive. But nobody kills for an apartment or a room, except maybe in Manhattan. In Manhattan they seem to be capable of killing people to clear spaces in a fancy kindergarten. But not here. Did Fletcher have a motive? Clearly, he didn't like Andrew (who did?). There was Andrew's behavior to Lydia, but she gave Andrew the cold shoulder, or at least that's what they said. This too seemed far too weak to constitute any sort of real motive. I couldn't see them as killers, either one of them. For that matter, I couldn't see Chuck as a killer. We chatted for a while. They talked about the night Andrew died—they had gone to a movie, they said. And then they left the room. Leaving not much more light than when they entered.

7

Carmen was the next to enter. She was a striking woman, about 40, I would say, with dark hair, a round but strong face, high cheekbones, deep-set eyes, and a look about her that seemed somehow pained, almost ravaged. Her features were vaguely Asian-American. I thought she was rather elegantly dressed. I'm not much of a judge—Celia could have given a better opinion—but I noticed what she was wearing, which I rarely do, except when there's a maximum of cleavage. She was wearing a kind of pantsuit, with a striking black and white jacket, decorated with flowers.

"I'm not sure why you're here," she said, "or what we're supposed to talk about."

"I'm not sure either," I said. She smiled, and twisted her fingers nervously. There was a short silence. I felt it was up to me to pick up the conversation. "I've been talking to people about Andrew's various schemes," I said. "On this business of bringing in cameras, I understand you were in the minority. Other people have talked to me about this. They said you were really against it."

"Yes, I was."

"Can I ask you why? I mean, in some ways it's completely natural. Believe me, if I lived here, my vote would have been no no no."

"The real question," she said, "is why so many people said yes."

"And what do you think?"

She shrugged her shoulders. "He had some kind of hold

over them."

"And not over you?"

There was a long, pregnant silence. Then she said, "I don't know why, but I feel I can trust you, and I want to talk to *somebody*. I'm.... scared. I'm really scared, Mr. May."

"Call me Frank."

"I'm scared, Frank."

"I don't blame you. The idea that somebody here might be a killer...."

She shook her head. "No. It's worse. Look: I've had a problem, most of my life. Like a lot of women, I get attracted to the wrong men.... I'm naïve, or ... I don't know what. I was married once. When I look back, I don't why I married him. He was depressed. He yelled a lot, and he drank and even hit me. I got a divorce. Anyway, how this happened—how I wound up with him—I was living in Daly City, trying to pull my life together. I was lonely. I met this guy, at the office where I worked. His name was Garth Winter. He was good-looking and a real charmer. I was making good money. I was working for one of those dot-coms, I had stock options. He seemed so sweet. He said he loved me. We starting seeing each other all the time. He said he was lonely. He wanted to get married. I wasn't sure. He lost his job, he seemed lost. He seemed to *need* me. So we got married. I'm such a fool. My family never liked him, but they're far away. My mother warned me against him, but I thought, she's wrong; she just doesn't know him. I told her, Mother, when you get to know Garth, you'll see he's a real sweetheart. I should have listened to her. We went to Las Vegas, and we got married. He got a job in the LA area. We moved down there and rented an apartment....

"Then things began to change. I found out things I didn't know about him. He lost job after job. He used to blow up at work and get himself fired. He began to show me a side of him I never saw before. Mean, cold-blooded, abusive. He had a terrible temper. He started drinking a lot, and when he was drunk he ... he hit me. Sometimes he really hurt me. I was humiliated and afraid. Then he would cry and say he was sorry, give him another chance. Said he really loved me, that kind of thing. I tried, I tried to make it work. I tried to believe him. I didn't want another failed relationship, but he never did change.... Finally, I couldn't take it. I said, Garth, I can't stay with you anymore. But he couldn't accept that. He had always been terrifically jealous. Any time I looked at anybody, and mostly it was his imagination, he'd have a fit. Well, when I said I was leaving, he said, you met somebody else. I swore, no Garth, that's not it. But he didn't believe me. You're screwing around. I'm not good enough for you. He was in this kind of insane rage. Then he started cursing and screaming and hitting me, again and again. I was crying. I was hysterical. I ran out of the room, I shut myself in the bedroom, I called the police. Then he was all sorrowful again, with tears running down his cheek.

"I found out he had a criminal record. Attempted rape. He had been married before to a woman who divorced him. I found out he had beaten her so badly she had to go to the hospital. She wasn't the first one.... He had a trail of battered girlfriends.

"The police warned him. He even spent a night in jail, but what difference did it make? He was drinking more and more. He was disintegrating, and so was I. I had to get out. I just packed my bags, and I ran away. I came up here, from LA, got a job, and moved into this house. I have an unlisted number. I don't want him to find me, ever. I think he's capable of ... killing me. He scares me to death. And here's the awful part. He's living in the Bay Area. I actually saw him one day.... He didn't see me, it was in a shopping mall. My heart sank.... I got out of there and came back to the house. I couldn't sleep that night."

"Maybe he was just here on a visit."

"No. He's living here. He has family here. A brother. I asked Fletcher to snoop around. Fletcher is a really good guy—Lydia's a lucky girl. Fletcher got a kick out of it, playing detective. He found out Garth had been in jail in LA, a month or so, maybe for drunk driving or something. When he got out, he packed his stuff, came up here, and moved in with his brother. But that didn't last. Maybe the brother kicked him out, I don't know. Garth seems to have a job again, and he's living in an apartment in San Carlos. That's only ten miles from here, maybe a bit more. I'm terrified he'll find me. He was living with some woman for a while, then she dumped him. I'm sure he abused her, he can't help himself. He's a sick guy, but danger-ous. Frank, that's why I'm so scared. Can you imagine what it's like? I was thinking, I'll move away, I'll go to Australia, anywhere, just to get him out of my life. But I need to save up some money.... You can imagine what I thought when Andrew started talking about cameras, and I thought, my God, my face will be plastered all over TV."

I said, "Of course. I understand. The last thing you want is publicity."

"Absolutely," she said. "After the meeting, I went to see Andrew. I told him why I was so opposed to the whole idea, I told him all about Garth. He said, look, you'll be famous. That's the best protection. I said no, no, you're wrong. He's not a rational guy. He'll kill me, I know he will. He won't care about getting caught or anything. Andrew said, come on, Carmen, I want you to stay. You're important to the whole scheme. I said, I am? Why? He said, we have to have some attractive women here. There's Lydia, but she isn't enough. There's Sheila, sure, but I want you too."

"But you still said no."

"Naturally. He said, well, Carmen, I don't think it's a good idea, you moving out. I said, what do you mean? He said, I mean, I can find out where this guy lives. Garth. You told me his name, and you told me enough. I could locate him in a jiffy. Now just suppose he found out where you were living. Acci-dentally, Carmen. You know what I mean? My blood turned cold. I said, Andrew, what is this all about? Am I understanding you? You're threatening me. He said, oh, no, no. I just want you to think it over, that's all. But I knew damn well what he had in mind."

I thought: what a bastard.

She went on: "Frank, I'm at my wit's end. I'm thinking of running away. I have a job, I have friends, but what good does it do? My name was in the paper. You know, in connection with the case. The local paper, they listed the people who lived here.

I pray to God Garth never saw that story.... But sooner or later, he's going to find me."

"Maybe he's forgotten about you," I said weakly. "It's been a while."

She shook her head. "I don't think so.... People like that, they're vindictive. They never forget, and they never give up. Frank, can you help me? I need a restraining order, something. Tell me what to do."

I had to explain to her, patiently, that I was not a criminal lawyer. I told her I did some family law work, especially trusts and wills and that kind of thing, and once in a while a divorce, but no restraining orders. I felt she should go to somebody else who might help her. I gave her some names. She thanked me and wrote them down on a small pad of paper.

As I watched her, I felt a wave of sympathy. But it occurred to me that this woman was the first person who had a real motive, a strong motive, for killing Andrew Wright. On the other hand, I simply couldn't imagine Carmen as a murderer.

When Carmen left, Sheila came in again. "Want some coffee, Frank?"

"Absolutely."

"Give me a minute." She came back with the coffee, and said "Cream and sugar?"

"No thanks. I'll take it black."

"How's it going?" she asked.

"OK, I guess. I don't know where it's supposed to be going, to be perfectly honest. I haven't seen everybody yet, either."

"You've seen everybody but Billy and Kurt. I'm sorry to say, Kurt refuses to talk to you. I don't know what's eating him. I have to tell you, Kurt has been acting very strangely.... This was even before the, uh, murder. About a week ago, I found him in the living room, crying. If you knew Kurt, he's a tough guy, the idea of him crying? I said, what's the matter Kurt, but he said something really sweet, like screw you, and he left the room. He seemed ... terribly depressed. Now he said, he doesn't want to talk to you, period. I can't force him, can I? Billy will be down in a few minutes. He was making a phone call or something."

"Well, there's Angelica. I haven't seen her."

"She's not having one of her good days," Sheila said. "There isn't much point."

As if on cue, Angelica herself appeared in the doorway. She was a tiny woman, with snow-white hair. She was thin, and had the kind of spindly fingers with big spots on them that old people have. She was wearing a floral housedress and slippers. She had a more or less dazed look on her face.

"Angelica," Sheila said, "This is Frank. He was Andrew's lawyer."

She stared at me blankly. She seemed not to hear the question. Sheila repeated it. But Angelica had other things on her mind. She said, "Max is so angry at Andrew."

This caught my attention. Sheila said, "Max? Angelica, who is Max?"

If she expected some sort of rational answer, she was doomed to be disappointed. The old woman went on, "I told Max I didn't want him here. I said Andrew's my friend. I don't like people shouting at Andrew, really, it's very upsetting. But he paid no attention. He was always like that. I really don't like Max."

Sheila seemed to be as much in the dark about this as I was. She took Angelica's hand, and sat her down on the sofa. She said, "Is Max somebody we know, Angelica? Is he a friend of yours?"

Angelica said, "I was afraid he was going to hurt Andrew. Max can get very angry. He was always that way. Even when he was a child."

She was clearly lost in some world of her own. Something from the past, I supposed. I fidgeted in my seat. She went on talking, as if she and Sheila were the only people in the room.

"I don't know Max," Sheila said.

"Oh, but you do, dear. You were here, weren't you? The other day."

"The other day?"

"Yes. Max came by. I do wish he'd call in advance. He came to see me."

Angelica's grip on chronology was not very strong, to say the least. Who knows what "the other day" meant to her. It could mean something that happened thirty years earlier. Still, I couldn't help wondering about this mysterious Max, who shouted at Andrew and was very angry. If this was something that took place years before, then it had nothing to do with Andrew at all. Maybe it was just something that emerged from the fog of poor Angelica's brain with its tangle of aluminum or whatever lies behind Alzheimer's.

Sheila patted Angelica's hand. "It's OK. Max isn't here now, is he?"

"Oh, no...."

"Maybe he isn't coming back."

Angelica said, "I hope not. Unless he behaves."

Clearly, we were not going to find out more about Max. The old woman now seemed completely lost. "I'm tired," she said. She got up and slowly drifted out of the room. I heard the sounds of her slippers as she went up the stairs. I said, "I gather, Sheila, you have no idea who this Max is."

She said, "Not a clue. It could be anybody. Or nobody. Angelica has her good days and her bad days. Sometimes she doesn't seem to understand that Andrew's gone. At other times she does. This Max—who knows where or when? I wouldn't pay any attention."

"Sure," I said. But somehow I thought that Sheila was hiding something. I can't explain where this feeling came from. Something in her tone, something in the way she said what she said, some little catch or pause in her voice, some body language. Did she know Max? Naturally, I had no way to confront her, or to check it out. Just another one of life's little mysteries.

* * *

I had seen everybody now, except Kurt, who I wasn't going to see, and Billy. Sheila left the room to get Billy. There was a coffee table in front of me, with a small pile of magazines: *National Geographic*, *Newsweek*, *The New Yorker*. I picked up *The New Yorker*. I wondered which of the people in the house subscribed to *The New Yorker*. I thumbed idly through the magazine, looking mainly at the cartoons. None of them struck me as particularly funny. Maybe you had to live in New York City.

Billy came in a few minutes later. He was slight, and very pale, almost ghostly in appearance. He might have been somewhere in age between 30 and 40. He had thin, light brown hair, which he combed over a bald spot. His eyes were a very watery blue. He was wearing chino pants, and a plain tan sport-shirt. He seemed to avoid eye contact. He wore glasses, with thin, dark rims. He gave me the impression of somebody sick and fragile. But he also seemed sweet, gentle, and perhaps depressed. I'm certainly no expert in human psychology; but something about Billy said to me that life had defeated this guy. Of course, the world is full of losers. Some of my law school classmates, the ones who are partners in Wall Street firms and pull down millions a year, might regard me as a loser as well. It's a large and flexible category.

"How's it going?" he asked. "The conversations?"

I said, "OK, I guess. I'm not sure what I'm supposed to be getting out of this. Or what you people are getting out of this. People haven't told me much. I mean, nothing really big."

"Well, I'm different," he said, with a kind of wry smile. "I *can* tell you something big."

That caught my attention. "I'm listening, Mr., uh...."

"Oh, call me Billy. Everybody calls me Billy."

"OK, Billy. And call me Frank."

He was sitting on the other sofa, across from where I sat. He looked around, a bit furtively, as if he was afraid somebody was listening in. He spoke in a low, flat voice. "Sheila told you, I'm sure, about this house meeting. The one where she told us about this crazy scheme of Andrew's, you know, the cameras, and somebody getting killed on camera. And how everybody was so shocked...."

"Yes."

"Well, I wasn't shocked," he said. "I knew all about it. Maybe I wasn't the only one. I don't know—maybe not. Anyway, I pretended to be surprised. But I wasn't. Me and Andrew, we had had a long talk about it."

"You talked about it? How come?"

He paused and pursed his lips. He looked down at the floor, and then up again. He took off his glasses, and wiped them with a small, fuzzy cloth. He looked at me. It was as if it was a struggle to talk. "I knew because ... because I had a part in his little drama. I was going to be one of the players."

"Players?" I asked, somewhat bewildered.

"A starring role," he said. "For once in my life, I was going to have a starring role. I was going to be the victim, Frank. The guy who gets killed on camera."

8

I sat there, flabbergasted. "You? You … you knew … that some-body was supposed to kill you? You were going to *let* someone kill you? I don't understand."

He said, "Well, I've got to explain. I met Andrew in Los Angeles. It was in connection with this other scheme, you know, *The Earth Moved*. The fact is, I'm a dying man. I don't want to dramatize things. I have a genetic condition. It's incurable, and it's invariably fatal. It's in my family. I had a brother, he had the same thing. He's dead now. And two cousins, none of them made it to age 40. I've known about this for a while. I've been to all sorts of doctors, and they all say the same thing. There are certain symptoms, but I don't want to go into the gory details. When these symptoms start appearing, well, then you know you're running out of time.

"There are people who can handle this sort of thing. Dying. They're brave. They make the best of it. I wasn't one of them. It was devastating to me. When I began to get the symptoms, I … I went to pieces. My marriage broke up. OK, it wasn't such a great marriage to begin with, maybe it would have ended anyway; but she couldn't take it anymore. My ex-wife Hilda, I'm not blaming her. But there it was.

"So then, the earthquake. I was divorced, I was on my own, and I was with this woman…. In fact, we were in bed together, having sex, and … the whole place started shaking—you have to understand, I didn't know anything about earthquakes, I'm from Dayton, Ohio. So … I thought, oh God, this is it, this is the thing I've been dreading…. I'm about to die. I've got to explain:

this woman, the one I was with, well, she wasn't a girlfriend or anything like that. I'm not exactly great with women, never have been. She was somebody I met in a bar. I somehow got the nerve to talk to her, and, well, she came to my apartment, and it wasn't a relationship or anything like that. I haven't seen her since that day.

"Anyway, I'm rambling. The whole thing freaked me out totally. I was in a terrible state. I think I kept saying over and over, Jesus, I'm going to die; and she thought I was just scared out of my wits. She said, you jerk, it's an earthquake, and nothing happened. The house didn't collapse. She told me to calm down and don't be a baby, what's the matter with you? Then I told her, I thought I was having an attack, and I've got a disease. She started laughing. You, you thought you were dying, you thought the sex was killing you, and it was an earthquake, you loser, she said. It was embarrassing. You can imagine how I felt."

"And you told this story to Andrew?"

"No way! Why would I? I'd sooner die.... But Elizabeth— that's the woman—she did. She read the ad in the paper, and she went to Andrew with this story. He was offering $200 to people who were willing to tell him what he wanted to hear. I thought this was disgusting. Anyway, she went to him, with this weird story, telling him I'm with this jerk: he's screwing me, and the earthquake starts, he thinks it's some sort of medical crisis, he gets totally freaked out, and isn't that just the funniest thing you ever heard? Well, Andrew loved the story, as you can imagine. Then, he got this other great idea, or what he thought was a great idea. He got in touch with me. I didn't want to see him, talk to him, but.... Andrew could charm the pants off you, believe me; you have to give him credit for that. Meanwhile, I was getting sicker and sicker. I was terrifically depressed, because my time was running out. But Andrew had this proposition for me; I quit my job—I was going to, anyway—and I moved up here."

"Why did you do that, Billy? Was it for the scheme?"

"Yes, sure; but not only that. I had nothing going for me down there in LA. I felt I had to get out of there, I wanted a change. I went on disability. It keeps me going, the money. And here, they've got some great doctors, specialists—at Stanford, you know, or U.C., in San Francisco. Big hospitals. Not that there's any hope, really."

"There's no treatment at all?"

"I take some drugs. They don't do much. I'm ... a dead guy. I don't want to be dramatic about it, but I can feel ... there isn't much time. I've got nothing to look forward to. And I'm lonely and miserable. Wouldn't you be? I go for walks, I see my doctors, and I read books; I like to read about history, I was a history major in college; God, it seems so long ago. I try to keep my mind off what's happening. It doesn't always work."

"Do you have ... family?"

"Yes and no. I told you, I'm divorced. I have a child, a daughter. My ex-wife has custody. Hilda moved away, took a job in Pittsburgh. Look: it's only human. She didn't feel like hanging around watching me die. She never loved me. Don't get me started. I don't care about her; that's water under the bridge. She isn't worth a damn. Now she's hooked up with some creep. She's pregnant, she'll have more kids, and where will that leave my little girl? Susanna, that's her name. I always called her Sparrow. My little sparrow. I'd like her to have a good life. I talk to her on the phone, but it's painful. She tells me, she hates her mom's boyfriend. But what can I do?"

"Do you have parents? Brothers and sisters?"

"I had a brother; he's dead too. Same business, same disease. I told you that. I've got a mother, she's in Trenton, New Jersey. My father's dead. Mom isn't well. She's old and she's got a heart condition, diabetes, you name it. She doesn't know how sick I am. I don't want her to go to a nursing home. She already needs care. She's in assisted living, you know what that's like. She's got some money from my dad, but it won't last much longer. Those places cost an arm and a leg. I'm telling you all this to explain why I agreed to go along with Andrew. He said I'd get a bundle. He offered me more money than I ever dreamed of. I'm a dead man, anyway. You'll be the victim, he said. And I figured, why not? What have I got to lose?"

He paused. I looked at him. He was staring straight ahead,

talking in a monotone. His pain was palpable. I felt awfully sorry for him. He stopped talking. I was afraid he was on the verge of tears.

His story *was* important. It filled in a lot of gaps. Andrew had solved one of the problems I was sure he couldn't solve. He had found himself a victim. But that was only half the battle. Maybe less than half. I waited a bit so that Billy could get hold of himself. He said, "Sorry," and dabbed at his eyes with a handkerchief. "I get emotional," he said.

"I don't blame you. Billy, can I ask you some more questions? What else did Andrew tell you? Did he tell you who the other one was going to be? The ... uh, killer?"

"He wouldn't tell me. He said that would spoil it. I really don't know. Maybe Andrew himself. That's one possibility, though I really don't think so."

"And ... how were you supposed to be killed?"

"I'm not sure about that either. I told him I didn't want something painful. I've had enough pain. Something quick, with no suffering. He promised. We talked about poison. But then he said, no, poison wouldn't work. He said we'd try something else. Something painless."

"And ... sudden?"

"Quick, but not sudden. He promised that too. No surprises. He'd let me know when it would happen, and how."

I said, "Do the others know? I mean, how sick you are? I know you didn't say anything about the scheme. But do they realize your medical condition?"

"I don't think so. I didn't tell anybody. Maybe Fletcher knows, I saw him at the clinic once. Maybe he guessed, or asked some of his doctor friends. I'm not sure. I think people realize I'm not in perfect health; all you have to do is look at me. And I'm running to the doctor all the time. But the details, no."

I was silent for a while, chewing this over. I felt I ought to say something comforting, something empathetic. But what? It was an awkward situation. I mumbled something inane, about how life isn't fair. He said nothing. I guess he had to accept how people reacted to him, just as he was forced to accept his fate.

How would I react myself, I wondered, if I had this kind of

death sentence? Badly, I'm sure. The silence was oppressive. I pulled myself together and asked him, why he was confiding in me. Why was he telling me his story, if he was keeping it secret from the people whose house he was sharing?

He paused. His eyes looked even sadder and paler than before. He said: "Two reasons. First, I just had to talk to somebody. I felt, well, I don't know how I felt. But I wanted you to know. People said you were sympathetic. And you're a lawyer. You know how to keep secrets. But there's another reason, something a lot more crass, Frank. Andrew said he had an advance. He said he had a backer, somebody who was going to finance the whole deal, and he had $100,000, cash—and half of it was mine. There would be millions, but later on. Right now, though, he said he had this much cash. And ... he said ... he had a lawyer, and the lawyer was holding the money."

"Oh God."

"That's what he said, Frank. He said you were going to draw up a contract, so that when the rest of the money came in, it would go in a trust, my share, and that would pay for my kid, in college, pay for my mother's care, and so on. There would be plenty of money. Subsidiary rights, too. He talked about a book, about magazine articles, all kinds of things. All I had to do was sign a piece of paper, a contract. He said you were a big guy, a fancy lawyer, that you had the money in escrow, and you were going to draw up the papers. Half of the escrow money— $50,000—was mine, whenever I wanted. It was a kind of signing bonus like they give basketball players. The big money came later. Well, of course there isn't going to be any big money. He's dead. But the $50,000; I was wondering, do you have it?"

The more I learned about the late Andrew Wright, the more I realized the world was better off without him. I said, "Billy, I hate to break the news to you, but all this stuff about the money, it's a total fabrication. I don't have a dime. Andrew made it all up. There's no contract, no money, no papers, no big backer; it was just plain lies."

He blinked. He looked even more pained. His eyes seemed to tear over. He said, "Why am I not surprised? I was afraid of that. I had a feeling.... Andrew was such a liar. But I couldn't help hoping...."

"I'm sorry, Billy, I wish it was true."

"He was an out and out scoundrel," Billy said. "You know, at some level, I was thinking, maybe it's not true; but that guy, he had the gift of gab. I had the feeling, maybe this was all a pack of lies; but still, he seemed so, well, sure of himself. There were so many details, he spelled it all out, so I felt it can't all be just hot air. Well, now I know better."

Billy was quiet for a minute. Then he said, "Maybe he said the same thing to the other guy."

"What other guy?"

"I was lined up as the victim. Whoever he had lined up for the other role. The guy who was supposed to kill me."

I said, "Maybe. Do you have any idea who that could be?"

"Not really.... If I had to guess...."

"Yes?"

"No. I better not."

"I wish you'd tell me," I said. "Or better yet, you should tell the police. If you have some idea. Anything at all. Billy, I can understand why you agreed to be the victim. But why would somebody agree to take the other role? Why would anybody agree to kill you?"

"Maybe somebody would do it for the money. People will do anything for money. Who knows?"

"But presumably the person would get caught. Millions of people would see it. He'd be arrested, tried for murder. So what would happen then?"

He shrugged his shoulders. "I don't know. All I know is ... something went wrong."

"In what way?"

"It's obvious," he said. "The scheme never happened. Instead Andrew got himself killed."

"And you think the person who was supposed to be the TV killer actually turned around and killed Andrew?"

"Well, I think it's possible. Like I said, maybe Andrew was going to do the killing himself. Anyway, I have a feeling," he said, "that there's somebody else who was in the know. Not just me. But if there was, Andrew never told me about it."

"And you have no idea? Not even a guess?"

"I've got a guess," Billy said, "but I don't want to tell you what it is. I hope you understand. It's a hunch. It's not based on anything. Maybe *you* know something. Maybe somebody came forward, like I did, and told you about it? Somebody saying, hey, I knew about the scheme, and I was supposed to be the star, the killer guy."

"No...."

"And you talked to everybody?"

"Not Kurt. He wouldn't talk."

He raised his eyebrows. "Kurt!" This information seemed to have meaning for him. I asked him more questions, but now he turned reticent, shy, holding something back. We talked for a little while, mostly about nothing much; and then he left the room.

I sat in the living room for a while. Sheila came back in. I asked her again about Kurt, but she said, he was adamant—he was in his room and wasn't coming out.

I said goodbye and drove back home.

9

That night, I had trouble falling asleep. I tiptoed out of bed, so as not to wake Celia, and sat in the family room, turning things over in my mind. What had I learned at the house? Not very much. I had a better sense of the layout of the place, and I had met the people who lived there—well, almost all of them. I hadn't met Kurt. Perhaps I never would. The most enlightening conversation had been the one with Billy. It told me at least *something* about Andrew's scheme. But the most important bits were still shrouded in mystery.

I read *National Geographic* for a while. I got engrossed in a story about Peruvian mummies, left over from the days of the Incas. Then I went back to bed, and I fell fast asleep.

I was at the office the next day, hard at work on a trust agreement, when I received a call. It was Chuck. He wondered if we could have lunch together. "There's some stuff I want to get off my chest."

"OK," I said, "I'm free for lunch. Why not?"

He said, "We work all kind of crazy hours at Quisquad, nights, holidays, weekends. We're pretty much into flextime, during normal hours. Generally speaking, normal isn't normal with us. Not at Quisquad."

He mentioned a Thai restaurant, in downtown San Mateo, saying, "They've got lots of vegetarian items on the menu. Do you know the place?" I did, and I agreed to meet him there at 12:15.

It was a beautiful day, typical of California. The restaurant, King of Siam, was walking distance from my office. Celia says sunshine at midday is good for mental health. I'd enjoyed about four blocks of this natural therapy by the time I arrived at the restaurant.

Chuck was there already, waiting in a comfortable booth. "I don't normally eat Thai stuff," he said. "Too greasy. But this place is different. They've got some killer salads here. And soups. A lot of lemongrass. It's great for your insides."

I ordered pad thai. I'm a little wary about lemongrass. I mean, what is it, really? How could grass be lemon? The name puts me off. Another name that bothers me is coconut milk. Maybe I'm a dirty old man at age 45, but it makes me think about milking a coconut, and that brings all sorts of weird images to mind. At least to me.

Chuck attacked his soup with great gusto. "I bet you're wondering, why I called you," he said.

"I have to admit it. Yes," I said.

"You remember, I told you, I thought I knew something. But I wanted to check it out. Well, I did check it out, and I wanted to let you know about it. You're investigating this thing, right? OK, OK, I know you say you're not, but I don't believe you."

"Really, Chuck, I swear to God...."

"Don't swear to God. I don't care if you're lying. You're a lawyer. Really, I know how these things are."

I had no idea what "things" he was referring to. But I kept my mouth shut. He was convinced I was some sort of investigator, and no matter what I said, he would go on thinking that way. Denials were pointless. Maybe I should try to act the part he wanted me to play. If I only knew how.

"Sheila told me," he said, "that you came by the house. The day Andrew died."

"Oh, dear."

"Frank, don't worry: I won't tell anybody. You didn't kill Andrew. I know that. And, anyway, you weren't the only one who came by. I was in the back yard, oh, sometime in the evening. I don't know exactly when. It was after dinner though. I didn't have my watch on. I'm trying not to be a slave to time. Time should just flow—you know what I mean? Anyway, I have some exercises I do outside, when the weather's nice, which it almost always is. These exercises are kind of halfway between martial arts and some other stuff. They're originally from Cambodia. The monks do them, they chant and all that. It makes them calm. It's kind of a way to get yourself into a sort of spiritual state. Whatever. That's what swimming does for me, but you can't swim all day now, can you? Anyway, I was there, and I saw this man coming out of the side door, which is the door Andrew used."

"A man. Can you describe him?"

"Well, not really.... I didn't pay that much attention.... Of course, I noticed. It caught my eye. You know, I thought, oh, Andrew had a visitor. Nothing wrong with that. I just noticed it, that's all. The guy was middle-aged, I'd say. Wearing a business suit. Guy in his late 40s, maybe 50...."

"Nobody you actually knew?"

"Never saw him before. Complete stranger. Just came out of the room, walked around the house, and drove away, I suppose. I didn't see where he went."

I remembered the old man in the house next door. I said to Chuck, "There's an old man, lives in the house next door. He says he saw somebody that night. He was looking out the window. I suppose this was the guy."

Chuck said, "I guess. Maybe. I'm not saying this guy killed Andrew. I don't know exactly when this happened, but ... anyway, Andrew was still alive. I know that because Sheila told me he was.... She said she was with Andrew, later."

"Maybe the man came back."

"Maybe. But who knows? Maybe he was some kind of a salesman or a religious nut. Maybe he was trying to convert Andrew. Man, would that ever be a waste of time!"

Somehow, I doubted this mysterious stranger was a salesman. Or a missionary. But then, who was he? I liked the idea of a killer from outside. It was too uncomfortable thinking that somebody in the house killed Andrew. I had *met* them, after all. (Well, all except Kurt). Once you're introduced to somebody, once you talk to somebody, you don't like to think they go around batting somebody else in the head, then smothering

him with a pillow. Especially if the person smothered is somebody you knew personally.

Chuck was talking again. He said, "I came to talk to you
about something else, too. Something I didn't tell you last time.
It's about the, uh, crazy scheme. You know, the murder thing.
Well, when we heard about it, you know, when Sheila broke the
news, I pretended to be surprised, just like the rest of them. But
that was just an act. I didn't say anything, but, to tell you the
truth, I knew all about it.... I was in on the plan."

"You were?"

"Right. And that's what I want to talk to you about. Andrew came to see me, and he told me what he wanted to do. He
said it was very hush hush, and he made me swear not to
breathe a word of it. See, he needed money, financing. He said
that the idea was a gold mine, that it was going to make
millions. But he needed seed money. That's where I came in.
He wanted me to get money from my boss—Joe Strapazzo. You
know who he is?"

I had to confess I had no idea.

"Wow. Well, he's the founder of Quisquad. He's a real ge-
nius. He's an amazing person. And he's a billionaire. Maybe
mega-billions. He started this company. He was a college
dropout. After a few years, he put it on the market, you know,
an IPO—you know what that is—and the market goes wild.
Later, a big corporation bought him out, all his stock. Now
we're a division of something else. I think it's called Hyper-
ventricle. Joe, he walked away with billions. And it's not just
Quisquad; he's got real estate, he's into venture capital, and he
makes money hand over fist. He's a good guy, too, Joe is. He's a
vegetarian. Almost vegan. He puts a lot of money into organic
farming. Tomatoes especially. He doesn't like to wear leather
shoes. Anyway, he's really great. I knew him in college, and
we've been friends forever. Actually, we have a lot in common.
We work out together. He's got a private gym in his house. I'm
pretty thick with Joe.

"Andrew wanted *me* to put up the money. He thought,
seeing as how I worked for Joe, and I was his buddy, I must
have money myself. He thought maybe some of the millions

trickled down my way, stock options, whatever. Well, I had some money once, but my ex-wife got it all. That's another story. Andrew should have known better. If I had millions, why would I be renting a room in Angelica's place? I had to break the news to him, I don't have a dime to spare. Then he asked me to get it from Joe. He said, look, what's a few hundred thousand to a billionaire? That's all I need to get going. Hey, to a guy like Strapazzo, it's lunch money."

"What did you say?"

"I got to tell you, and I'm not proud of myself, I told him I'd try; but I had no intention of doing any such thing. I thought, I'll say I asked Joe, and he turned me down. It'd be a lie, but so what? You see, we're friends, me and Joe, even though he's got billions, and I've got nothing. But if I started in asking him for money, that'd be the end of our relationship. You don't know Joe Strapazzo. I do. Ask him for money, and you're history."

"So you just played along."

"I did," Chuck said. "And, then, he had to go into a lot of details. He knew that Joe Strapazzo wasn't going to give any money, unless Joe was clued in. He'd have to know exactly what was going to happen to the money. Now, maybe Andrew was telling me the truth. Or maybe he wasn't. He wasn't exactly a straight-shooter."

"Boy, do I know that," I said.

"But anyway, here's what he said. This was the deal. He was going to pretend it was something like the game, Clue, you know, a murder mystery game. Not real. Colonel Mustard in the library with a rope, or whatever. It would be a kind of reality show, a game, eight people in a house, and they're playing this game. But it isn't a game. It's a real murder. The victim is really dead."

"Poisoned?"

"Who said anything about poison? Well, maybe. Or he's smothered to death with a pillow."

"And the network was going to broadcast this?" I asked, incredulous.

"The network? You see, they don't know it's real. They just

think it's this sort of game. Then the guy is dead. By then, it's too late. They can't back out."

"And … you went along with this?"

"Frank, I just strung him along. I'm not proud of what I did. And yes, I tried to talk him out of it; but that was useless. He made me promise though, not to say a word to anybody. Only to Joe Strapazzo."

"Did he tell you who the killer was going to be?"

"Ah! No. He wouldn't say. He said, Chuck, I've already told you a lot of things I didn't want to tell. I had to tell you, he said, because of the money. But I'm not going to tell you *that*, you know, who does the smothering job."

"The audience would know," I said.

"No, they wouldn't either. He said the cameras would be fixed up so that you'd see the murder, but you wouldn't see who did it. Just a shape, you know? You'd see the victim. You'd see these hands, you'd see the guy smothering the victim. The victim is squirming, fighting a little, but it's no use…. Maybe he's gasping, gurgling, can you imagine? These hands, maybe wearing black gloves, real creepy. People would be horrified. But who was it? Who's the killer? We don't know. So that would be an extra bonus, something to keep up the interest, even later, even after that first program."

"And you don't have any idea who it would be? Do you think it might be Andrew himself?"

Chuck shook his head. "I doubt that somehow. Not the type."

I wondered: who *was* the type? Nobody I had met in the house. Maybe the mysterious Kurt. I asked, "What about the victim?"

"Oh, I knew about that. That was going to be Billy."

"Did Billy tell you that?"

"Oh no. We didn't even know he was sick. I mean, we knew he was in poor health. I talked to him about it a lot. I recommended stuff for his diet, exercises, all that. No, Billy never complained…. It was Andrew; he told me about it, said it was a secret. He said the defense was going to be euthanasia. They would reveal the secret that Billy was dying, that he was in pain—not that he was actually in pain. He takes a lot of pills, but he isn't really suffering. Anyway, the pain part, you could make it up—and it would be a mercy killing, to put him out of his misery."

"Chuck, if you had to guess about the killer, I mean the role of the killer, do you have any idea?"

"I don't know. Hey, how about Fletcher? The medical connection. He's practically a doctor already, so he'd have some kind of poison or something, like you suggested, and he could claim it was a mercy killing, he could say Billy begged him to take him out of his misery. So if the police arrested him, he'd have a defense. OK, at least it's a theory."

I said, "Fact is, mercy killing, it's not really a defense. I remember that from law school. Whatever the motive, it's still murder. Mercy killing, there's no such legal category."

He said, "Maybe Andrew didn't know that. It's actually murder? Honestly?"

"Well, technically. Actually, juries don't like to convict people in those cases, the pathetic ones. I remember one in particular, the guy was 80-something. His wife was in desperate pain, and so on. Why they even arrested the husband I'll never know, but the jury recommended mercy and the judge gave the guy probation. Or maybe I'm not remembering it right."

Chuck nodded his head. "But still," I said, "it doesn't make sense to me. And if the networks ever got wind of this, it'd never see the light of day."

"Oh, Andrew didn't think that would happen," Chuck said. "Anyway, he had it all figured out. He'd have the tape, the video, and he'd sell it to a magazine or a news broadcast. You see, it would be fabulous *news*. Murder on TV! It would be news, big news, a major story. They'd simply *have* to broadcast it, or at least broadcast something about it. It would be worth millions. He thought it would make him famous. Give him a tremendous career."

"And you told him, don't do it?"

"Yes. I certainly did. I thought it was awful. But I didn't really insist. Andrew, you couldn't really talk him into anything.

Like I said, he made me swear, made me promise I wouldn't say anything. He was disappointed about the money. But I did keep my promise, not to talk. Till now. I haven't said a thing to anybody. In a way, you have to hand it to him. He knew every angle."

"Well not quite," I said. "After all, *he's* the one who got bashed in the head and smothered with a pillow. There were no cameras around, and we don't know who did it. So that was one angle he definitely hadn't taken care of. Otherwise, he'd be with us today."

10

I had learned something, of course, from Chuck. There were pieces of the puzzle falling into place. I knew and understood more about Andrew's plan. It was on the brink of crazy, but not quite. It is just possible he might have pulled it off. Billy's story, and Chuck's, added information. But of course something had gone wrong. Seriously wrong.

I have to admit I was intrigued by the whole affair. No, of course, I'm not a detective. No forensic skills whatsoever. But I couldn't help pondering. Daydreaming. Thinking about the case, in my spare moments—in the shower, dawdling over breakfast, and the like.

Who could have killed Andrew Wright? And why? Two things kept running through my head. I thought about the people in the house. I had met them all, with one exception. None of the ones I saw seemed a likely suspect to me. I just couldn't picture Lydia, or Carmen, or even Sheila in the role of a murderer. Or Billy. Or Chuck. Or Fletcher. Then there was Kurt. He seemed much more likely. Maybe it was because I had never met him. It came down to him by a process of elimination—and why was he so reluctant to talk to me? But of course this was pure speculation. I had never laid eyes on the man.

Another possibility was the mysterious stranger. The man who had come to visit Andrew. Nobody seemed to know anything about him, or who he was.

Why did somebody kill Andrew Wright in the first place? What was the motive? That too wasn't clear. Andrew had a collection of files, tapes, notes for his book. Now this material was gone. Presumably the killer had taken the stuff. But why? Some of it was probably embarrassing, no doubt. But was that a motive for murder?

Or was it something to do with the scheme for murder on TV?

At the rational level, I knew I had no business even speculating. This was a job for the police. They had laboratories, detectives, and all the rest. They had experience. They had ways of getting information. They could look for fingerprints, scraps of evidence, anything they could send to their lab. They could quiz everybody in the house, and the neighbors to boot. Including the old man. That weird man who watched me come up to the door.

* * *

My blood turned cold when, the very next day, I had a call from a police detective. He said he had a "few questions to ask me." He was quite polite. He came to see me at my office, and I prepped myself carefully. I tried to be calm, matter-of-fact. I was terrified that somehow the police had found out about my visit to Andrew's house. But the detective clearly knew nothing whatsoever about this. He knew only that Andrew had consulted me professionally, and he wanted to know why.

I told him as little as I could without lying outright. I said he was thinking about his project that grew out of the earthquake, which I assumed the detective already knew about. It turns out he did. Andrew had asked about incorporation and so on. I'd said that I had very little advice for him; the project was not advanced very far, and I was not a specialist in the kind of contacts and contracts that might be useful to him.

Yes, I had dinner with Andrew Wright, but it was mostly social. No agreement about representation had been finalized, I said. I told him nothing about the scheme to broadcast a murder. Apparently nobody in the house had mentioned it either. The conversation then turned to a somewhat embarrassing subject. Apparently, he had learned a bit about at least *some* of Andrew's lies—for example, Andrew's story that somebody had given him a fat advance, and that he deposited the money with me. I told him that this was simply a lie, that I found it outrageous, and that the police were free to check my financial records and so on. I'm pretty sure he believed me—no doubt he had already learned what a liar and a cheat Andrew was. The conversation lasted about an hour; and then, to my great relief, he left.

* * *

I told Celia about the call from the detective. We were having dinner together, at home, eating leftovers. The girls, as often happens, were away visiting friends. At least that's what they said. I'm actually quite worried about my older daughter, Amanda. She's 16, a dangerous age. She has been seeing a lot of this Ryan person, who couldn't possibly look scruffier. Were they having sex? God forbid. But of course this was a completely forbidden subject. There must be some adolescents who confide in their parents, but I haven't met any of them yet. Sometimes I wonder: do I *want* my girls to confide in me, or for that matter in Celia? At some level, I think I don't. I want the day my daughter loses her virginity—which might have happened already—to be and remain a dark secret.

This Ryan was at least a shade better than the last boyfriend, who had the improbable name of Sylvester, wore nothing but black, and looked to my jaundiced eye like an apprentice ax murderer. His reign was mercifully brief.

Celia is the sensible one in the family. I am reasonably intelligent, I think. I have a respectable professional life, and my judgment, on legal matters, is quite sound. On the home front, Celia is the one with sound judgment. The trouble is, nobody really listens to her, at least not consistently. And that includes me.

"That detective," she said. "That's a warning, Frank. As much as you can, stay out of this whole miserable affair. It's none of your business, and it will be nothing but trouble."

"Andrew was sort of my client," I said lamely.

"He never paid you a nickel, and besides, he's dead," she said. "Are you ready for dessert? I bought a pie on the way home from work."

She was right of course about Andrew Wright. But it was like her message not to eat between meals, to cut down on cholesterol, to avoid cheeseburgers, to lower the stress level, to do aerobics and so on—all very sound advice, and totally futile. Naturally, I didn't argue the point with her. I said I totally agreed. I said I rued the day I met Andrew Wright. And, yes, I was true that we never really got around to any legal business, or any firm arrangement. In fact, I had consistently told him no. Therefore I have absolutely no reason to concern myself with him or his affairs.

I broke this vow, if it was a vow, the very next day.

The pie was cherry pie, and completely delicious.

11

I was at work the next day, doing what I should be doing, when Sheila called me on the telephone.

"Frank," she said, "This is Sheila."

"Yes?"

"I need to talk to you. I'd like you to come over, OK?"

"What for? Really, Sheila, I'm quite busy these days," I said. "I just don't have the time...."

"You're lying, Frank."

"Sheila, I'm not lying. I have clients, remember? Clients who pay me a fee. I have work to do."

"You can make time—if you want to. You've got to come to the house. I need to talk to you, I said."

"Sheila, I'm through with this business. I wash my hands of it. If you need a lawyer, I can recommend some good ones. Especially criminal lawyers—if that's what you're after. Are they hounding you again, the police?"

She didn't answer. She insisted I come to the house; and when I declined again, she reminded me gently about the note I left behind, under Andrew's door, and how she had done me this enormous favor by tearing it up. She said: "You owe me one."

"Sheila, that's blackmail. I can't believe you're saying this."

"I need your help, Frank. Just do what I ask. Blackmail, you say. A nasty word. In a way, that's what I want to talk to you about, if you must know."

"Blackmail? Somebody's blackmailing you?"

"I'm not going to talk about this over the phone. I mean it. You've got to come over."

I sighed and agreed to pay her a visit. She had me over a barrel. The last thing in the world I wanted was for her to tell the police I had been to the house. I called Celia and told her I was going to be late for dinner. I didn't tell her why. I never lie to Celia—well, almost never, but sometimes I do a little editing and filtering of information.

At about six o'clock, I had gotten rid of my last client, so I got in my car and drove through rush-hour traffic to Palo Alto. At that hour, it's murder on the freeway, so I drove through city streets. It was stop-and-go all the way. By the time I arrived, struggling through the herds of cars that clogged El Camino Real, I was not exactly in the best of moods.

I rang the doorbell. The door opened, and I found myself looking at a dark, rather thin man, in a t-shirt and jeans. He was in his late 30s, I would say, with coal-black hair, and a square, rather ominous face. His arms were bare, and I thought I saw the edge of a tattoo above the elbow, just at the point where the sleeves of the t-shirt ended. He said, "Yeah, what do you want?" in a grim, gruff voice.

"I'm looking for Sheila."

"Wait here," he said. He disappeared for a second, and then Sheila came out. She said: "Frank, you're a bit earlier than I expected. Come in. Sit down in the living room. We're just finishing dinner. I'll be with you in a minute."

I sat quietly, on the sofa, thinking. I heard a clock ticking. I felt vaguely nervous, for some reason. After a moment or two, I heard a slight rustling noise. I turned and I saw Angelica. Her hair was somewhat askew, and she had that distant Alzheimer's look. She stared at me.

She said, "Oh, I didn't know you were here. I'm looking for Andrew. I can't seem to find him anywhere, but I just know he's in the house."

I didn't quite know how to react. I said, "Mrs. Finster, I'm sorry, I guess you forgot, but Andrew's, uh, dead."

There was some sort of faint awareness now in her eyes, like a far-off light blinking on a dark night. A pinpoint of reality was creeping into her brain. She said, "Oh, yes. I do remember now. He's dead. It's just like my nephew Oscar. They all do die, don't they?"

"Yes, they do, Mrs. Finster."

She said, "Andrew ... they told me, somebody killed him. Well, that wasn't a bit nice. Not nice at all. Andrew was terribly sweet to me. Like Oscar. I do miss Oscar."

I said, "Yes. I know." Not that I knew anything at all.

"They shouldn't have done it. I don't mean Oscar. The doctor said it was Oscar's heart. I was so alone after that. Then Andrew came along, and the house was filled with people, and we have a cleaning service. There was so much dirt in the tub before. Did you know that? I just didn't have the strength to clean it. So it was really bad when they killed Andrew. I'm really ashamed of him."

"Ashamed? Of who, Mrs. Finster."

"The man. He came out of the house, the side door. Andrew's door. I was in the garden. He talked to me. I said, do I know you? He said, don't you recognize me? I said, oh, of course, and I was a little frightened. I'm afraid of strangers. But he wasn't really a stranger. That's the funny part. I did think I knew him. And he called me Angelica."

I sat bolt upright. "Do you know his name, Mrs. Finster?"

She said, "Do I know *you*? Are you one of the people who lives here?"

I said, "No, I'm a friend. This man. Was it somebody who lives here?"

She said, "What man?"

I said, "The man you saw. When you were in the garden."

"I'm so bad at names. I get confused."

"And when did this happen, Mrs. Finster?"

"I'm sorry. When did what happen?"

"This man. Who called you Angelica, and you think you knew him...."

She had a strained look on her face, as if she was struggling to get somewhere, fighting desperately to bring something up to her consciousness. But it was really no use. "Oh, I don't really know. Was it yesterday? No, yesterday, the police were here. Or were they? Oh dear, it's hard. I have so much trouble remembering…. That man did come again…." But here her voice trailed off, and she drifted out of the room.

I was mulling over what Angelica said, wondering if it had any meaning or importance. Of course, times, places, and people were totally beyond her; she would be a completely worthless witness in a courtroom, for example. And yet…. I stared at the walls. Chuck, too, had seen somebody. And Angelica *thought* she knew the man.

Sheila came in, apologizing for how long it had taken. I decided to say nothing about my conversation with Angelica.

I said, "Who was that guy, the one who answered the door?"

She laughed, "That was Kurt. The mysterious Kurt."

"He's avoiding me. Why do you think he's avoiding me?"

She shrugged her shoulders. "How would I know? He's an odd duck to begin with, and lately, he's been acting even more peculiar. The police spent hours talking to him. He seemed extremely angry and annoyed. He's a pretty strange guy. Lately, he's been like a recluse. Stays in his room all day, only goes out at night."

"Doesn't he have a job?"

"He does. I mean, I suppose so. At least he has *some* source of income. He pays the rent after all. I think he said he was a programmer. But for sure he hasn't gone to work lately. Maybe he was fired…. But look: I don't want to talk about Kurt. That's not my problem. I want to talk to you."

"Talk away."

"OK," she said. "Here's my question. What's the legal definition of blackmail? Suppose I have information about somebody, say I know something, and I use this information, not for money, don't get me wrong, but more or less to hold it over their head—to use it as leverage, if you know what I mean…?"

I said, "What are you getting at, Sheila. Somehow I feel this isn't just a hypothetical question. Is this something about you?"

"No. About somebody else."

I didn't believe her. "OK, have it your way," I said, "somebody else."

She looked me straight in the eye. I didn't flinch. She was quiet for a moment or two, then she said, "Alright. It's about me. So tell me: is that blackmail?"

I replied, "Sheila, I tell you, I tell everybody, I'm not a criminal lawyer. I took criminal law in law school. That was twenty years ago. Anyway, the professor never said a word about blackmail. I know there's something in the California Penal Code. I could look it up. But off the top of my head, I just don't know. It certainly sounds like blackmail. I don't think blackmail has to be about money. That's my guess." And I added: "You could be talking about you and me, after all."

"You and me?"

"Sure. You're blackmailing me, aren't you? You threatened to tell about the note, about my visit to Andrew, all those things, unless I did what you wanted. Now, isn't that blackmail?"

"Don't be an asshole, Frank."

"OK, OK. But, admit it: You know something, and you want to use this information, strategically. Am I right?"

She seemed pensive. Then she said: "Well, yes. You're right. This information—I haven't actually used it. But I might. Or I might not."

"My advice, if you want my advice, free of charge, is just don't do it. Don't play games. It's dangerous and it's morally obnoxious."

"I don't give a crap about morally obnoxious."

"Suit yourself," I said. "But anyway, what sort of information? Exactly what are we talking about? Or can I assume you aren't going to tell me?"

She was quiet for a moment or two. Then she said: "No, you're right. I'm not going to tell you. Not all of it, anyway. It's information about Andrew."

"About Andrew? *What* about Andrew?"

"It's complicated. But maybe it's about who killed him."

Now it was my turn to look her straight in the eye. I said,

"Sheila, this is no joke. If you know something, anything about this case, about Andrew and who killed him, go right to the police. I'm not going to talk about civic duty...."

"That part is right, Frank," she said. "I'm not big on civic duty."

"Then I'll make another point. It's downright dangerous. Somebody was willing to kill Andrew, God knows why; and this somebody isn't exactly confessing and throwing himself on the mercy of the law, if you know what I mean. If he thinks you have this information, and could use it, maybe he'd be willing to kill *you*. You're playing with fire, Sheila."

She said, "Don't get so melodramatic. It's not that big a deal. Anyway, for now, I'm not doing anything. But I do want to entrust this information to somebody. I don't want to hold on to it, by myself. I want you to have it. After all, you're a lawyer."

"Sheila, I don't want to get involved. I told you that. I'm telling everybody that. I'm trying to mind my own business and stay out of this."

"You can't stay out. You *are* involved. You know that."

"I don't know that."

"Frank, do I have to remind you about the blackmail, as you put it? The note I tore up? I hate doing this. And I'm not asking you to do anything drastic; I just want you to hold on to something, in case—well, never mind. It's just some documents."

"Documents? What kind of documents?"

She had a big wicker tote bag with her. She reached in, and took out a thick, sealed envelope. "It's this," she said. "Just hold on to it."

"What the hell is it? And where did you get it?"

"It's things I got it out of Andrew's room. Now don't ask me anything else. Put it someplace that's nice and secure. You've got a safe deposit box for your clients, for wills and things.... I asked around, people told me that lawyers like you have these safe deposit boxes. So I assume you do too."

"Actually, I do."

"Take it then," she said, handing me the envelope. "And

don't open it. Just store it until I say something. I'll pay you something. A fee. That makes me a client, then. And then you can't say anything, to anybody, about this, right?"

I should have refused. But I didn't. I said no a few more times, but Sheila was not inclined to let things stand in her way. I really had no principled objection, and so I ended up taking the envelope. Sheila seemed pleased with herself and glad to be rid of it—whatever it was. She left shortly afterwards. I sat for a bit, staring at the envelope. I was tempted to open it, but I knew that would be wrong. It ended up, as she had requested, in my safe deposit box.

12

The next day, when I came back from lunch with two clients—the lunch lasted until almost two o'clock—I was surprised to find Fletcher standing in the hallway outside my office, waiting for me. He was wearing the loose white coat I associate with doctors. No, there was no stethoscope hanging around his neck.

He said. "Do you have a minute, Frank? I need to talk to you. About this situation, you know—about Andrew, this mess...."

"Sure. Come on in," I said, trying to sound friendly. I opened the door to my office. After Fletcher sat down, I said: "OK: let's have it."

"I hope you don't mind," he said. "I felt I had to talk to somebody. I've got something on my mind.... I got away from the hospital, told them some story. I just had to get this off my chest. It's about.... a suspicion."

"A suspicion?"

"It's more like an idea. You know, I spend a lot of time at the house. With Lydia. I know everybody there. I've been going over this stuff, over and over, and talking to Lydia, and ... well, I came to a conclusion. That's what I want to talk to you about."

"Why me? Why not the police?"

He said, "I don't want to go to the police. I don't think they'd listen. And I didn't want to get all entangled.... But you, you're a lawyer."

"And you're a doctor. An intern, anyway. That's a doctor, isn't it? You know: there's eye doctors, foot doctors, stomach doctors, psychiatrists, and oncologists and who knows what else? Well, lawyers are like that. There's patent lawyers, divorce lawyers, personal injury lawyers, and all sorts of lawyers. And then there's criminal lawyers. That isn't me. I don't have anything to do with criminal law, and I don't want to. I can't tell you how many people I've had to say that to. You want a will, you want a divorce, a real estate closing, fine, I'm your man. But defending criminals, prosecuting, doing anything with crime or criminals: no thank you."

"I have to talk to somebody."

"I'm not a therapist either."

"Listen, Frank," he said. "Don't you want this cleared up?"

"I do, Fletcher," I said. "But mostly because I'm a good citizen; I want criminals caught and punished. This case is really none of my business, although everybody seems to be conspiring to drag me into it."

He said, "*You* don't want to be dragged in. We don't either. Can you imagine what it is for us? The fear, the suspicion...."

I said, "Suspicion? But nobody suspects you, Fletcher. Or do they?"

"I suppose they don't. I mean, not me personally. But the atmosphere in the place is downright poisonous, and then there's the police, the questions, the reporters. I'm there a lot, as I said; and I was there earlier that night. Me and Lydia. But we were at the movies when they say Andrew was killed. So, we're not exactly suspects, but the police think *somebody* in the house knows something. Anyway, the movies, that's not a real alibi. We said we were at the movies but we can't prove it. We paid in cash and didn't keep the stubs. We could be lying to protect each other."

"Didn't somebody see you at the movies?"

"Who? It was one of those multiplexes. Twelve screens. Who saw us? Some kid with acne, who sold us the tickets? You think he remembers? A girl who was chewing gum, and who sold us nachos and a Diet Coke?"

"Granted. But you don't have a motive," I said. "Why on earth would you want to kill Andrew Wright?"

"I told you. He was coming on to Lydia. She wouldn't give him the time of day, but the police, they don't trust anybody. They haven't got a good suspect, and that makes them edgy and nervous. Aren't you involved, too? You were Andrew's lawyer."

"Not really," I said. "He consulted me, that's all. We never finalized anything. When the police called, I had to answer a few questions, sure; but nothing serious. I'd like to keep it that way."

"Well, won't you at least listen?"

"OK, Fletcher, if you really want me to, I'll listen."

He leaned forward. "I think it was Kurt."

The mysterious Kurt. "Why do you think so?"

"I'll tell you. First of all, by process of elimination. Who else is there? Sheila? Carmen? Lydia? Ridiculous. Chuck? Not the type. Billy? No way. The old lady? Completely absurd. That leaves Kurt."

"Or an outsider."

"Maybe. But I don't think so. What outsider? And why? Anyway, there's more to my suspicions; it's not just that I can't picture anybody else but Kurt. This Kurt, you don't know him I guess; he's a real moody guy. He seems, well, smoldering. Like a volcano about to erupt, you know? A lot of suppressed violence. Brooding. OK, that's no proof. But I overheard a conversation, not long before Andrew died. I don't remember the exact date. Him and Andrew. They were in Andrew's room, and they seemed to be arguing. I was going by on my way to the kitchen. Kurt was yelling something, but it was incoherent. And then he said, 'you bastard,' plain as day. And, 'I'll get you some day.' Honest to God, that's what Kurt said.

"I have to admit, it intrigued me. I stopped. I was quiet, and I tried to listen. Nobody else seemed to be around. Andrew was saying in a very calm voice, 'I wouldn't advise it, Kurt. Not with your background. Not with the things I know.' And Kurt said, 'You wouldn't dare.' Andrew said, 'You know I would, Kurt. I absolutely would. So on the one hand, there's a chance to make a million dollars, and on the other hand—well, let's just say, San Bernardino, May 2009.' Then I heard Kurt say, 'you bastard' again, very loud, and slam something down, and he rushed out of the room. He nearly collided with me, and—well, that was it. So *now*, what do you think?"

"It doesn't prove anything."

"No, it doesn't. But somebody killed Andrew. Here's a guy we don't know much about. He's strange, he's moody, and he had a fierce argument with Andrew. Sort of threatened to kill him. Doesn't that tell you something?"

"He didn't exactly threaten to kill Andrew."

"Not in so many words," Fletcher said. "But that's what he meant, isn't it?"

"I don't know. I wasn't there. Why don't you tell this story to the police? That's what I would do, Fletcher."

"Like I told you before. I don't want to be involved. That's why I need your advice. Is there some way I can tell them ... anonymously? Or through you? You could say, I have a client. He has some information, but he prefers to remain anonymous. They can't make you reveal your source, right? So I'm asking you to do this. Would you?"

"Absolutely not," I said. "I told you, I'm staying as far out of this as I can."

"Look," he said. "I need you to do this. For Lydia. She's all on edge. We want to move out, and we're going to. But meanwhile, we're there. Please, Frank. You've got to help us."

"You asked for advice," I said. "Here's my advice. For now, don't do anything. Let the police investigate. If Kurt really did this thing, they'll probably get him. Give it a week. If after a week, nothing's happened, then let me know, and we'll think about what to do next."

"And what about us? Me and Lydia? Living in the house with a murderer?"

"If you feel that way, you should leave," I said. "Go to a motel. Go on vacation. If you can."

He seemed unhappy; disappointed in my response. "It's not that easy to get away.... I've got a job, Lydia has a job. We'll think about it," he said, and left my office.

* * *

But afterwards, as I sat there, his story reverberated in my mind. This argument between Kurt and Andrew. It *was* potentially significant. But what were they quarreling about? San Bernardino, May 2009. What did that mean? I think, despite all my intentions, fate meant for me to get involved. I was hopelessly curious, intrigued, caught up in the mystery. San Bernardino? That's this huge county to the west of Los Angeles. Part of the metropolitan area. Suburbs, mountains, deserts. What could it have to do with this case?

They could have been talking about something purely personal. Or maybe not. Could the local newspapers shed some light on this affair? On Saturday morning, I went to our local public library. It was, as usual, quiet, except for the little kids squirming on the floor of the room with children's books, while a gray-haired lady read them a story about a hungry little caterpillar. I asked the librarian if they had a file of San Bernardino newspapers—I wasn't even sure San Bernardino *had* a newspaper. Whether San Bernardino had a newspaper or not, the San Mateo library had no such thing. The librarian suggested I try a university library. They did have the *San Francisco Chronicle*, would that do? I decided to look at May 2009 in the *Chronicle*, and, as it turned out, they had bound copies, not microfilm, which was a surprise. I thought everybody threw these things out and replaced them with that despicable invention of the devil, microfilm. I hate microfilm. I can never get it to wind properly. When I have to look at some legal records on microfilm, I always get it backwards or upside down.

The *Chronicle* is the leading newspaper of San Francisco. Maybe by now the only one. I rather like it. It has a lot of local news, some good foreign news, and a wonderful nose for prurient and titillating local stories. Of course, the foreign and national news tends to be somewhat second-hand; it's mostly cribbed or bought from *The New York Times*, but so what? *The New York Times* is fine in its place. I like to read it once in a while, but it doesn't tell you what's playing at the local multiplex. And a sex scandal has to be really big and of national importance before it can crash *The New York Times*. I was hoping that whatever was going on in San Bernardino—*if* there was something going on—would be reported in the *Chronicle* as well. I started reading, and pretty soon I found myself deeply engaged. I love to read old newspapers, not that 2009 really qualifies as old. Yet in some ways it seemed downright quaint. New news becomes old news so quickly these days.

I soon realized, though, that this was going to be a frustrating, and probably pointless search. After all, what on earth was I looking for? Something about Kurt. Or Andrew and Kurt. But I didn't even know Kurt's last name, and I had seen him only once, and fleetingly, so that I really had no clear idea what he looked like. The *Chronicle* was full of all sorts of stories, but I doubted somehow that upheavals in the Middle East, or corruption in China, or a coup in some African country I never heard of, or rumblings about elections in the good old USA was what I was looking for. There was a juicy local scandal in Vallejo, with local officials helping themselves to public funds. Nothing new there. There were stories about bus problems in San Francisco. The only thing that concerned San Bernardino at all, at least as far as the *Chronicle* was concerned, was the final days of a huge and sensational trial. A man named John Gruber was prosecuted for killing his pregnant wife. Turns out he had a girlfriend on the side, whose name was Crystal. I vaguely recalled this trial. It was big, big news, for some reason, at the time; it even made the front pages of those trashy magazines you see in the supermarket. ("John Gruber's Confession! Why I Killed Her!" and "Crystal: He Lied to Me! I Never Knew He was Married," and "Gruber's Secret Love Nest," and so on.)

I've always wanted to buy one of those magazines, but I'm simply too embarrassed. The other day I was particularly tempted. Some of them specialize in celebrity gossip and crime stories, and others, in supernatural claptrap. I wish I could read them, such wonderful stories, like "Devil's Face Appears in Cloud over Baghdad," followed by "My Mom was an Alien from Outer Space," and "I Lost 200 Pounds on a Diet of Chocolate and Peanut Butter." But what if somebody saw me putting down my money for this trash?

Basically I was getting nowhere. I should have realized that—since I had no idea what I was looking for. But I don't give up easily. I called Sheila the next day, around dinner time. "What's Kurt's last name?" I asked.

"It's Schmidt," she said, "why do you ask?"

"Never mind that. I'm just curious. What do you know about his background, who he is, where he comes from, what he does for a living, and so on?"

"I don't know anything," she said. "I'd say the same thing about some other people here. We don't do an FBI check before we rent out rooms. If you can pay the rent, and you don't have obvious body odor, you're in. What's this all about?"

"Can you get me a picture of Kurt?"

"A photograph? You think I carry a picture of him around in my wallet? You think I try to make sure he's in the background of my selfies? Be serious, Frank. And what is this all about?"

"Sheila, I'd like to meet him. Talk to him."

"But he doesn't seem to want to meet *you*," she said. "Look: I'm busy. If you don't want to tell me what this is all about, I'm hanging up." Which she did.

* * *

For a while, at least, I was at a dead end, as far as Kurt was concerned. I knew I should just drop the subject, but as I've already confessed, I was simply unable to mind my own business. On an impulse, I called Lydia and asked whether Fletcher was around. She said he was on call, and unavailable. "Can I assume he has a smartphone, with a camera?"

"I guess so. I do. Doesn't everybody? But why are you asking?"

"Never mind." My plan was to enlist Fletcher, persuade him to take a photo of Kurt, and give it to me. Armed with a picture of Kurt, I might be able to make more sense of the newspaper stories. Already I had a vague idea, vague and fantastic. As it turns out, it wasn't quite as fantastic as I thought.

Dinner that night was a dinner for the whole family. That didn't happen very often. My daughters, devout teenagers, preferred eating with people of their own species or having a pizza in their room. We had almost given up having them at the table. To tell you the truth, sometimes it's better without them. First of all, they're usually sullen and they talk in monosyllables. Or they look at the food and say yuck. At other times, they babble on to each other. Or bicker. We live in different worlds, I guess. I'm an alien in their world, and they're an alien in mine.

Amanda, the older daughter, was going on and on this particular evening. First, it was about something "totally sick," but then it was about something else at school. "Daddy, I want you to hear this," she said. "The principal, he's acting like a real jerk."

"He *is* a jerk," her sister said.

Then Amanda let loose. "So this Tiffany and she's, like, a total slut; I mean, who can stand her? And she's got this boyfriend, Christopher. He's on every sports team, and the two of them, I mean they're like *animals*, the way they carry on. I mean, like, who cares—but it's annoying. And somebody took a video, how they were making out in the parking lot. He's got his own car, his parents are filthy rich. And everybody saw this video, and she complained to the principal and we had to listen to this dumb speech in assembly hall, I mean, it was like beyond boring, about how to behave and privacy and blah blah blah. I mean, everybody takes pictures of everything, I read that in a magazine, and so what? Daddy, you're a lawyer, and don't we have a constitutional right to stuff like that?"

I wasn't sure what she meant by stuff like that. I actually don't t remember what advice I gave her about the Constitution of the United States and the crisis at her high school, but it does seem as if nowadays everybody is taking photos of everything twenty-four seven. I have heard that the kids, at least the post-puberty kids, send naked pictures of themselves to their friends, and I meant to ask Celia if she would please warn the girls not to do anything of that sort—Celia would have a better chance at that than I would. Like so many other things, these phone cameras have their good points and their bad points.

You have to wonder about a world in which there are cameras watching you wherever you go: government cameras, but also private ones. Still, they are awfully convenient devices; and they were going to give me what I wanted right now, which was a photograph of Kurt. True, I had seen him when he answered the door, but that was only a glimpse and the light was bad. I needed a second look.

13

I couldn't wait to talk to Fletcher. It frustrated me that I failed to connect with him when I wanted to. A day or so later I finally got through to him, and he agreed, somewhat reluctantly, to take a photograph of Kurt or ask Lydia to do it—and to be as unobtrusive taking it as possible, which I guess would not be so easy. As luck would have it, I was tied up with clients all morning and part of the afternoon, but I made an arrangement to meet Fletcher when both of us were free, in the evening.

It was about 4:00 in the afternoon. I was just cleaning up some matters in the office, when I had a visitor. I don't usually get clients off the street. Lawyers almost never do. Some lawyers advertise on TV, of course; they're looking for people arrested for drunk driving or who are in trouble with immigration officials. I don't do drunk drivers. I don't do immigration law. The lifeblood of my practice is referrals, usually from satisfied clients. When I hear a knock on the door, it's usually some kind of delivery service. This day, when I opened the door, a man was standing there who was, I would guess, about my age. He was wearing a dark blue business suit. He had a receding hairline, which he tried to hide, as most people do, by combing a few pitiful wisps of hair over the bald spots. He was pudgy, but not extremely so. I noticed two large rings on his somewhat fat fingers. He had small, squinty eyes, partly hidden behind tiny steel-rimmed glasses. I noticed his shoes, too: very shiny shoes that looked expensive. Not that I'm an expert.

I said, "Can I help you?"

He said, "You're Frank May?"

"Guilty as charged."

He reached into his wallet and took out a business card. "Let me introduce myself. I'm Max Appleby. Angelica Finster is my aunt."

I looked at the card. It had his name and phone number, and the name of his firm: Wortman, Appleby and Biggs, Certified Public Accountants. They were located on LaSalle Street, in Chicago.

I shook his hand, which I found rather clammy. We went into my office, and I waved my hand at a seat, which he took. I said, "What can I do for you?"

He said, "Am I right in presuming that you represent the estate of Andrew Wright?"

"You are not right."

He seemed surprised. "I was told you were his lawyer."

"He consulted me, yes. We talked about certain things. We never reached agreement, so it's wrong to say I was his lawyer. And I certainly don't represent his estate. I don't know if he *has* an estate. To the best of my knowledge, Andrew Wright didn't have any money."

"And his will?"

"If he had a will, I don't know anything about it. I never made out a will for him. I'd be surprised if he had one."

Appleby made a face. "But you did handle his affairs...."

"No I did not," I said, quite firmly. "I never handled anything for Andrew Wright. Yes, he consulted me. Yes, I discussed one or two things. But that's as far as it went. In fact, I specifically declined to represent him."

"And why was that?"

"I really don't care to say."

"May I ask, then, even though you didn't represent him, exactly what did he consult you about?"

"You may ask, but I'm not going to answer, Mr. Appleby. What we talked about is entirely confidential."

He said, "You're going to make things difficult. I can see that. Let me make myself perfectly clear. I'm Angelica Finster's closest blood relative. My late father, Richard Appleby, was

Mrs. Finster's brother. Her only brother. My father had two sons: myself and my brother Oscar. My brother, Oscar, had a lot of problems. He never married, and he wasn't employed for many years. He lived with my aunt, and more or less looked after her, I suppose, but unfortunately, he was never in good health, and he died some years ago."

"Go on."

"My aunt is a wealthy woman. Or was, until she met this creature Andrew Wright, who of course has been robbing her blind. I don't know how much of her assets are left, after he pillaged them. There's the house, of course. It's worth, I believe, more than three million dollars. I presume, since you're a local lawyer, you're aware of the staggering prices of real estate in this area. That house would sell for a fortune."

"This is all very interesting, Mr. Appleby, but I don't see where I come in."

He said, "You deny the existence of an estate. Then can you tell me who the heirs are? Andrew Wright's heirs? And who will handle his affairs?"

"I don't think he has any heirs. Or, for that matter, any 'affairs' as you put it."

"I'm not a fool, Mr. May. If he stripped my aunt of assets, they're part of his estate, and I can assure you I will sue the estate for every penny."

I shrugged my shoulders. "It's a free country, Mr. Appleby. I really have nothing to do with Andrew Wright's estate, as I told you quite plainly."

"Do you represent a Sheila Donnelly?"

"I'd rather not answer that."

"My understanding is that you do. I've heard a rumor that she is Andrew Wright's heir. In which case, yes, indeed, you most certainly have a lot to do with his estate."

"Really, Mr. Appleby. Let's assume I do represent Ms. Donnelly. And let's assume she is indeed Andrew's heir—which I know nothing about, since as far as I know, he died intestate, and she isn't a blood relative, or a wife, or anything like that. And let's assume further that he did have certain assets. Are you saying that they're rightfully yours? That they were stolen from your aunt?"

"That's exactly what I'm saying. Aunt Angelica, by the way, had made out a will at one time. I have a copy of it in my possession. After Uncle Morris died, and Oscar moved in with her, I made arrangements for her to see a good lawyer, here in Palo Alto. Do you know Foster Gilpin?"

"I've met him."

"Well, he drew up the will. She made a few bequests to charity, she left the house to Oscar, and the remainder of the estate was for Oscar and me, the two of us, share and share alike. Then unfortunately, my brother died. He had no will, and I'm his closest relative. Oscar himself left nothing, or next to nothing. Once he was dead, as I understand the legal situation, I stand to inherit the whole estate. The house, and whatever else there is. That is, that was the situation before this schemer got hold of Aunt Angelica."

"There's no estate," I said, rather waspishly. "For one thing, your aunt isn't dead."

"I know that, of course. Yes, she's very much alive. A bit frail, but considering her age.... I don't see her very much. I'm a busy man, I have a family, you understand, and my professional life keeps me on the go. But I try to stay in touch. It isn't easy. Aunt Angelica has been confused, mentally. Suffering from dementia. It's not easy to communicate. But I did find out, that she has made out a new will...."

"Really. May I ask, *how* you found out?"

"Well, she called me, to be perfectly honest. She said, Max, I've met the loveliest man, and he's going to take care of me now that Oscar is gone. Of course, I asked her, who is this? But she was quite incoherent; she said, oh, I just can't remember his name. And then—I know somebody was in the room with her—she said, oh, yes, his name is Andrew, and he's so nice to me, and we're making out a new will. I'm giving Andrew the house. He'll take good care of the house. I'm so pleased with this arrangement. I said, Aunt Angelica, you can't do that, and she said, oh, but Andrew wants me to, and he's so terribly nice.... Well, I immediately realized, she was under duress. This Andrew, he was standing right there, when she made the phone call. I should have known that. Aunt Angelica is much too far gone to make a long-distance call. It's totally beyond her. Obviously, this man put her up to it. I'm sure he actually dialed the number."

"And was she right? Did she make out a new will?"

"I believe she did. I called Gilpin, but of course he knew nothing about it. So she must have gone to another lawyer. If she went to a lawyer at all. Anyway, I called Andrew Wright, and I demanded to know if all this was true."

"And what did he say?"

"He laughed. He was very impudent, and he said, well, what's it to you? She has no obligation to you. I said, I'm her nephew, and he said, so what? What's a nephew, anyway? She barely knows you. Right then and there I realized he was taking advantage of her, robbing her. I made some inquiries and found out he had turned her beautiful house into some sort of rooming-house, perfectly disgusting. I'm sure it's a violation of the zoning laws. There's who knows what kind of people there, and I'm sure they're doing drugs in the house or worse. I thought to myself, poor Angelica...."

"And the will? If there is one?"

"It wouldn't be valid. I've consulted my own lawyer, in Chicago. It's undue influence. That's what he said. Anyway, she wasn't competent to make out a will. If you'd met her, you'd know that. She's got Alzheimer's disease. Dementia. It's perfectly obvious. She's been incompetent for years. Anyway, I want to see that will. I have a right to. I'm her flesh and blood. I'm the closest living relative. If somebody tries to probate that will, I'm going to fight it tooth and nail."

"That's your privilege," I said. "But I don't know anything about it. Not her will, and not Andrew's. Anyway, nobody is going to show you anything, especially while your aunt is alive."

To me it was as plain as day he cared nothing about his aunt. He was a vulture, attracted by the smell of money.

"I have an attorney here, in San Carlos," he said. "My attorney back home referred me to this gentleman. Winston Grace, that's his name. He specializes in will contests. I flew out here to meet with him."

"Really? How long have you been here?"

"I've been here something over a week. I had other business to transact as well."

"You've been here a week? So you were here, in town, the night Andrew died?"

"Well, yes, as a matter of fact. We had a meeting, the day before this unfortunate event. We met in my attorney's office...."

"And you saw him the day he died, too."

"I beg your pardon?"

"I said: you went to see him the day he died. In fact, that very evening."

"I have no idea what you're talking about," he said. But he was lying. It was written all over his face. He was fidgeting and coughing and giving himself away by his tone, his body language, everything.

"Somebody saw you," I said.

He was silent for a minute. He took off his glasses, and rubbed them with a tiny piece of cloth. He seemed to have poor eyesight, because he squinted badly when his glasses were off. I could almost *feel* his embarrassment.

"Suppose, for the sake of argument," he began, but I interrupted him.

"Don't say 'for the sake of argument,' Mr. Appleby. You were there. At the house. You were seen going in and out. Or rather, a person who meets your description. Nobody knew your name, but I'm sure they could identify you in a lineup."

"A lineup? What on earth are you talking about? Are you insinuating...? No, you can't be serious."

"I'm not insinuating anything."

"Yes, you are," he said, raising his voice. "Talking about lineups.... I resent that bitterly. You're insinuating that I killed Andrew Wright."

"No, I'm not," I said. "But you're the first person I've heard about that actually had some reason to kill him."

"A reason?"

"Well, yes," I said. "You accused him of stealing, or practically stealing. You said he took advantage of your aunt. I suppose that's a motive, isn't it?"

"This is intolerable," he said.

"Moreover," I went on. "You had an argument with Andrew Wright. You actually yelled at him. Didn't you know that you'd be overheard?"

"Overheard?"

"Your aunt heard you. She told us about an argument between Andrew and somebody named Max. We had no idea who she meant. Now we know."

I was amazed at my own nerve. Why was I doing this? Was it because the man was so obnoxious? I waited to hear what he would have to say. But he was clearly taken aback. He was trapped and clearly surprised that his little secret was out. He felt it was better, no doubt, to say nothing at all. "This conversation is over," he said, peremptorily. He stormed out of my office.

Actually, it never entered my head that Max Appleby was the man who crept into Andrew's room, hit him on the head with something hard, then smothered him with a pillow. He just didn't seem the type. I looked at his business card again. He was a partner in Wortman, Appleby and Biggs, certified public accountants. I probably was just indulging in stereotypes, but I simply didn't associate CPAs with murder. Tax evasion, maybe, but murder, no.

But then who *was* a likely suspect? None of the people I met in the house struck me as the murdering type. Possibly Sheila. She was tough as nails. But why would she kill Andrew Wright? Also, according to her, she had sex with Andrew an hour before he died. I couldn't picture her as a kind of black widow spider, devouring the male of the species after mating with him.

I don't hang around with murderers, so maybe I just don't know one when I see one. It happens, sometimes, that some psychopath is arrested—with a trail of dead bodies, maybe buried under the basement—and the neighbors say they never guessed, they're shocked, he was so quiet, so polite, never any trouble, and so on.

There was always the mysterious Kurt. The man was hiding something. He was deliberately avoiding me, for some reason. *He* could be the one.

Or some stranger. A homicidal maniac, prowling around Silicon Valley. If you read enough novels that you buy at airports, the woods are full of such people. Insane people who kill for fun. Maybe one of these people killed Andrew. Maybe this monster escaped from a mental institution, and is right now stalking the next victim of his insatiable blood-lust.

Or the old man next door, who finally gathered up the energy to come down from his duck blind and do something useful.

Or a werewolf, frothing at the mouth, and waiting for the full moon to come, which would turn him into a murderer with fangs and huge hairy paws. Why not? There was a full moon the night Andrew died. I remember it distinctly. A big fat moon was hanging in the sky like a huge white balloon.

The werewolf theory was fun but unconvincing.

No, it had to be Kurt.

* * *

I had arranged with Fletcher to meet him at the house that evening. I said I would be there at 8:00, hoping that I could already have the photos. Actually, the traffic was lighter than usual—it happens every once in a while—and I got there a bit early. Sheila answered the door when I rang. "Frank," she said, "what the hell are you doing here?"

I told her I had something to talk to Fletcher about. She said, "To Fletcher? Come on, tell me. I hate these secrets." I dodged the question. I said I also wanted to talk to her, and would she be around? She looked at me suspiciously, but said yes, she would be.

Fletcher wasn't in the kitchen or the living room or any place obvious. Sheila said, "He's upstairs in Lydia's room; I'll go get him." She went upstairs, and came back down in a minute or so, saying, "He'll be with you in a second." A short time later, Fletcher and Lydia came down the stairs. They were both wearing white t-shirts and jeans, and she was adjusting her long hair, winding it around the top of her head, and fastening it with something.

There was something about the look on their faces—I can't describe it—a certain breathlessness, or something about the way he fiddled with a button, and she fiddled with her hair, or something about the way they looked at each other, that made we think—no, made me sure—they were in the midst of sex when I arrived ahead of time. Or was I just a dirty old man? Anyway, why shouldn't they have sex? I'm not an abstinence freak. Except when it comes to my adolescent daughters. Fletcher and Lydia were young. The young have a lot of sex. At least that's the impression we middle-aged people get. But do they have a lot of love? Maybe we old folks have more love than the young folks. That would be a comfort.

On the other hand, there's the high divorce rate. Love is hard work. Or it's like a big test, a final exam. Lots of people flunk.

My business with Fletcher and Lydia didn't take very long. We went into the study. There was nobody around. They hadn't yet taken any photographs.

"We don't see much of Kurt these days," Fletcher said, and Lydia nodded. "But then I'm not here that much myself."

"He comes to some of the meals," Lydia said. "He seems awfully depressed. I get the feeling he's got something on his mind."

Something on his mind? Could that be guilt, I wondered? Or fear?

We talked a bit. There had been no chance of sneaking a photograph, but they were still willing to do this. Lydia offered to email the photos to me when they got them; but I preferred actual prints. She had a friend at work, she said, who owned some sort of device that would print the pictures well. "Fletcher's got a busy schedule," she said, "But I'll see Kurt, when he comes around. I should've done this already, after your phone call. I'm sorry that I've been busy too. But I will definitely do it. Kurt knows I'm always talking on my cell phone, mostly to Fletcher, so maybe he won't be suspicious. Either Fletcher or I will find a way to take his picture on the sly. At least we'll try."

I thanked them for their help. They said they'd call me when they had results. Then they went back upstairs, maybe for an encore or for unfinished business, or just for conversation. I went into the living room. Sheila and Carmen were sitting there. Sheila had her arm around Carmen, who was crying.

"Carmen," I said. "What's the matter?"

"It's Garth," she said. "I actually saw him again.... I don't think he saw me; it was on University Avenue, not four blocks from here. I don't know what he was doing there. He doesn't live around here. Frank, I'm just plain terrified. I think he must have figured out that I live in Palo Alto. Maybe he's got my actual address. Frank, what should I do? I can get one of those protective orders, but the man is crazy; he wouldn't let that stop him. I told you that. I can't get the police to arrest him, because he hasn't done anything yet. I've got to get out of here. That's all there is to it. But I'll lose my job...."

She began sobbing uncontrollably. I said, "Maybe it's not so bad. You can't be sure he was looking for you."

"Oh yes, I'm sure," she said. "You don't know Garth."

Sheila said, "You should go away for a few days, Carmen. Can you get some time off?"

Carmen nodded. "I've got some sick leave coming.... And I called my sister in LA," she said. "I'm going to go down there. For a few days anyway. The police don't want us to leave town, but I'm going to do it anyway."

"Great idea," I said.

"But that won't solve my problem," Carmen said. "Garth won't give up. And I can't stay long at my sister's. She's got kids.... Her house is crowded. What can I do?"

We talked for a while, and she seemed to calm down. Eventually she went up her room, and Sheila and I went into the study to talk.

"I've got a new theory," Sheila said. "Maybe it was Garth all along."

"Garth?"

"Maybe he killed Andrew Wright. How does that idea strike you?"

"Sheila, did he even *know* Andrew?"

"Look: Andrew was threatening Carmen. He was using Garth's name to force her to stay. He said he'd tell Garth unless she cooperated—Carmen told me that herself. Maybe Andrew actually saw the guy, talked to him. He obviously knew where Garth lived."

"How did he know that?"

"Well, Fletcher had traced him...."

"Why would Fletcher tell Andrew?"

"I don't know," she said. "Maybe he didn't. Maybe Andrew just overheard something. Who knows? So suppose Garth knew about this place...."

"But he wants to kill Carmen if he wants to kill anybody. What did he have against Andrew?"

"Oh, a lot."

"Like what?"

"Look," she said, "The man is nuts. Garth, I mean. He's homicidal. And there's a history here."

"A history?"

She hesitated. "Did Carmen tell you why she was living here?"

"No," I said. "Well, she said she had to get away. She left LA. I guess she just answered an ad or something."

Sheila laughed. "It's never that simple. Everybody in this house is here for a reason. They're not randomly selected, believe me. Andrew *found* her. He recruited her."

"Recruited her? What do you mean?"

"Remember, Andrew was collecting these weird stories about sex during the earthquake, OK? Well, there was this woman who came to Andrew with a kind of hair-raising story. She met a man in a bar, he seemed charming, attractive. They went to her house, and it was Dr. Jekyll and Mr. Hyde. He turned into something really scary. He wanted sex, which was OK with her in general, but he seemed really creepy and wanted to tie her up to the bed, or do something with chains, who knows? A real pervert. She was sure he was going to hurt her, so she pretended she was hot for his body, and she said, yum, that's sounds just great, I love it, just let me get ready, you wait here, I'll be in the bedroom. She got a knife from some-place, and put it under the pillow. He came in and started undressing and doing weird things, she didn't specify what, and he took out a pair of handcuffs or something like that. She was getting ready to pull the knife, and then came the earthquake. He went totally bananas, and pulled up his pants and ran out the door with his pants at half-mast, hollering and carrying on. She locked the door. He had left his shoes behind, and he pounded on the door; but she never let him in. The guy was Garth. She knew his name. He had been dumb enough to tell her his name, where he lived, who he worked for."

"And she gave this story to Andrew?"

"Exactly. It was a choice morsel for his collection."

"OK," I said, "So Andrew knew this story, but where does Carmen come in?"

She said, "I'm not exactly sure. I think Andrew checked up on this guy, Garth, and found out he was married. To Carmen. He talked to her, and she said they were separated, that she was afraid of him, said he was violent and an abuser. Andrew induced her to come up here to get away from Garth. Mean-while, he kept in touch with Garth. I think maybe he was playing a double game all the time, when he arranged for Carmen to move in. Maybe he was holding this over her head, as a kind of leverage—he wanted to use it for his own purposes. He was a bastard, Andrew. A regular first-class A number one bastard."

A bastard she slept with, I reminded myself. But I kept quiet. Instead I asked, "I'm wondering, though, how do *you* know this, Sheila? I can't believe Andrew told you. And Car-men, she doesn't know the whole story. Is it just a guess? I can't believe that."

"Never mind how I know."

She seemed a bit upset. I think I knew why. I think I knew, too, the answer to my question. But I had other fish to fry at the moment.

* * *

Actually, some of the fish I had to fry were clients. Clients can be an annoyance, but they pay the rent. They put food on the table, and shoes on the feet of my kids. At least that's the expression. My daughters seem to wear mostly flip-flops, which can be bought at Target for a dollar or two. But I'll skip the details about my children's footwear.

A few days went by, and nothing much happened in the case of Andrew Wright. Then Lydia called me at work. It was about 3:00 in the afternoon. She said she had the photographs.

"Good going. Was it hard?"

"It took some maneuvering. I didn't want to seem too obvious. But I did it, and I don't think he noticed. Some of them are pretty good. I've got mostly profiles, but some of them show his whole face. Fletcher took some of them, too. I printed them out."

I asked her whether she knew of any progress on the case. She said, "I don't think so. There's a detective who came around and asked more questions, but frankly I think they're completely baffled."

"What's the atmosphere in the house?"

"Sort of grim. We all feel trapped. It's hard on all of us. I think we all want to get out of here. Move. Go somewhere else. But right now, well, we can't. We're all reacting in one way or another. Chuck is swimming twice as much as ever. And Billy ... he's always been sickly; the tension doesn't help. I asked Fletcher to talk to Billy; but Billy has his own doctors. He doesn't want to talk to Fletcher. Carmen is a real basket case. And then there's Kurt himself. He's more secretive, more distant than ever. And morose. Other times, it's like he's going to explode, like he's just barely keeping it all in. Whatever the 'it' is. I mean, the tension in the house, it's major."

"I can imagine."

I promised to come get the photos as soon as I could. I asked whether I could come after work that same day, but she said no, she and Fletcher were going to visit a friend. So we put it off for a while. I went back to my normal work. I was drafting a trust agreement for one of my better (that is, richer) clients, who owned two apartment buildings and a Greek restaurant, plus various stocks and bonds. I was in the midst of it when the phone rang.

It was a guy named Steve Stern, a lawyer, a solo practitioner in Palo Alto, who did mostly estates work. I knew him, more or less. We had some dealings once, with regard to a case. I represented an older woman whose sister had died and left behind a very complex estate. Steve was handling the sister's estate. Steve was older than I was, and perpetually looked thin, tired, and gaunt. He had a little goatee, which was speckled with gray. He seemed perfectly competent, though a little tense and pushy. He was a graduate of Stanford's law school, which is ranked "almost as high as Harvard, maybe higher. Look at the ratings." He never let people forget this. He said, "Hi, Frank. How's it going?"

"Oh, you know. Comme ci comme ça."

"I thought I'd check in with you about something. Client of yours, who got himself murdered. Andrew Wright."

"Well, not really a client. At best an ex-client. I guess anybody who's dead is an ex-client. Everybody says I was Andrew's lawyer. It's positively amazing. Sure, we talked, but we never really came to any agreement, and I never did agree to represent him. Anyway, what's on your mind, Steve?"

"I guess you answered my question. I wanted to know if you wrote a will for him, or anything like that."

"Nope. Never did."

"Here's the deal. I've got a cousin in Omaha, and he lives next door to this guy, Lucas Grove, who is a high school teacher. Apparently, he and his brothers—he's got three brothers—are the closest relatives of this dead man, Andrew Wright. They hardly knew him—met him two or three times—and had nothing much to do with him, didn't like him in fact, but they found out he was murdered. I guess the news somehow penetrated all the way to Nebraska; and they got to wondering, if he had some money, you know, inherited something from his parents. This Lucas, he's no fool, he figured a young man like Andrew wouldn't have a will, so the money would have to go to the Grove brothers. Well, my cousin said he knew a lawyer in the area—me—and so Grove gave me a call. I spoke to some woman, Sheila, who was his girlfriend I guess. She said probably there wasn't a will, but to check with you, Frank."

"No, no will, as far as I know. Probably no assets either, Steve. I think Lucas Grove is going to be very disappointed."

"That'll make two of us," Steve said, and hung up the phone.

* * *

I've been telling people that Andrew's estate had no assets. But was this really true? And what about a will? I had a most uncomfortable feeling. Sheila had gone through the room, had rifled through Andrew's papers. She had taken some of them. She claimed that she couldn't find the material for *The Earth Moved*, that the material was already gone. But was she telling the truth? Then she gave me a thick envelope, with papers or documents inside, asking me to keep them in my safe deposit box, but not to look inside.

Was I doing the right thing? I had visions of the Ethics Committee breathing down my neck. Accusing me of suppressing evidence, or something along those lines. I couldn't be sure I was suppressing anything; I had no idea what was in the package. But was that an excuse? I wasn't a safe deposit box company. If you gave a lawyer something and asked him to hold it, keep it safe, what did that mean? Did that put him on notice that there was something suspicious going on? Papers taken from the room of a man who had just been murdered? Not a good idea.

So was I breaching legal ethics? I wish I knew the answer. I took legal ethics in law school. It was a required course. Boring beyond belief. And that was so many years ago. I wonder if the rules had changed.

I felt nervous and uneasy. I had to get in touch with Sheila and clear this matter up. I called her that evening. Carmen answered, and she put Sheila on the line. We made an arrangement to have lunch, in Palo Alto, during her lunch hour. We met at a Thai restaurant on University Avenue, which was close to her workplace. It is one of my favorite restaurants. I like the atmosphere. Pictures of the King and Queen of Thailand hang on the wall, smiling benignly. The menu is full of delicious and mysterious things.

Sheila was reasonably prompt. The restaurant was not crowded. We sat in a booth near the back, where we had a decent amount of privacy. "Sheila," I said, "I've got two matters I have to discuss with you."

"Alright."

"First of all … about Andrew: did he have any money, as far as you know? Bank accounts, that sort of thing?"

"How would I know?"

"Well, you two were, uh, lovers…."

She gave me a withering glance. "Lovers? Frank, don't be so old-fashioned. Really. I thought lawyers were tough-minded. We weren't lovers. We had a relationship, of sorts. That's all. And we never talked about money. Besides, it's none of your business, is it?"

"Yes and no."

"What's the yes part? Oh, never mind. But since you ask: he did have some money. Not a whole lot. But some."

"Family money? I thought he spent all of that."

"If you must know, he skimmed it from Angelica's income. She had dividends, a pension; and then we all paid rent—well, all except Andrew. He felt he earned what he took. Maybe he did. She'd be drooling in some godforsaken nursing home, if it wasn't for him. He kept her alive."

"I guess."

"Naturally," she said, "he did it for a reason. It wasn't out of the goodness of his heart. His heart didn't have much goodness, in case you hadn't noticed. Anyway, he had a bank account somewhere. I don't know where. Some local bank. Mind you, we're not talking millions. Maybe $20,000. Of course, he was always bragging that he was going to make millions someday. He sang that song all the time."

"Did he ever talk to you about making out a will, or anything like that?"

"When we were together, he usually had sex on his mind,

or was bragging about what a great guy he was and how much money he was going to make. *Going* to make. No, we never talked about wills. Anyway, why would he tell me?"

We were interrupted by the arrival of heaping platters of food, noodle dishes and meats that looked totally delicious. For a while I was silent, concentrating on the food. Sheila only picked at hers. I like women who have reasonable appetites. Finally, after I had cleaned my plate, I said, "Sheila, I've got something else on my mind.... I think we have a problem."

"*We*? Meaning me?"

"No. We, meaning both of us. That package you gave me...."

"You didn't open it! I told you not to open it! Damn it, Frank!"

"Don't get excited," I said. "No, I didn't open it. But you said these were things you took from Andrew's room. Now, you had no right to do that. It was wrong. Suppressing evidence, or something like that. And if I'm aiding and abetting you...."

"How do you know it's evidence? Frank, I believe you *did* look inside."

"I swear I didn't. But are you saying, inside the envelope there *is* some kind of evidence?"

"Evidence of what, Frank?"

"Well, who killed Andrew Wright. Or, at any rate, some-thing relevant to the investigation. Look, Sheila, I'm just worried about the ethical aspects...."

"The what?"

"You know. A lawyer's ethics, our oath. My obligations as a member of the bar."

Another look of withering contempt. "Give me a break, Frank. Spare me the Sunday sermon. You just don't want to get into trouble. Believe me, there's nothing in that envelope. Well, I don't mean nothing. I mean nothing incriminating. But I don't want you to open it. Do you hear me?"

I heard her.

Suddenly she said, "I've got to go," and she swept out of the restaurant. I was left sitting there sheepishly, staring at the bill, which the waiter had just deposited on the table. I had to pay it, of course.

Had I learned something? Andrew was stealing money. That in a way didn't surprise me. But was that connected to his death? It was hard to see a connection, unless the connection was Max Appleby, and that seemed unlikely.

What on earth could be inside Sheila's package of documents? But I had promised not to open it. I sighed, and resigned myself to the fact that I would probably never know. I was wrong. Within a week, Sheila would change her mind. We're coming to that. Things were heating up in the case. And very soon, there was going to be another murder. In fact, it happened that very night.

14

I had a quiet evening at home, a good night's sleep, a nice big breakfast, then I drove to the office. I had no idea that during my tranquil, humdrum night at home, reading the newspaper, watching some mindless show on TV, a killer was at work. I was in my office, plugging away at my work, when the phone rang. It was Carmen. I hardly recognized her voice. She sounded almost hysterical. Her sobs and cries almost obliterated her words.

I said, "Carmen, calm down. I can't understand a word you're saying."

"I've got to see you, Frank, you're the only one who can help me. I don't have anybody else; nobody to turn to. I'm in terrible trouble."

"What kind of trouble, Carmen?"

"They think—Frank, I know you don't do criminal law, but I need somebody. Can you help me, or tell me what to do, where to go?"

"Of course, I can. But what's this about?"

"Can I come see you?"

"Sure...."

She said she'd be at my office as soon as she could. Not half an hour later she appeared. Fortunately, I had nothing vital scheduled for that hour. She was clearly a mess. Her eyes were bloodshot; her hair was uncombed. Obviously, she had been crying. She was trembling all over.

"Sit down," I said. "Can I get you something? You look

really upset."

"I am, I am.... Oh Frank, it's ... it's Garth...."

"Oh my God. He found you? He tried something?"

She shook her head. "No, not that. Frank, he's dead...."

"Dead? But that's.... I hate to say this, but isn't it a relief? What happened, Carmen? Was it an accident?"

"Frank, no; it wasn't an accident," she said, wiping her eyes. "He was killed. Murdered. And that's not all.... I'm so afraid they'll arrest me. I'm terrified, Frank. That's why I need a lawyer. I'm afraid they're going to come after me."

"The police?"

"Yes. They've already been asking questions.... I don't want to go to prison, Frank, I couldn't bear that."

I said: "Carmen, get a grip on yourself. Nobody's going to arrest you. How could anybody imagine you could do a thing like that? I mean, kill a guy. It's totally ridiculous."

"I couldn't kill anybody, hurt anybody, you know that," she said. "But the police, they're tough, they're cynical, they're suspicious.... And I don't have an alibi. Why would anybody kill Garth? Except me...."

"Lots of people," I said. "You haven't been in touch with him. You think you're the only person he's brutalized? There might be a long list of people who might want to get rid of him."

"I don't know," she said, "Maybe, maybe not. If only it didn't happen last night! If only things had been different...."

She was crying again. I handed her a Kleenex. "Tell me what happened," I said.

"I was supposed to go to Los Angeles, last night, to spend some time there with my sister, with the family. I was going to visit them. You were there when I talked to Sheila about going away. I was so terrified of Garth. I just had to get away. And all this awful business about Andrew. So I told everybody I was going, and I had a ticket and everything. I packed a bag. I put it in the car, and I was actually on Highway 280, on the way to the airport. Well, my cell phone rang. It was my sister. She said, I'm so glad I caught you before you got on the plane. I said, what's the matter? She said, oh, a bunch of things. Nothing serious. But Jacob—that's the five year old—he's got chicken pox; and my mother-in-law is here, and my sister-in-law, they just came, just invited themselves, and Bob—that's her husband—he's such a wimp, he never tells them, it's not a good time, or we're expecting company. So what are you saying, I asked my sister. She said, Carmen, it's just not a good time. You know I love you, I want to see you, but we don't even have a spare bed. So I said, of course, I don't want to be a burden. I'll just cancel the ticket. I'll use it some other time.

"Well, there I was, two miles from the airport. I was really disappointed, and I didn't want to go back to the house. I even thought about going on, to the airport, getting on some other plane, just going anywhere, somewhere, I didn't care, just to get away. But where? I just couldn't wander off. I had reached Daly City. There's a big shopping center just off the highway, with a multiplex, you know, a movie theater. I parked the car there. I called the airline and canceled my ticket. Then I went to a movie. I was so upset I hardly remember what I saw, something stupid, but it killed a couple of hours. I had coffee some place. I don't even remember where. I got home after midnight. The house was dark. Nobody saw me come in....

"That night, somebody killed Garth. It was around 11:00, I guess. I got a call this morning, from some detective. He told me about Garth, and he said, where were you last night, around 11:00? Well, I could have lied, but I knew it was no use. I told him I was watching a movie. I was so unlucky, Frank. Can you believe it? If my sister hadn't called, then I would have been landing in LA, 400 miles away from Garth's place, at 11:00. But I wasn't in Los Angeles. I was in Daly City, watching a movie. And I was all alone."

"Didn't anybody see you?"

"Frank, I'm sure lots of people saw me. It was crowded, but I didn't talk to anybody. I didn't even buy candy. I just got a ticket—with cash—and went in. I sat next to an elderly couple.... But I don't know who they are, or how to find them. Would they even remember me? You go to the movies, Frank, do you remember the people you see, the people who sat next to you? It would be a miracle if somebody remembered me."

"The kid who sold you the ticket?"

"Sure. Like he'd remember me out of the hundreds of people. Did he even look up at me? I don't know. Just a kid. I wouldn't recognize him, and he wouldn't recognize me. No, Frank, I haven't got anything to prove I didn't do this horrible thing. I can hardly tell them the name of the movie, or what happened. I'm the one with the motive, and I was in Daly City myself, only a couple of miles away from where it happened.... Frank, I used to dream about Garth dying, and I used to say to myself, how great it would be, not to be scared; and here he's dead, and I'm still terrified...."

"It's OK, Carmen," I said, "You're innocent. Why would you go to Garth's place, when everybody knows you were scared to death of him?"

"Lots of women do crazy things," she said. "They get beaten, kicked, burned, and they go back for more. So maybe I was still in love with Garth. Or maybe I went there to kill him, first claiming I wanted to get back together. Anybody who knows me knows that doesn't make sense, but these police, these detectives, they don't know me...."

"Carmen," I said, "Believe me, you have nothing to worry about. There's no proof. You weren't there, so there's nothing to pin on you, no fingerprints, nothing. The movie theater, maybe they have you on security cameras, the police will check that. The main thing is, you didn't do it. You'll just tell the truth, and it'll come out OK. I'm sure of it: Carmen, everything is going to be OK. Besides, maybe the police know who did it. Maybe they already have somebody under arrest."

"Frank," she said, "There's something else."

"Something else?"

"Garth.... The way he died.... That's what's going to make them so suspicious. Somebody hit him with something, maybe a baseball bat, something hard, and then smothered him with a pillow. Just like Andrew. It can't be a coincidence. That's going to lead them right to my door. Who else in the house had a motive? Nobody even knew Garth except me."

"Are you sure of that?"

"Well ... maybe Chuck...."

"Chuck?"

"He's been a real friend. Of all the people in the house. Chuck, well, he's asked me a couple of times ... if I'd be interested.... What I mean is, he's very fond of me, he's told me that. He's said, Carmen, I really like you, I admire you. I said, Chuck, I like you, but I'm not ready yet for that kind of thing. He said, I understand. But I've told him all about Garth, about what Garth was like, and how scared I was of him."

"Including where you think Garth lived?"

"I can't remember."

"And where was Chuck last night?"

"I don't know," she said. "But ... won't they think of me, first? I have no witnesses, nobody to back up my story."

"But you can prove you were on the way to the airport. You can prove that your sister called you."

"Sure, Frank, I can. But so what? I was on my way to LA; then the trip fell through. I felt trapped and desperate and, you see, I was already in Daly City, so maybe I just drove on to his house and got rid of Garth, once and for all."

"You were taking a baseball bat with you to Los Angeles? Or something like that? It doesn't make sense, Carmen. They won't think it's you, trust me. It's all going to turn out OK."

"I hope so," she said. "But there's even something more."

"Something more?"

"I have to explain something," she said. "We all have cell phones, I suppose, but there's also a phone in the house, a landline, actually two or three of them. They're kind of for general use—and for Angelica, of course. Not that she ever uses the phone, poor thing. Andrew had an extension in his room. I think he used it all the time; but we all did, if we were lazy, or didn't have our cell phone with us, or something like that."

Where was this going?

"Anyway," she went on, "The police asked if I had been in touch with Garth. I said, absolutely not, I was terrified of him. I was hiding from him. Why would I be in touch with him? They said, well somebody was. I said, what do you mean? It seems there were phone calls to the house from Garth's phone, and phone calls to Garth's house from our house. So they said, did you make those calls? I said no, I swear, no, it wasn't me. They said, well, that's what everybody else says. We've checked with everybody in the house, and they all deny it."

"When were these calls made?"

"A couple of weeks ago, I think. Or ten days, I'm not sure. Frank, this is another thing that's driving me crazy. I know I never called Garth. The idea that somebody in the house was calling him, talking to him.... Who could it be? And what for? It's a nightmare.... And, of course, the police think it's me that made the calls. They probably figure Garth found out where I lived, that he called, I called, we talked, maybe he threatened me, then we got together, and I killed him. That's why I'm terrified, Frank."

Poor Carmen. I didn't think for one moment that she had killed her ex-husband. But then, who had? She was right about one thing: nobody else had a motive. Nobody in the house, that is. To be sure, there might be dozens of people anxious to get rid of a creep like Garth. Other women he had abused, for example. I never met the man and knew nothing about his life. He might have had a list of enemies a yard long. But the way he was killed—hit on the head, then smothered with a pillow—that was just too much of a coincidence. Of course, maybe somebody just happened to know about the blow on the head and the pillow thing. Was it in the newspapers? I couldn't remember. If so, then maybe somebody used this method to suggest a connection with Andrew Wright, to throw people off the track.

That was possible. Yet it was hard to believe the two murders weren't connected. And the phone calls from the house, what did that mean? If nothing else, it suggested some sort of relationship.

For the life of me, I couldn't imagine what this might be. That, I suppose, was the danger for Carmen. To somebody who didn't know her, she did seem a prime suspect. She had the motive to kill Garth, and she was living in the house where Andrew was killed in the very same way. And there were those phone calls that had to be explained.

OK, but why would she kill Andrew? Or were there two

separate murderers floating around?

I couldn't make head or tail out of any of this. Meanwhile, I had Carmen in front of me, and I had to help her out. I tried to calm her down. I recommended a couple of good criminal lawyers, but suggested she shouldn't rush into anything. "Wait and see, Carmen," I told her, "Chances are, the police are going to arrest somebody today, maybe tomorrow. That's what usually happens. Then you'll be off the hook. Most criminals are dumb. Maybe somebody left fingerprints all over the place. There's all sorts of possibilities, Carmen. Don't panic."

She seemed calmer. She liked the idea of waiting a day or so. She was worried about how much it would cost to hire a lawyer. "I don't have much money," she said. "Billy said he'd help me out. We talked about it this morning. But I don't think he's got much himself."

"Think positive," I said. "Think about the chance somebody's already been arrested."

She thanked me and left. I think she was in a slightly better mood.

15

Celia had warned me, again and again, not to get involved in the case. But I was like an alcoholic who couldn't walk past a bar without going in and having a drink. I had a call in the morning, from Lydia, about the photos of Kurt she and Fletcher had taken, which I was supposed to pick up. She volunteered to come by the office and drop them off, in a plain white envelope. She was as good as her word.

After lunch, armed with the photos, I marched over to the public library to do more research on San Bernardino and the mysterious Kurt. I felt twinges of guilt. After all, I have nothing to sell but my skill and my time, and nobody was paying me to go through old newspapers, looking for whatever it was I was looking for.

But I was more intrigued than ever, after I took a look at those photographs. I had had only a quick glimpse of Kurt. I do remember thinking he looked vaguely familiar. The photos were amazingly clear. He had a striking look—dark, brooding, and rather handsome. He had large eyes, and a strong, square, imposing chin. His black hair was thick and wavy. Somehow it looked dyed to me; it didn't fit the rest of him at all. What struck me most was the sense that I had seen him somewhere before, or at least his picture. In the newspapers, or on TV. And not just from my fleeting look at him, briefly, at the Finster house.

The minute I went back to the newspapers, I found what I was looking for. It was shocking and dramatic. I should have known! I should have recognized him earlier, when I saw him in person, even though it was so quick and casual. Now I knew, for sure. Kurt was not Kurt at all. He was John Gruber. He was the defendant in a big, sensational trial. He was accused of murdering his pregnant wife, Tracy. It was the talk of the town—indeed, the talk of the whole country. The instant I looked at the first photo of John Gruber, leaving the courtroom, I knew that I was looking at Kurt. The biggest difference was the hair. John Gruber had light hair. Kurt had darker hair. He had lost weight since the trial; that seemed clear. But the identification was unmistakable. My instincts were correct: he was obviously dyeing his hair—probably so people would be less likely to recognize him.

The Gruber case was exactly the kind of story newspapers loved. It was front page news, for months. I can't believe I hadn't picked up on this before. The newspapers practically slobbered over this scandal. Gruber worked for a paint company. He was some kind of glorified salesman. He lived in San Bernardino, in a tract house, probably the same as a hundred other tract houses, except that it was painted pink instead of purple or purple instead of pink. Tracy, his wife, was in the last stages of pregnancy. She had quit her job as a receptionist, and was staying at home, waiting for the baby to be born. It was a girl, and they had already picked out a name for the baby: Angela. Then Tracy disappeared. She went for a walk, he said, and she never came back. She used to go for a walk in the morning, he said, under doctor's orders, trying to keep in shape during the pregnancy.

From the very beginning, the police were suspicious of Gruber. He claimed to be all distraught, but he behaved in a peculiar way; and he told a story that just didn't add up. The day she disappeared, he didn't show up at work until 11:00 and said something about a dentist appointment, but that turned out to be a lie. At least according to the dentist. When the police questioned him, and asked him why he had lied, he said he wasn't feeling well. That's why he came in late. But why lie about the dentist? He had no explanation. Nobody believed him. He also left work early that day, complaining about a headache.

They never found Tracy's body, but they did find blood-stained clothes that belonged to her. The clothes had been dumped in a trash can, a couple of blocks from the house.

At first, he said, they weren't her clothes, but that story fell apart, too. Then Gruber said, his wife had cut herself the day before, chopping up onions for a stew, and that's where the blood must have come from. He said he had lied because he was afraid people would suspect him of harming his wife, and he had panicked. Of course, by now, everybody did think of him as a liar. Then the police got an anonymous phone call: Gruber had a girlfriend. He had been having an affair with this woman for over a year. The woman's name was Crystal Palmer. The media descended on her like locusts. She claimed Gruber had lied to her, she did not know he was married, said she was shocked when she found out. "Palmer said she never would have slept with a married man," said the breathless story in one of the newspapers.

More revelations followed. According to neighbors, Gruber and his wife had had a terrible row. She screamed at him so loud the neighbors could hear her voice. And she told a friend, a woman she played bridge with, that she knew her husband was "fooling around," and that she wanted a divorce. She was the daughter of a building contractor. Her parents were dead, and she and her sister had inherited quite a bit of money. She told the friend that she wasn't going to give him a penny. "He can go jump off a cliff as far as I'm concerned; I'm fed up with him." And she had an insurance policy worth $200,000 that was payable to her husband. She called the company, and asked how she could change beneficiaries. But she never followed up on this. Two weeks later, she disappeared.

Everybody was convinced Gruber was guilty. He had killed his wife and disposed of her body somewhere. Everything pointed in that direction. The neighbors started shunning him. The police were searching the neighborhood, dredging a pond nearby, but they found nothing. Then a dramatic witness appeared. It was a young man who worked for a boat rental company, in the Long Beach area—quite a distance from San Bernardino. He said he saw Gruber the day his wife disappeared. Gruber came in a pickup truck and rented a boat, a small but comfortable boat, with room for a few people, with a galley and a bed underneath. It was early evening, and it was already getting dark. Gruber paid cash, and said he was going to keep the boat overnight. In fact, Gruber took the boat out after it was dark, and returned it sometime after midnight. The witness remembered seeing Gruber get on the boat, carrying what looked like a large duffle bag; and he was walking as if there was something very heavy inside the bag.

Things were really looking bad for Gruber. The police began to search for the body in the waters off Long Beach and adjacent areas. Then Gruber seemed to panic. He took all the money out of a joint bank account, rented a car, and headed for the Mexican border. The police found him in a motel, in San Diego. They arrested him and charged him with murder.

It was headline news. Everybody was talking about the case. It took a solid week to pick a jury.

Gruber hired a really good lawyer, Sam Grapple, a man who rarely lost a case. Gruber had pleaded innocent, but the newspapers, the talk shows, and opinion polls all agreed that he was guilty, that he had murdered his wife and dumped her body in the ocean. Trouble was, there was no real physical evidence. Everything was purely circumstantial. No real eyewitness, no fingerprints, nothing whatsoever to tie him to the crime. Sure, there were the bloody clothes, but that was all. Above all, there was no body. The police never did find the corpse—if there was a corpse. The prosecution hammered away at Gruber. This fiend in human form, he murdered his wife, his pregnant wife. He killed her in cold blood. He killed little Angela too. Think of poor little Angela, never to be born.... Imagine a man who would kill his wife and his innocent unborn child, and so on.

But Sam Grapple laid it on with a trowel: where's the evidence? You have to believe a man is guilty, beyond a reasonable doubt, he told the jury. A man is innocent until proven guilty. And where's the proof? Maybe she ran away. Yes, they were having marital difficulties. Maybe it wasn't entirely John's fault. These things are usually not so one-sided. Maybe she was having an affair herself. Maybe she ran off with somebody else. What would you think if you sent this man to his death, and his wife turned up years later, with her new Australian husband?

He also undermined the prosecution's witnesses. He brought in friends of John Gruber, who testified that John Gruber loved his wife, despite the affair. A cousin of his, one Charles Lemmy, swore on the stand that Gruber was not a violent man, that he was a loyal friend, and had never been in trouble with the law. Gruber had no criminal record. No history of killing cats or that sort of thing. Crystal took the stand, and she was a sensation. She said that they weren't in love, that it was just sex, nothing more. "He was a very passionate man," she said. She told the newspapers that she felt he was becoming more distant, and strange, in the weeks before his wife disappeared; she repeated her story that she had no inkling he was married. Did she want to marry him? Maybe, she said. She was uncomfortable with their situation. She had had a strict Catholic upbringing, and she was pressing him to "make a commitment." Did they ever discuss children? He said (she said) that he did not want children. The defense went after her, hammer and tongs. Isn't it true that you've had affairs with other men? John Gruber isn't the first, isn't that true? But the prosecution objected, and the judge stopped that line of argument. Isn't it the case that you have been treated for depression and that you have a reputation for telling lies? More objections. She burst into tears on the stand. Grapple clearly saw a need to go slowly. Crystal was a very sympathetic, somewhat tragic figure. On the whole, she helped the prosecution more than the defense.

Gruber himself never took the stand.

The prosecution called as a witness the young man from the boat company. He stuttered a little, and seemed like a dimwit. Grapple cut him to pieces. The guy ended up saying "I don't remember" over and over again. How big was the duffle bag? Most duffle bags couldn't hold a woman's body. Gruber's wife was a tall woman, and she was in her eighth month, after all. What size was this duffle bag? "I don't remember." You said the duffle bag seemed heavy. He looked like he was carrying something heavy. How do you know this? Did you actually *see* what was in the bag? "No, no...." Well, how can you be sure it was full of something, that it was heavy? "I don't know. It was, kind of, an impression...." Oh, 'kind of' an impression. But you're not really sure, are you? "I guess I'm not." Let me repeat: was there anything strange or unusual about the duffle bag? Didn't many people carry duffle bags aboard their boats? "Well, sure." Did Gruber seem nervous, and was he acting strange in any way? "I don't remember." Didn't he bring the boat back early because there were storm warnings? "I really don't know." Isn't it a fact that later that night, it rained heavily, and that the water was dangerous? "I can't remember."

The prosecution did a good job summing up. But Grapple's final statement to the jury was a masterpiece. He explained everything away. The bloody clothes? How do you know that Gruber was lying about the blood? Wouldn't a guilty man try to destroy the clothes, or at least dispose of them much farther away? The flight to Mexico? Sheer panic. And quite understandable. Even an innocent man, caught in the web, might choose to run and hide. But most of all, over and over again, he pounded away at the concept of reasonable doubt. The evidence is all circumstantial. All inferences. Can you send a man to his death on mere inferences? Are we even sure this woman is dead? And then, the final touch, which (according to the press) must have had a powerful effect on the jury: he said, over and over again, "If there is no body, the case is shoddy."

If there is no body, the case is shoddy. Again and again, he hammered it home.

Despite Grapple's eloquence, the jury seemed to have a tough time. They were out for two weeks, arguing and squabbling. Twice they said they couldn't agree. The judge sent them back in. Finally, they announced that they had reached a verdict. The courtroom was jammed with people, reporters, TV cameras. The foreman of the jury, a high school soccer coach, seemed nervous, on edge. Then he announced, in a low monotone: we find the defendant, John Gruber, not guilty of murder.

Most people had expected a verdict of guilty. The commentators and talking heads and pundits had been more cautious. They admitted it was not exactly an ironclad case for the prosecution. Still, the verdict did set off something of an uproar. Newspaper and television polls showed that most people felt the verdict was a "tremendous miscarriage of justice." One or two jurors, who agreed to give interviews after the trial almost admitted as much. A third juror, who appeared on a TV talk show, voiced the same opinion. One juror at least was said to be writing a book about the case. The message of the jury, however, was practically unanimous: sure, he's guilty, and her body is in the ocean somewhere, but there was no real proof, and isn't the proof supposed to be "beyond a reasonable doubt"? All the evidence was just circumstantial, or just suspicious things the man did. We couldn't convict a man, send him to jail for life, or put him on death row, just because we *think* he did it. Sam Grapple told us over and over again that you can't find him guilty on hunches; where's the evidence? Admit it to yourselves, he said, there's more than a reasonable doubt. If there is no body, the case is shoddy.

Anyway, that wasn't the last of the story. His wife's family brought a civil suit, for damages. I think it was sheer anger on their part. At least this is what the newspapers thought. Gruber had little money to start with, and whatever he had surely disappeared into the bottomless pockets of the lawyers. The civil suit never went to trial. It was settled out of court. On what basis, I have no idea; and the newspapers had none either.

That was all there was. John Gruber was a free man, but of course the whole world thought he had gotten away with murder. For a while, there were echoes of the case in the newspapers and (I discovered later on) in the supermarket tabloids. "Gruber: The Untold Story." "'I Dumped the Body in the Pacific Ocean.'" "Psychic Offers to Locate Tracy's Body," "John and Crystal's Secret Tryst," and more of the same sort of thing. Then the fuss died down, as it usually does.

I came away from the library with my head in a whirl. John Gruber had tried to put the past behind him. He left town, morphed into Kurt Schmidt, and moved to Palo Alto. He dyed his hair, and was trying to live in obscurity. Had somebody recognized him? That was not at all unlikely: his face had been on TV (which I rarely watch) for days on end. In any event, I had to label him the number one suspect in the murder of Andrew Wright. For one thing, wasn't he already a murderer? Even the jury that acquitted him thought so.

What was to be done? One obvious answer was: nothing. In the first place, all this was basically none of my business. In the second place, I had no idea what I should or could do about the situation. Confront Kurt? That seemed idiotic. Or suicidal. One thing was clear—I had some sort of duty to report what I had found to Fletcher and Lydia. After all, I had enlisted their help with the camera. I dialed Lydia's cell phone. Fletcher answered. He said, "Well, did you find anything? Did the pictures help?"

"They certainly did. Do you know who Kurt really is?"

"What do you mean? He's Kurt Schmidt. Do you mean to say he's somebody else?"

"I do," I said. "His real name is John Gruber."

There was a pause. "John Gruber. Am I supposed to know who that is?"

"If you don't, you're just about the only person in the United States of America. John Gruber.... San Bernardino. Does it ring a bell? Guy whose pregnant wife disappeared? Everybody was sure he murdered her, but he got acquitted a couple of years ago. Remember the mantra: 'If there is no body, the case is shoddy.' For a while, the whole world was saying that. Admiring the lawyer, but at the same time, convinced the guy was guilty."

Silence. Then Fletcher said, "My God. Of course I remember. You couldn't read about anything else.... And that's Kurt? John Gruber? But that means the guy's a killer! Wow, I felt it in my gut. I knew something was wrong with that guy. It's got to be him, Frank. It's Kurt. Or John, whatever you call him. He's the one. The one who killed Andrew. It has to be him."

"You didn't recognize him?"

"I didn't follow the case, I mean, not all that closely. Are you sure, Frank? He did look vaguely familiar, but...."

"I'm sure. He's dyed his hair, lost some weight, but otherwise, it's the same man. And I agree with you, he's got to be a suspect here…. But why would he kill Andrew? What reasons could he possibly have?"

"I don't know. He's trying to build a new life. New name. You say he's dyeing his hair. He doesn't want to be recognized. Maybe most people have forgotten about the whole business. It's not like he's been in the news for the last couple of years. Now here's comes Andrew with that scheme with the cameras. Millions of people would be watching. They'd see Kurt…. For him, it'd be a total disaster."

"I see the point," I said. "But Sheila told me, when you guys had your meeting, and Andrew brought up the camera idea, she said that Kurt voted yes."

"Sure, sure," Fletcher said. "But maybe that was a lie or a trick…. Andrew knew who he was. That wouldn't be much of a feat. Now that I think of it, his face was in every newspaper. He was all over TV. It was in the *National Enquirer*. It was in *Time* magazine, in *People*. It's actually amazing none of the rest of us recognized him. Here's my theory: I think Andrew must have been blackmailing him."

"But he doesn't have any money."

"Oh, money wasn't the issue. Maybe Andrew was trying to force him to go through with this crazy scheme with the cameras and the murder on television. Maybe he was supposed to be the killer…. That would be logical, wouldn't it? Kurt couldn't say no, but he dreaded the idea; he didn't want any publicity. So he killed Andrew. Why not? He killed his own wife, after all, his pregnant wife…."

"You think he'd kill Andrew, just to stop the scheme?"

"Andrew was a risk to him. Andrew was going to dredge up the whole dreary business, ruin his chances for a fresh start…. It's a motive."

"Enough to kill somebody? If he killed Andrew, that would generate publicity, too, wouldn't it?"

"He's a killer," Fletcher said, "they're not always logical."

"But you don't have any proof."

"No, I don't. But can you think of anything else that makes sense?"

I couldn't. But I said, "Still, you're assuming a lot. You call him a murderer. I don't want to sound too much like a lawyer, which I am after all, but a jury did acquit him."

"Come on. Get serious. We all know about that. He was acquitted, sure. But that doesn't make him innocent, does it? He did it. That's what everybody thinks. It's as plain as the nose on your face."

"And Garth? Did he kill Garth?" I asked.

"Who knows? Maybe they knew each other. Maybe they had an argument. Look: I've got to get Lydia out of here. We're not staying one night more under this roof. The man is dangerous. Who knows who's next? He must be getting desperate. Frank, tell me, can I spread the word? In the house I mean. People have to know."

I felt a little awkward. I didn't want to start a stampede of people out of poor Angelica's house. "Maybe not ... for Angelica's sake."

"Angelica?"

"If you all desert her...."

"We won't all desert her. Chuck will stay. He's fond of her, and he's a good guy. But Sheila and Carmen, they have to know. And Billy."

I had no argument. If I was in his position, I'd do the same thing.

After I hung up, quite naturally I kept thinking about Kurt—I mean, John Gruber—and the whole Andrew Wright affair. One thing puzzled me. Surely the police knew who Kurt really was. They would have been on to him immediately—that is, even if he didn't tell them himself, when they questioned him. Yet nobody had made a move to arrest him. As far as I knew, he hadn't been grilled any more than the rest of the people in the house. He was an obvious suspect. But it was equally obvious that the police had no evidence, or not enough evidence, to tie him to the death of Andrew Wright. If Gruber was the killer, he seemed to know exactly how to cover his tracks. For the second time, it appeared. Even the third.

16

Right after my conversation with Fletcher, the news about Kurt and his identity spread rapidly through the house. The next day, I had a phone call from Sheila. I think it would be fair to say that I heard panic in her voice. Any trace of toughness was gone.

"Frank, I've got to see you."

"What about?"

"I'm at the house. I'm not working today. I called in and said I was sick. I'm afraid to talk, somebody might hear me, and ... I'm really scared...."

"Scared? Of what?"

"There's two people dead! This is getting dangerous, Frank. I don't know what to do. You remember those documents I gave you?"

"Sure."

"Can you get them? Are they in a vault somewhere?"

"Yes, but that's no problem," I said. "If you want them back...."

"No, I don't want them back," she said. "I changed my mind about them. I want you to give them to the police. Anyway, I want to talk to you about it."

"Why? What's in that package?"

She said, "I think they're evidence. I think they're important. They're things I took out of Andrew's room."

"Evidence? What sort of evidence?"

"Frank, I really don't want to talk about this on the phone.

When can I see you? Can you get the documents? Right away?"

"Not right away…. I have clients."

"How soon then?"

"Sheila…."

"Please!"

"OK. I can do it over lunch hour. And I can see you late afternoon."

I'm sure she wanted instantaneous service, but it just wasn't possible. I was tied up all morning with clients. I did manage to find a half hour at lunch to go to the bank where I keep a safe deposit box for my clients. It's full of wills and trusts, for the most part. Wills of people whose estate—I hope—will fall into my lap when they pass on. Not that I wish them dead.

Sheila's package was right on top, where I had put it.

She appeared promptly at 3:30. She looked pale. I offered her a cup of coffee, but she turned it down. "Do you have the stuff?" she asked.

"Right here," I said. "Tell me what this is all about."

"They were in a drawer. In a desk in Andrew's room. Not the file cabinet, where he kept the earthquake stuff. I didn't lie to you about that. Somebody else stole that material. I looked for the paper—the files—the earthquake material; but I didn't find them."

"Can I ask, Sheila, exactly *why* you were looking for those papers? Seems a little odd, a man's been murdered, and you're rummaging around in his papers."

That came out a little harsh. But she didn't seem to show any resentment. She said, "I thought, well, they might be useful."

"Useful?"

She hesitated, then said, "I thought, he had material that might be embarrassing to people, and…."

I couldn't help it. I said, "Sheila, are you saying you were going to use the earthquake material for your own purposes?"

"Well, maybe selling some of it back to … certain people."

"You can't be serious. You're talking about blackmail."

"That's an ugly word."

"It's an ugly *thing*."

She said, "You said it, not me. Maybe I would have changed my mind. Maybe I'd end up destroying the stuff, to save their reputations."

I said, "I hope so. Anyway, you didn't find anything. So exactly what's in this big envelope here, and why do you think it's important?"

She said, "Look for yourself. Open it up."

I opened the envelope. There was a lot of financial material in it—a bank book, and a small black notebook with financial entries. The rest was a collection of newspaper clippings.

"OK, Sheila," I said, "What's this all about?"

She said, "The bank book, the financial stuff—I think that could show what he was doing to Angelica's money. That's what I wanted to hide. He was a bastard, but I didn't want this part of it to come out. Look: she had no real family. The nephew, he's a bastard too. He never paid any attention to Angelica until he thought somebody was going to deprive him of his precious inheritance. I think Andrew—sure, he was milking her, he was exploiting her—but he was also good for her; he really was."

"So that's why you took the stuff? So nobody would know? Sheila, they'd find out anyway."

"I wasn't thinking. But it's not important now. What's important is the rest of the stuff. The newspaper clippings. At the time, I didn't pay any attention.... I thought it was peculiar. I wondered, why did Andrew keep these clippings? But now, I see why they're so important. Just take a look."

I did. They were stories in the *Chronicle* and elsewhere, about the trial of John Gruber. And his acquittal. There was nothing particular new about any of it, especially to me—I had spent hours myself poring over this material. But then something struck my eye. It was the two most recent clippings.

They were stories buried inside the paper, and I hadn't noticed them before. But Andrew had. The headline of the first was "Girlfriend of Accused Killer Dies in Accident." The story recounted the death of Crystal Palmer, 29, in an auto accident. "Palmer, a legal secretary, achieved notoriety in the trial of

John Gruber, who was accused of murdering his wife Tracy Gruber and an unborn child. Palmer was considered the 'other woman' in the case." The article went on to describe her testimony at the trial. Then it said: "Palmer was driving her car, a 2012 Toyota, on a narrow road in the canyon country outside Los Angeles when, rounding a bend, the car plunged over a cliff."

The second clipping, a day later, began with news about "funeral arrangements for Crystal Palmer, 29, who died in an auto accident." It talked about "speculation" that John Gruber might attend the funeral, but the Palmer family—Crystal's mother and stepfather, and her two sisters—said "he would not be welcome. Crystal hasn't seen him since the trial." The article added more details about the accident. It happened at night. The car and the body were not recovered for several hours. The wreck was not visible from the highway. "Palmer appears to have died instantly. Police cite a report that an anonymous caller informed them about the accident. Late yesterday, an eyewitness came forward, a construction worker named Trenton Blore, who may have seen the car moments before the accident." Crystal Palmer—if it was indeed she—was apparently going quite fast. This eyewitness, who was driving in the opposite direction, did not, however, know about the accident until the next day, when it was first reported in the newspapers. The paper also reported speculation that Crystal had been drinking.

I read the material carefully. I said, "Frankly, Sheila, I don't see why this is so important. Why does this upset you?"

She said, "Don't you see?"

"Really, I don't...."

"I didn't either," she said. "At first. I didn't even ask myself, what is this all about? And I didn't connect Karl with John Gruber. I had too many other things on my mind."

"Well, what *is* it all about?"

"Andrew obviously knew all about Kurt, I mean, John Gruber. He was using him for something, but don't ask me what. And why did he clip the story about Crystal Palmer? I'll tell you. It's because Kurt killed this woman. Don't you see? I'm

100% sure of it. He did something that made her go off the road, maybe he strangled her, or something, and then crashed the car, and then he just ran off. Nobody would think it was anything but an accident, nobody would investigate. He'd be home free.... Or maybe he went down to the car, made sure she was dead, then he went to a phone booth, called the police. That must have been him."

"But why, Sheila? Why would he do that? She was his girl-friend once."

"You said it: once. She was his girlfriend once. Maybe he found out she was screwing around with other men. He's violent, Kurt. He's a jealous guy, so he killed her. But he's clever, too. He knows how to cover up."

"Still," I said, "if he did that, you know, if he was in the car, or somehow managed to get rid of her in that accident, wouldn't there be fingerprints? Evidence against him? Fibers or whatever?"

"Who would think to look for fingerprints, or fibers, or hairs, or anything? It was an accident. A drunken woman, driving too fast, spins out of control; it happens every day. End of story."

I said, "But this is all just speculation, Sheila. Some news-paper clippings. Andrew was interested, maybe that's all it meant. Kurt was living in his house. Andrew knew him, and he clipped out the story, so what? Anyway, the accident was in Los Angeles, not here."

"And where was Kurt?"

"You tell me."

"I will. Kurt was not in the house when this so-called acci-dent happened. And where was he? He was in LA. I know, because he told me he was going. He was scheduled to make supper that day. It was his turn, but he said, let's switch. I have to go to LA. And he came back the day after Crystal died."

"OK, but it could be a coincidence," I said. "Lots of people go to LA."

"Frank, are you listening to me? I don't believe in co-incidences. Not in this case, anyway. Besides, ever since that time, Kurt's been different. Acting different, I mean. He's been just plain *weird*. OK, he was always weird, but now he seems weirder to me. He's more morose, more into himself.... And then, the day before Andrew died, I heard the two of them arguing about something, then Kurt came out of Andrew's room and slammed the door. His face was ... I don't know what you'd call it, it wasn't even human. I never saw such rage, such anger.... Frank, everything fits together. He's a killer. He killed his wife. He killed his girlfriend. Andrew somehow knew about this. They had a huge fight. Maybe it was because Andrew told him what he knew.... And then Kurt decided to get rid of him. Listen: he's almost a professional killer. He's got *experience*. He knows exactly how to do it and get away with it."

Fletcher had said much the same thing about Kurt. That he was a killer—and what's more, a killer who knew how to get away with his crimes. But I was still cautious—you might even call it lawyerly. After all, I *am* a lawyer. "Don't get me wrong," I said. "I see what you're driving at. I see the logic too, but still—"

She interrupted me. "You're not listening. Kurt killed his wife. We know that. He got off, he had—pardon me—some shrewd shyster who got him off. Andrew knew something, he knew some dirt, maybe he had real evidence, maybe he could show that Kurt was guilty. He knew about Kurt killing the girlfriend too. Or maybe he just put two and two together, like I did. So he was blackmailing Kurt. OK, I know Kurt didn't have money, but Andrew had *something* on him. That's probably why Kurt was willing to go along with the crazy scheme, the TV murder thing."

"Go along?"

"Frank, don't be dense. Andrew was forcing him to do it. Kurt was going to be the murderer, isn't that obvious? Who else? And then Kurt went to LA, and he had a quarrel with Crystal, and he killed her too. Then he killed Andrew. I tell you, it's the only thing that makes sense."

"But how would Andrew know?" I asked. "OK, let's say Kurt killed his girlfriend. The papers said it was an accident. Nobody was even suspicious of Kurt. Andrew was here, not in LA; so, even if he was suspicious, what could he know? Nothing. And this quarrel, we don't know what they were arguing about, not really. It could have been about something trivial, like loud music on Andrew's radio."

"Oh, Frank, give me a break."

"We can't prove—"

Suddenly she was crying. "Proof, proof! That's all you talk about. Frank, I don't give a damn about proof.... I'm living in a house with a serial killer. I've got to get out, me and Carmen. We can't stay there a minute more."

Mentioning Carmen reminded me of that issue too. "Sheila, what are you saying? And, by the way, do you think he killed Garth too?"

"Frank, I don't know. Why not? If you killed three people, why not four? Maybe he was in love with Carmen. Chuck certainly is. Chuck's constantly mooning and staring at her. That's common knowledge around the house. Maybe she's attracted to violent guys. Maybe she didn't go for Chuck. He's too flaky with his damn vegetables, but Kurt, there's somebody she'd have the hots for. And maybe he wanted her, too. I don't know. Or maybe somebody else did it, killed Garth I mean, somebody who thought it was heroic, or some total nut. Who knows? Who cares?"

I wasn't quite convinced. But I sympathized with Sheila. I would be uncomfortable, too, in her place. I told her I understood her situation entirely. "I'd move out too. So, you and Carmen, sure, get out. Unless the police want you to stay put. Anyway, what do you want me to do with these papers? They're just newspaper clippings. They don't prove anything, even if I showed them to the police. And if you show them, then they'll wonder, where did you get them? And you'll have to say you went into Andrew's room after he was dead. And that won't be good news for you."

She was silent for a minute. "I guess you better hold onto them, then," she said. "For now. Let me think about it. You know what I really want? I want you to find something on Kurt. Some real proof. Otherwise this thing is a nightmare."

I had to agree it was a nightmare. But I had no way of "finding something on Kurt," and I told her so. Wearily, I reminded her that she was asking for something that was just not in my line of work. I don't think she heard a word I said. Or rather, she heard it, with her ears; but it didn't penetrate.

17

When Sheila left, I spent some time just sitting and thinking. I stared at the window, at the cars passing by, at people on foot, hurrying along. It was a typically bright, clear day. The streets were crowded in downtown San Mateo. I thought: every one of those people is going somewhere. Everyone has a life, a story, problems, desires.

Me too. Right now, I couldn't get out of my mind the house in Palo Alto, and the strange death of Andrew Wright. And other strange deaths: Crystal Palmer—probably an accident, but who knows? And Garth Winter, Carmen's nemesis.

I wracked my brains for some insight. Why was it so easy for the detectives in mystery novels? There are times when I like to read mysteries; it relaxes me on airplane trips or when I have bouts of insomnia. Most of them are fairly trashy, but they're enjoyable trash. If you have a headache, or you're flying to Denver on a business trip for a client, or it's 3:00 a.m. and you've been tossing and turning, you're simply not going to turn to Wittgenstein or Aristotle. Or even *War and Peace*, I'm ashamed to say.

Mysteries are in a way so comforting. Those detectives— from Sherlock Holmes on—they're like trapeze artists. They make it seem so *effortless*. Holmes solves a case because he can deduce absolutely everything from a cigar ash. Miss Marple has her cutesy little insights from her boring little village and drinking tea at the vicarage. And Sam Spade, too, along with the other tough, silent guys, wisecracking and fornicating their way through the urban jungle: they get threatened, they get beat up, they soldier on through 200 pages of sex and violence. But they solve everything neatly in the end. All of them: they have a knack. Well, that's why it's fiction. In real life, half these things are never solved. If you don't find some drug addict, high as a kite, standing over the body, or a dumb kid who ran off with the victim's credit cards, you have to wonder: do the police *ever* solve cases of murder? Maybe not. So why should this case be any different?

But I couldn't help speculating. Thinking. Cogitating. The people in the house.... The more I thought about it, the more I was convinced it had to be Kurt. It just had to be. By the process of elimination. I just couldn't imagine anybody else in the role of a killer. Take Fletcher and Lydia, for example. Decent, clean-cut young people. Lovers, too. Young people in love. He was a budding doctor. A resident; or was he an intern? I can't remember. Do these young doctors kill people? I mean, yes, doctors do, but not sadistically. They do an occasional mercy killing. Speed up the process for somebody painfully dying. I suppose there's the occasional weird doctor or total incompetent who buries his patients. You read about this sometimes. But I didn't see Fletcher in this role. And Lydia? Impossible. Or was this just sexism on my part: you know, she's a pretty girl, intelligent, with a loving boyfriend, so how could she kill anybody?

Sheila: she just possibly might kill somebody. She was tough, cold-blooded; but somehow I couldn't see her in the role of a murderess. And why would she kill anybody? Why Andrew of all people? Carmen. Out of the question. Billy? Weak, sick, a classic nerd. Did he even have the strength, mental or physical? I ruled him out as well. And Chuck. He was in love with Carmen. Did that give him a motive? He was a passionate vegetarian. Do vegetarians kill people? I know they don't kill animals, but people? I found it inconceivable. If you were unwilling to make an oyster suffer, are you going to bash in somebody's head with a baseball bat? Still, wasn't Hitler a vegetarian? Maybe Andrew had something on Chuck, maybe he was blackmailing him. Maybe he had a secret video, showing Chuck in a steakhouse, cramming beef down his throat or eating a clandestine pork-chop, and drooling with lust for red meat. But no, this was just too absurd.

Then who else could there be? There was nobody else in the house but Angelica. That was out of the question. A woman in her 80s, who has no idea whether it's Tuesday or Wednesday—she is simply not a likely suspect. Did she have the strength to hit somebody over the head and knock them out cold? Moreover, she really liked Andrew. But maybe she thought he was somebody else. Still, I just had to rule her out. An outsider? Well, there was always Max Appleby. But he was a certified public accountant. I've already ruled out CPAs. They might cook the books, but that's a far cry from murder. No, they seem even more unlikely than vegetarians. Then who? A crazed stranger? A robber? It really did seem like an inside job. So that leaves me with nobody. Except Kurt. Everything points to Kurt.

Was my reasoning sound? Was I too quick to rule people out? After all, wasn't somebody just arrested in Wichita or somewhere like that, Kansas or Nebraska, one of those flat, Republican, church-going places? A mild-mannered, middle-aged guy, and, yes, a church-goer, married, family man—and it turns out he was a cold-blooded serial killer, who raped and tortured women, and maybe ate parts of them. I don't remember. There was always that cliché about those serial killers, as I said: good neighbors, quiet, polite, and so on.

But still, I couldn't get Kurt out of my mind. He had to be the one.

That's where I ended up in my reverie. Yet the very next day, something happened that—well, it didn't rule Kurt out, but it muddied the waters even more.

18

I woke up early in the morning, much too early in fact. I got into my robe and slippers, and went out into the driveway to retrieve the morning newspaper. There was my old friend, the *San Francisco Chronicle*. I know it doesn't have that high a reputation in the world of professional journalism; but, as I said, I like it. It's not really a bad newspaper. It has just the right amount of sex and scandal, for those of us who are gawking bystanders, as opposed to the people who are *doing* sex and scandal, and who presumably don't have to read the *Chronicle*.

Celia was still asleep, and so were the girls. They would get up in a half hour or so, at which point early morning bedlam would take over. I used to think two bathrooms was a luxury, but with teenage girls, it's a necessity, and in fact it's not nearly enough. Right now, though, it was quiet in the house. I made myself a cup of coffee, poured a glass of some low-pulp orange juice, heated up a frozen cranberry scone, and settled down at the kitchen table to read my paper in peace.

On page three, I was startled to see a story with this headline: "Body of Missing Victim Found." Underneath that, surprising news: the police had recovered the body of Tracy Gruber, "central figure in the sensational trial of her husband, John Gruber." The body had been positively identified through dental records. I thought to myself: what an amazing coincidence. That this should happen, at this particular time. Or was it a coincidence?

I read the story hungrily. The police had received an anonymous tip, according to reliable sources. Whoever gave them the tip was able to provide very precise directions. The body had been buried in a shallow grave, covered with rubbish and leaves, in one of the forested canyons on the outskirts of Los Angeles. The newspaper story did not give as much detail as I would have liked. It did say that Ms. Gruber had been apparently shot to death. It said her family had been informed, and it quoted her brother as saying that the family was "heartbroken by the confirmation of their worst fears," but that they had never harbored any hope that Tracy would be found alive, and that finding the body permitted a certain amount of "closure." The newspaper briefly retold the story of the trial, and explained that John Gruber had been acquitted. They even repeated the famous line, if there is no body, the case is shoddy. Now of course there was a body, so presumably the case was no longer shoddy; but the trial had been over for years. Efforts to reach John Gruber, said the paper, had been unsuccessful. It was believed he had changed his name and moved out of the Los Angeles area.

I showered and got dressed, all the while wondering what this meant. This was an unexpected development. An anonymous tip? From whom? And why at this point in time?

Who knew where the body was buried, except for John Gruber—Kurt—himself? Was *he* the anonymous caller? But if so, why?

When I got to the office, I had a message waiting for me from Sheila. She left a number to call, which I did not recognize. It turned out to be a motel in Redwood City. I asked for Sheila, and was connected to her room.

"Hi, Sheila," I said. "So you did move out."

"I did—as fast as I could. Can you blame me?"

"Not at all."

"I told you," she said, "I wasn't staying another night in that place."

"And Carmen?"

"No, she's not here.... Poor thing, she's in an awful state. Worse than I am, if that's possible. But she thought if she moved out, the police would think she was running away. You know, because of the Garth business. I told her to let them know where she was going. Or to go to her sister's house, but this time really go. Anyway, she was dithering, and I couldn't wait. I told her, Carmen, I'm out of here; you can come or not, it's up to you."

"I don't blame you."

"Frank, I've got to talk to you again. When can I see you?"

"I'm kind of busy.... I have clients to see...."

"Please, Frank. It's a matter of life and death."

I *was* busy; I wasn't lying. I had a pile of work on my desk, and several clients with appointments, include a new client, whom I was very anxious to please. "Life and death, Sheila? You're not serious."

"Not literally, Frank. Don't be a jerk, will you? It's something important to me. Your clients can wait."

"My clients can't wait, Sheila. They pay the rent."

She insisted. In fact, she wanted to come that very minute. "Redwood City is ten minutes from your office, Frank. Your precious clients can sit and wait while we talk. It's good for them. Make them think you're so busy you're just squeezing them in. They'll never know the difference." I refused to budge. She alternated between nastiness, and abject begging and pleading. But I held firm. In the end, though, I did agree to meet her for lunch. That way, I could keep my appointments with clients. It did mean, though, that I had to cancel lunch with a friend of mine, a personal injury lawyer who works in San Carlos.

We met at a Thai restaurant in Redwood City. That was another concession on my part; the restaurant was minutes from her motel. As soon as we sat down, she said, "Did you see the paper this morning? Did you see the story about Kurt's wife?"

"I did."

"How they dug up the body?"

"I read it, Sheila. I told you that."

"Didn't it hit you in the face?"

I said, "Nothing hit me in the face, Sheila. You're going to have to tell me what you're thinking. I'm not in the mood for guessing games."

"OK, it's this, Frank. If you had any doubt before...."

"Doubt?"

"About Kurt. That he killed Andrew. If you had any doubts, they have to be gone, Frank. This clinches it."

"Clinches it? Sheila, I don't see the connection. I don't know what this means at all. The whole thing is totally mysterious. What about all that stuff that came out at the trial—about the boat, the duffle bag, the ocean, all of that? I don't get it."

"You really don't see?'

"I really don't see."

"He's a clever bastard. He knew he'd be a suspect. When a guy's wife disappears, who's the first suspect they think about? The husband. That's Kurt. He's the husband. And he's cheating on his wife. So he knows they'll be swarming all over him. What does he do? He's got this clever plan. He convinces everybody that he killed his wife and threw the body in the ocean. He knew they could dredge and dredge and send down divers and all until they were blue in the face, they wouldn't find anything except an old tire or two; they'd spend months with these skin divers or whatever, and it was just a way to trick them, fool them royally.... And all the time, the body was buried in the woods. Meanwhile, he goes on trial, but there's no body, so there's no real case."

"But ... wasn't that awfully risky? Even without a body, the jury could decide, he must be the one. There was all that stuff, things that pointed toward Kurt...."

"Sure it was risky. Murder is risky. Kurt gambled that he could get away with it. He gambled, and he won. And now there's Andrew, his latest victim. Frank, he's a monster. You've got to do something."

"Me? Like what, for instance?"

We were interrupted at this point by the waiter, who arrived and took our order. I ordered pad thai. I knew Sheila was not going to eat. She ordered a salad, though. When the food did come, she looked so unhappy, it made me uncomfortable. I was wolfing down my food, while she sat there mournfully, like an anorexic at a banquet. I felt guilty enough to forgo one of my favorite dishes, a rice dish with mango, which was their special dessert.

As I ate, she said, "Here's what I want you to do, Frank."

"What?"

"Go to the police. Tell them about Kurt. Tell them you have some information."

"But I don't. I don't have information. I really don't."

"You do," she said. "You can tell them you were there that night, the night Andrew died ... and you saw Kurt."

"But I didn't. I didn't see him. Sheila, I'm not going to lie to the police."

She said, "Then call them. Give them an anonymous tip. Tell them that Kurt is John Gruber, and that he killed Andrew Wright. Call them from a public phone. Then hang up. They'll do the rest."

"But they must know already that Kurt is John Gruber. That's for sure. Remember, they spent hours questioning him. I'm positive that stuff came out. And we don't really know that he killed Andrew. It's just a hunch. I'm just not going to do it. I'm not going to call the police. If you want to, you can do it yourself."

"Bastard," she said, and stormed out of the restaurant. I was left, as usual, with the bill.

19

I went back to the office after lunch. She had upset me, I have to admit. I plunged into my work, and there was plenty of it. But later in the afternoon, I had a surprise visitor. I see people all day, most days, but very few of them, if any, ever drop in unannounced. I wasn't expecting anybody, so when I heard somebody knock at the door, I was curious as to who it might be.

When I saw who it was, I was startled, to say the least. I recognized the face immediately. It was Kurt—or rather, John Gruber. He was wearing blue jeans and a white t-shirt underneath a faded denim shirt-jacket. He looked like a man on edge, as tightly wound as a coiled spring.

"You're Kurt," I said, somewhat foolishly.

"Yes," he said. "I'm Kurt. May I sit down?"

"Of course," I said.

He sat down in a chair opposite my desk. He cleared his throat. He put his hands together and cracked his knuckles. He was silent for a few seconds, then he raised his head, looked me in the eye with a kind of a glower. He said, "I've been avoiding you. You know that. I didn't want to have anything to do with you, or this murder case. The other people—that's their business. They want to talk to you? Fine. But I thought: count me out. So why did I come here now? It's because—because you're meddling in things that aren't any of your concern. And I want to know why you're doing this, and who you're working for."

"Working for? Nobody."

"I know lawyers are smart. They know how to twist things. Don't play games with me. What I mean is, who are you representing? Who's your client here? Is it Sheila, or somebody else? And what's your angle?"

"I'm not representing anybody," I said, "And I have no angle, Kurt." Then I added, surprised at my own boldness. "Or should I call you Kurt? Your real name is John."

He scowled. "My real name is Kurt. I'm Kurt now. That's who I am."

"You used to be John."

"That's who I was. I'm not him anymore."

"OK, Kurt," I said. "It's up to you, what you want to call yourself. But I don't know what you really want. I'm not involved in this at all."

"You're lying," he said. "You say that to everybody, but it's not true. You *are* involved. You've got certain documents. They don't belong to you, and you've got no right to keep them."

"I have hundreds of documents," I said. "I'm a lawyer. My life is documents. I'm not sure I know what you're referring to."

He opened and closed his fist. His face flashed with anger. "An envelope of documents. You know damn well what I mean. You got them from Sheila. They don't belong to her, and they don't belong to you."

I said, "They don't belong to you, either."

"But you know what I'm talking about. You can stop lying to me. You've got them. And they're important to me. I want them back."

I said nothing.

He said, "You know what's in them. Let's not play games...."

All I could do was repeat: "They're not yours. I have no right to give them to you."

He said, "I want to see them."

"I can't do that," I said. "They're private. They were given to me for safekeeping. They're in a vault. If I turn them over to anybody, it's going to be to the police."

"The police? Why the police? They have nothing to do with

the police. They're personal."

"Well, maybe," I said.

He seemed desperate. "Those papers—you have to admit, they have nothing to do with Andrew, I mean, with whoever killed Andrew. You know that. They're about that damn earthquake, and his stupid plans to write a book and publish a lot of dirt, a lot of lies.... As if that scumbag could write a book. Those files and papers...."

I stopped him, and (foolishly I think) blurted out, "Kurt, we're talking about different things. You think I have the earthquake papers? No, I don't."

He seemed genuinely surprised. "Then what do you have?"

"Something else. I'm not even sure what. Papers that came from Sheila; but they're not the earthquake stuff. Somebody else has those. I don't know who."

His whole demeanor changed. It was as if a huge burden had been taken off his back. The anger drained out of his face. "You're sure? You're not telling me a bunch of lies?"

"A hundred percent sure. And I don't tell lies. I'm not in the business of telling lies."

He seemed to quiet down. He frowned, and appeared to be lost in thought. I screwed up my courage and said, "Kurt, the people in the house know who you are. Maybe they didn't before, but they do now. They know that your real name—I mean, your former name—was John Gruber."

"Doesn't surprise me. That was bound to happen. Sooner or later."

"Yes. But ... well, now they think maybe you killed Andrew Wright."

"They think so?" he said, and his voice regained its sharpness. "Well, screw them. I'll tell you who *doesn't* think so. The damn police. I've been questioned and questioned. You can be damn sure of that. As soon as they realized that I was John Gruber, they were practically salivating.... Aha! This must be the guy! But they were disappointed.... They have absolutely nothing on me. Nothing. I'm not even a suspect."

"Maybe," I said. "I hope so. Still, your housemates...."

"You're lying!" he said, sharply. "They're my friends. They trust me."

I didn't have the heart, or the right, to tell him that this was wrong, that Sheila had fled from him, in terror. I felt distinctly uncomfortable, and squirmed in my chair. He said, "Give me a name. Tell me who's spreading this rumor. I have a right to know."

"I can't do that," I said. "Look: life isn't fair. Let's say you're completely innocent. You're trying to start your life over. But you've got bad luck; somebody is murdered, and you're living in the house. People have prejudices, stereotypes, you know? They find out who you are—or were—it can't be news to you that, well, a lot of people, after your trial—what I'm trying to say is, they still thought, maybe you were guilty anyway, despite the verdict. I'm not saying anything myself, after all, there was a jury, they heard the evidence. I'm not hinting at anything. But people might say: this Andrew Wright, maybe he knew something, some evidence against you, maybe he was blackmailing you...."

He was silent for a few seconds, as if he was thinking of how to respond. There was something crafty, or shifty, in the way he looked. I couldn't quite put my finger on it. Then he said, "You're a lawyer, right? I was acquitted. You can't be tried twice. I'm not admitting anything; but let's suppose Andrew did know something about what happened to my wife. What good would it do him? And blackmail? That's a joke. I don't have any money. I never had any money, and then her family sued me, civil suit, and I had to settle with them. They took everything I had left, the house, everything, there wasn't much to begin with after the lawyers got done with me. Anyway, I'm broke. I've got a job now, yes, but the pay is a joke, so how much money could he squeeze out of me? And you knew Andrew. He was after big money. Not small change, but big, big money."

But I persisted: "Sure, that's all true. Still, let's suppose Andrew had some sort of proof.... You couldn't be tried again, but you'd lose your reputation."

"My reputation? Get real. I lost that at the trial. You know that. What the jury said and did made no difference. The way people looked at me, when I walked out of that courtroom. I'm not stupid. I know what they were thinking. I read the newspapers, I see the magazines. I'm not an idiot. I'm a marked man. For the rest of my life, that trial goes with me."

Oddly enough, I felt my attitude toward Kurt was changing. I was losing my fear and my sense that he was dangerous. He seemed defensive—but somehow sincere. My prejudices were receding. I was getting a strong but surprising impression of him. Not the feeling of a violent bully, but of somebody complicated and volatile; and also clever, sly, a guy who was very good at covering his tracks. Maybe this was the profile of a certain kind of killer: somebody who could kill his own wife and get away with it; somebody who could do so good a job on Andrew Wright that the police were baffled and had to dismiss the idea that he was the killer. If he *was* the killer.

"One more thing, Kurt," I said, surprised at my own nerve. "Your friend Crystal. There are those who think you killed her too."

Now the mood changed again. All the suppressed violence came out again. He sprang from his seat, with his fists balled. The veins in his temples stood out. His voice was close to a shout. "That's a lie," he said, "A damn lie. How dare anybody say that! She died in an accident. An accident!"

"You were in LA at the time...."

"I was. So what? There are millions of people in LA."

"What were you doing there?"

"None of your damn business. Alright. I went there to see somebody. Meet somebody. A woman, actually."

"Her name?"

"Mary Ann Nobody. I'm not going to tell you. Damn it, you have no right to ask. And Crystal, she was drunk and driving like a crazy woman...."

"Drunk? How do you know?"

He was shouting again. "What are you insinuating? I read it in the papers. Good god, they'll never leave me alone. Never. Never. You're as bad as the rest of them."

I withered under the attack: "OK, OK, I'm sorry."

After his outburst, he seemed overwhelmed with other emotions. He slumped back in his chair. The haunted look was replaced by a look of defeat, even despair. Then he sat up. "You won't believe me, I know. You think I'm a killer. I can't talk you out of that. I know that from bitter experience.... But listen: I didn't kill Andrew Wright. Why would I do such a thing? You said you thought he could be blackmailing me. I told you that was ridiculous—I explained why it couldn't be true."

"Well, maybe. But you did have an argument, a real one, with Andrew Wright. You two had a fight...."

"A fight?"

"I don't mean physical. As I said, it was an argument. People heard you shouting. What did you argue about?"

"If people heard me," he said, "why don't you ask them? I have nothing to say."

"They couldn't make out the words. They only heard the shouting."

"Well, then, I guess you'll never know."

"But that makes people suspicious, Kurt, doesn't it? If you only told me—us—what it was all about...."

"It's none of your damn business. If some busybody heard something, they can tell you; if not, let's leave it at that."

I plunged boldly on. "Did you know about Andrew's schemes? His plans? His idea about the cameras in the house?"

"Sure. Everybody did."

"And the real scheme? About staging a killing?"

He looked at me, as if trying to decide whether to tell the truth or not. In the end, he decided on a dose of candor. "Yes. I knew all about it. He talked to me about it."

"What did he say?"

Kurt gave a kind of choked little laugh. "Oh, he was something, Andrew. He wanted me to kill Billy. Just like that. Kill him. When he first mentioned it, I said, you're out of your frigging mind. He said, look, it's not really murder; it's assisted suicide. The guy's got some fatal disease. He wants to die. Ask him yourself."

"And?"

"I said, I don't care. If he wants to kill himself, fine, that's his business. I don't want anything to do with it. *You* do it, Andrew, I said. If you're so hot for this sort of thing, then go right ahead. No, no, he said, it's got to be you. I said, look, I already went through one damn trial. I'm not about to go through another one. He said, they won't catch you, it's not going to be a problem. You'll get away with it."

"He said that?"

"Sure, but I wasn't buying. He kept saying, I have a plan. But I knew better. That guy, he was a congenital liar. He wasn't fooling me. I was going to be the fall guy, take the rap. The police would be all over me like maggots."

"So you told him definitely no."

"Exactly. I told him once, I told him twice, I told him three times," he said, "But you know, Andrew. He never took no for an answer. He kept at me till ... well, till he died."

"Why did he think you'd do it?

"Ask him yourself," he said, and laughed maliciously. "Oh, I guess you can't; he's dead."

I tried once or twice more to learn something about the argument, and about the conversations he had had with Andrew, but without success. We had reached some sort of an impasse. I had made it clear I was not going to give him the documents, and I had no intention of telling him what they consisted of. This made him uneasy, but not tremendously so. He obviously came with the thought that the papers posed some sort of danger to him. He had no idea that the "papers" were nothing but some financial data, dangerous to the late Andrew Wright, but to nobody else, and a collection of newspaper clippings. These were, in fact, relevant, since they were about Kurt's trial, but it was impossible to tell *why* they were relevant. So long as they had nothing to do with the earthquake project, he seemed to accept the situation.

When he left, I had to see a client, then I went for a walk. It was late afternoon, and the sun was beginning to set. A beautiful time of day. But my mind was far away from weather and landscape. I was trying to sort out in my mind what, if anything, I had learned from my session with Kurt. Did he have a motive, or didn't he? If he had a motive, it wasn't obvious. Yet the two of them had quarreled, and the quarrel was apparently serious. Was it about Kurt's refusal to take part in the murder game? Did Andrew threaten to expose him? Ruin his chances of a new life, a new identity? Or what?

I could sense some vague, shadowy motive, and yet nothing seemed tangible enough to justify a planned, cold-blooded murder. Why was he worried about the earthquake papers? Who had them anyway? Had Sheila taken them? If so, she would have given them to me, instead of a mess of clippings. Or would she? Obviously, I couldn't trust Sheila to play with an honest deck. But why take the earthquake papers? Why would *anybody* take them? What was in those papers that was so important?

One thing was clear: the more I learned about Andrew Wright, the less I liked. What a bastard! Nobody could claim his death was a loss to humanity. Maybe, in fact, a net gain.

20

Of course, life went on—clients, family, the usual stresses and strains of daily life; a dead car battery, daughters who had to be grounded for a while, Celia's problems with the incompetent principal at her school—but in between crises, in the spare quiet moments or lying in bed at night trying to fall back asleep after waking up at 4:00 a.m., I found myself thinking about Andrew Wright and his mysterious death. Somehow I felt—I had an intuition—that we were approaching some sort of climax. I felt that something was going to happen, that something would break it open and let the light of day shine in.

The more I puzzled about the whole affair, the more it made no sense to me. People like me find it troubling when things don't make sense. *Why* did somebody feel strongly enough to kill that guy? OK, he was a worm, and lots of people had some vague sort of motive, but none of the motives seemed particularly compelling. There were other things, too. The missing papers. Who took them? Either Sheila or—more likely—whoever dispatched Andrew to another world. But why were they taken?

Andrew's two schemes: the earthquake book and the future staged murder. They were clearly the key to the whole affair. If I could only figure out why, and how they were linked. Curiously, the earthquake book seemed more dangerous to somebody than the murder scheme did; the murder scheme probably had no chance of actually coming into existence, when all is said and done.

Then there was Kurt, the dead wife, and the dead girlfriend, as well as the mysterious discovery of his late wife's body. And Carmen ... and the copycat murder of Garth Winter, her ex-husband. Oh yes, and the phone calls to Garth from the house. Who made these calls?

I tossed everything around in my mind; I got nowhere. And yet, as I said, I had the feeling, irrational I suppose, that something was going to break. This was not going to be a cold, unsolved case, a file that would gather dust on the shelves of the police department, slowly forgotten and sinking into oblivion. Something would happen. It *would* be solved.

As it turned out, I was right.

At 5:00 or so, I finally fell back asleep, exhausted from all this thinking and puzzling. I woke up at 8:00, which was much later than usual. I had to scramble to get dressed, shower, grab a mouthful of breakfast and a glass of orange juice, and make it to the office by 9:30, the time of my first appointment of the day with a client. When I got there, I found a message on my answering machine from Sheila. After I finished with my client I called her. She was no longer in Redwood City. Now she was at the Pink Peony motel on El Camino, in Mountain View.

"How are you doing, Sheila?" I asked.

"Wretched. I have a headache. I skipped work today. Look: I need to see you. Can you come here?"

"Why'd you change motels?"

"This one is cheaper," she said. "I'm low on cash."

"I'll take you to lunch," I said.

At noon, I drove to Mountain View. The Pink Peony was on El Camino Real. It was one of those sad motels, cheap, reasonably clean, but utterly depressing. Pink-colored stucco, two stories, a few pickup trucks parked in front, a tiny pool with traces of algae, women from places like Tonga or El Salvador shuffling along the halls to change the linen. The pool would be just great for lap-swimming, if you happened to be a midget. There was a neon sign outside that said "Vacancy." I imagine they rarely needed to change it to "No Vacancy," but I could be wrong.

I never got to see Sheila's room. She was waiting for me outside the tiny office. Inside, I could see a young woman, sitting behind the counter, chewing gum and watching a small TV set. No doubt a soap opera.

Sheila got in the car. "I hate it here," she said.

"I don't blame you. Do you have to stay?"

"It's so cheap. I don't have much money. I think I'm going to lose my job," she said. "I've called in sick too many times. My nerves are shot."

I resolved not to eat too much. She said she wasn't particularly hungry, which didn't surprise me. She looked somewhat thinner. "I just want a salad," she said.

I took her to a rather smart café. It was called Café Santa Rosa, for no particular reason. It served "California cuisine," which meant it had an eclectic menu. It mixed together every known cuisine, except I suppose Polish or German—cuisines that nobody will ever miss, unless you happen to come from those countries. The menu included ratatouille, Chinese chicken salad, and a rabbit-meat burrito, among other delights, plus various dishes that claimed to be "drizzled with rare oils." Sheila ordered an undrizzled green salad and left most of it uneaten.

I won't tell you what I ordered. It isn't relevant. It wasn't the rabbit-meat burrito; that much I can reveal.

"What can I do for you, Sheila?" I asked.

"I want to know, how you can get one of those protective orders, you know, like Carmen had, not that it did any good."

"You're thinking of Kurt?"

"Who else?"

"Well, first of all, I can't help you, myself, but I can refer you to a good person. It's going to cost you, though. And second, why on earth do you think you need one? Why should Kurt be out to get you?"

"Because of the papers I gave you. Kurt knows about them."

"Exactly what does he know?"

She said, "He knows I know who he really is. He knows I took some papers from Andrew's room; and he knows these papers have something in them about him...."

"How did he find out, Sheila?"

"Chuck told him."

"Chuck? And how did *he* know?"

"I confided in him. It was stupid. He was sitting there, eating his bean sprouts or whatever, and flexing his biceps. He's ridiculous, a real nut-case in some ways, but, you know, his biceps *are* impressive. He's a strong guy, and I felt, maybe he might protect me—and, oh yes, Carmen. He's in love with Carmen, but he doesn't dare make any moves. He's too shy, I think. Or maybe he has some sexual hang-up. I think all these body-builders and vegans are crazy. They're in love with their own bodies. Maybe they're all impotent, despite the muscles; who knows? Sometimes he gets on my nerves, but I was scared out of my wits, and as I said, he's in love with Carmen, or whatever. Maybe it's just puppy love, but it's intense. Anyway, I starting talking to Chuck, and I don't know why, but the whole story came tumbling out...."

"And he told Kurt? How do you know that?"

"It was about an hour later. Chuck came to see me, I was throwing some stuff in a suitcase. He asked me where I was going. I said, anywhere, just out of here. He said, Sheila, you don't need to do that; you're safe. I said, right, I'm safe. Tell me about it. I'm living in a house with a serial killer. You call that safe? And he said, you're making a mistake. I said, what kind of mistake? He said, Kurt, you don't understand him. I said, what's to understand? He said, well, I told him what you told me and—I interrupted him, I think I screamed at him: I went, you did *what*? And he went, let me explain."

"And did he? Explain?"

"Frank, I didn't wait to find out. He started to say something, but I couldn't bear it a minute longer. I thought I was having some sort of panic attack. I grabbed the suitcase, half-full, and ran out of the house. I got in my car, and I drove like a crazy woman. I found that motel in Redwood City, and I checked in. I had to go buy a toothbrush later on. I had been in such a hurry that I didn't even pack a toothbrush."

I thought for a minute, pondering how much I should tell her. Then I said, "You know, believe it or not, Kurt came to see me the other day."

She was wide-eyed with surprise. "He came to see you? What for?"

"It was about those papers. The ones you gave me."

"Oh, God. You didn't show them to him, Frank? You couldn't do that!"

"No, of course I didn't. I made you a promise. But really, you're worked up over nothing. I didn't show him the papers, but he knows they're harmless...."

She looked at me suspiciously. "How does he know that? They're not harmless. Frank, you're lying to me."

"Honor bright, I'm not lying, Sheila. OK, I can't swear he knows they're harmless. Or even if they *are* harmless. But that's not what he was interested in. He thought you had the earthquake book stuff. I told him you didn't. That's all he cared about. When he found out you didn't have those particular papers, that you didn't take them, and give them to me, it more or less took a big load off his mind."

This news seemed to have a benign effect on Sheila as well. She seemed to relax a little. She even took a few forkfuls of romaine lettuce and cucumber. But then she said, "OK, OK, that's good news. But he's still a cold-blooded killer. I still don't want to stay there. He's still a dangerous man."

"Well, I'm not sure," I said. "He didn't seem—I mean, I thought...."

"You thought what?"

"He seemed—I don't know, Sheila. He just didn't seem like such a monster to me."

She gave me a look of total disgust. "Honestly, Frank, sometimes I think you're a complete fool. What kind of lawyer are you? You're so damn gullible. What did you expect? 'Hi, good afternoon, my name is Kurt, I mean my name is John Gruber. I happen to be a serial killer, but underneath it, I'm a nice guy.'"

"I'm just saying what I think," I said.

"I wouldn't advise you to get into some dark alley with Kurt," she said. "You might not come out alive."

I changed the subject. "Sheila," I said. "Why was he interested in that earthquake stuff? What could possibly be in them that concerned him?"

"I have no idea," she said. "Who knows? Something incriminating, I suppose. You think his wife was the first person he killed? Maybe there was something there, other stuff. People he killed when he was a kid, whatever. Or some other crime. Anyway," she said, "I've changed my mind about those papers. I want you to take them to the police. I don't care if it gets me into trouble."

"Go to the police?"

"That's what I said, Frank. Don't act stupid. The police."

"But why, Sheila? I don't know what use they would be. These papers, they don't prove anything at all. They show that Andrew was a crook, that he skimmed off some of Angelica's money, but do the police care about that? The clippings show that Andrew knew Kurt's real identity and so on. Big deal. The police were aware of all that. They can't be that dumb."

"Don't argue with me, Frank. Just promise me you'll go to the police."

It was the last thing in the world I wanted to do. I would rather face anything: root canal work, chaperoning my kids at a rock concert, listening to a lecture on insurance—anything. So far, I had kept my name out of the newspapers. I had concealed the fact that I was at the Finster house the night Andrew died. I didn't want to promise Sheila anything. But I was in a bind. Sheila could always unleash the "nuclear option"—she could threaten to tell them about my visit to the house, and about the note under the door. Not that the police would suspect me of killing Andrew, but I would have to answer hours and hours of questions.

"Sheila, please. I really don't want to do this. Let me think it over."

"There isn't any time," she said.

"Yes, there is. You're safely out of the house. You're in a motel. Nobody's going to bother you. You can take it easy for a while. Cool it. Take a dip in the pool. Read a book. Relax."

"Relax? While that man is running loose?"

The waiter appeared at this point, and collected the plates. I signaled to him that we wanted the check. Sheila was silent until he left with the dishes. Then she said, "Frank, I'm begging you.... If something happens to me, or Carmen...."

"Nothing's going to happen, Sheila."

"That's easy for you to say. Please, Frank. I don't want to make threats, but you owe me something."

What could I do? I was over a barrel, so I agreed. "But not today Sheila. Not today. Maybe tomorrow."

"Make sure you do it," she said, and then, in a tighter tone: "Or else: no more Mr. Nice Guy, on my part. You know what I mean."

I did. I knew all too well. The waiter deposited the check. I paid the bill and we walked out of the restaurant together. "You won't forget," she said.

"Forget? How could I?"

Yet, despite the promise, I never did go to the police with the documents.

21

My instinct was correct. This was not destined to end up as a cold case. There were never going to be those yellowing papers filed away in a rusty box, in a warehouse. The truth was about to come out.

The day after Sheila's visit, Chuck came to see me. He came unannounced. Meanwhile, I had done nothing about the papers. They were out of the safe-deposit box and locked up in a drawer in my desk. But I had not taken the next logical step: I hadn't called the authorities. I was gearing up mentally to do that; it was terribly hard for me. To tell the honest truth, I was procrastinating.

Chuck was wearing chino pants and his usual faded t-shirt, a size or two too small so that his first-class muscles were clearly outlined. He had a large paper bag in his hand. It was just before lunch, and I was on my way out, hoping to grab a bite somewhere before my afternoon appointments.

He said, "Frank, you got some time? I need to talk to you."

I offered to take him to lunch, but he shook his head. "I don't eat lunch like you do, Frank. I bring my own stuff." He opened the paper bag. "This is my lunch." I saw a large plastic container, filled with greens, bean sprouts, and some mysterious leaves of unknown origin. It was a meal that would no doubt delight the palate of a lesser kudu or a pronghorn antelope—but definitely not mine.

"Can we just talk for a few minutes?" he said. Reluctantly, I sat down and waited. He said, "I wouldn't bother you, Frank, if this wasn't so important."

"I don't mind," I said, lying.

"Sheila wants you to turn over some documents. To the police. I know about this. She thinks—maybe it's better to say she *hopes*—that the police will do something about Kurt. Arrest him, basically. She thinks the documents are sort of incriminating."

"I'd rather not say."

"Frank," he said, "I know you're a good man. You wouldn't want to do something to hurt a guy. A guy who didn't deserve to be hurt, now would you?"

"No, of course not. When you put it that way."

"I'm thinking of Kurt," he said.

"I figured."

"Listen to me," he said. "I know Kurt. Sometimes we go to the gym together. He works out, he goes swimming too. He's not a bad swimmer. Kurt hasn't had an easy life. I know all about the trial and stuff. He's trying to get his life together. Me, I've been trying to work on him, make him take better care of himself, take care of his body. Not so much the muscles, but, you know, what you eat, keeping the poisons out of your system, that sort of thing."

Where was this going?

He went on: "He's not a bad man, Frank. Whatever you think. Whatever Sheila thinks. I'm sure of it. We're none of us perfect, you know? You think he killed Andrew Wright? I don't."

"Well, somebody did," I said.

"Right. Somebody. And I think I know who that somebody is."

That caught my attention. "You do? Who?"

He said, "How about Garth? Garth Winter. The scumbag."

"Garth? How does he get into the picture? Anyway, he's dead." Sheila had once floated this idea, but I dismissed it at the time. And ever since Garth became a victim himself, the whole idea seemed even less likely.

He paused for a minute, scratched himself, and said, "I don't know how much I should tell you.... Is everything here confidential?"

"I guess."

"I think Andrew planned to ask Garth to, uh, play a role in this murder thing. I think he wanted Garth to be the actual killer. An outsider. Nobody would suspect him. That was the reasoning, I think. In a way, it broke the rules of the game. People were supposed to think one of us did it, the guys in the house. But Andrew never played by the rules. He was going to sneak Garth into the house."

"And did Garth say yes?"

"That's the part I'm not sure of. But I think so."

"Then why would he get rid of Andrew?" I asked.

"Here's what I figure, Frank. Andrew had something on Garth. What it was, I don't know. I'm just guessing here. Andrew, you know, had no scruples. He had no respect for anything. I guess he was born that way. I talked to him a lot, about cleaning himself up, getting his mind and body sort of aligned. He was, well, twisted—out of whack. I don't give up on people, even somebody like Andrew. I thought, hey, maybe yoga, something, even religion, I don't believe in it generally speaking, but some of the Eastern religions, well, they could turn him around I thought; anyway, never mind. I know it works for some people. But it was useless to talk to the guy."

"Chuck, get to the point. What about Garth?"

"OK, he was putting the squeeze on Garth. So here was this guy, Garth, and he was stuck. He was kind of at a crossroads. Either he went through with this scheme, dangerous scheme, maybe he thought, I'll end up in jail; or if he said no, Andrew would go ahead and tell whatever it was he knew, some secret...."

"What secret?"

"Who knows? OK, here's some more. I'm friendly with a guy, he's with the police. We swim at the pool together, you know, we work out. He's really interested in nutrition too. Anyway, he's a lonely guy, divorced, sees his kid once a week, takes him to the zoo on Sunday, that's no life. He knows a lot about this case; and, like, he got really interested, because he and I are so tight. I live in this house where the murder took place, fantastic coincidence. I'm kind of a suspect, so he has to be careful, but he did tell me they're sure the Garth thing and the Andrew thing are connected. You know how they know?"

"Beats me. How?"

"Phone calls. From the house to Garth, from Garth to the house. Now, *who* in the house? That's not clear. Could be Carmen, they thought, but we know she'd sooner die. Then who else? That's why I say: Andrew."

"I still don't see why Garth would agree to do something. You think it was blackmail?"

"I do. Or money. Andrew was always promising people money. Not that he had any. Or he could offer him something better. Carmen."

"Carmen? He'd betray her?"

"He'd betray his grandmother. In a heartbeat."

I thought about it. It didn't compute. I certainly agreed with the assessment of Andrew's loyalty to his grandmother—or anyone besides Andrew himself. But something essential was missing. For one thing, OK, suppose Garth did kill Andrew—I wasn't convinced—but then who killed *him*? And why?

Chuck had no answer.

"Chuck," I said. "Now I'll tell you a kind of secret. The night Andrew died, I was at the Finster house. I came to see him. He invited me. Andrew told me he had things figured out, how to pull off his crazy murder scheme. He said he wanted to talk to me. But I think he was already dead when I got here. I rang the bell, I knocked on his door. No answer."

"And?"

"Don't you see? He said he had something *figured out*. Was that why somebody killed him? To stop this thing dead in its tracks? And what *was* the scheme? How on earth was he going to manage it?"

Chuck had no answer to this one either. But he said, "Think it over, Frank. It's not going to do any good, going to the police. Leave Kurt alone. And think about Garth. He's very important. I still think he got rid of Andrew. Then somebody turned around and got rid of him."

"But why?"

"Isn't that part obvious?" he said. "He was killed because of Carmen. That's where the answer lies."

But that means you, I said to myself. You were in love with her. And if Andrew was really scheming with Garth, you had a motive to kill him too.

Was it possible, after all, that a vegetarian could kill?

22

More time went by. I was busily engaged with clients and had no time to think about the case. Every morning I reminded myself about my promise to Sheila. My promise to go to the police with the documents she left. Every day I said: today I have to do it. But I never did.

On the third day after my discussion with Chuck, I was sitting in my office. It was about 10:00 in the morning, a bright, cheerful day, when there came a knock on the door. I opened it to discover I had a package delivered by Federal Express. I signed for it, and put it on my desk. It was completely unclear to me, from the return address, where it came from and from whom. I was curious about the contents, but before I could open it, the phone rang. I did not recognize the caller's number. I debated whether to answer it, but it could've been a client, so I picked up the phone. It was Fletcher.

He sounded quite excited: "Frank, is that you?"

"Right. What's up? You seem worked up about something."

"I am, I am. First of all, I have some very bad news. Billy. He's dead. He was admitted to the hospital a few days ago. He was having some sort of attack."

"That's awful," I said. "But he knew it was coming."

"Yes, poor guy; eventually, it was going to get him. But Frank, he didn't die of his condition. He died of a drug overdose. It could be an accident, it could be suicide, but, Frank, I don't think so."

"You don't think so? You think somebody killed him?"

"Frank, I do. I think it was Kurt. That's my other news. He's gone. Kurt's gone. Disappeared. He was the last person to see Billy. He went to the hospital to visit him. Lydia was there in Billy's room, talking to him.... Then Kurt came in. Lydia had to go somewhere, so she said goodbye, and Kurt was there alone, with Billy.... An hour or so later, a nurse found Billy dead. We got the news, and I went to tell people. I told Chuck, then I called Sheila, and I told Carmen. So then I knocked on Kurt's door. No answer. I went in. He was gone. Packed his bags, took clothes, and left. No word to anybody, not even Chuck, and they were sort of tight. No forwarding address. Frank, I'm afraid he killed Billy. I didn't know he would do something like that. Maybe he's just a psychopath."

I didn't know what to say, so I mumbled something incoherent. Finally, I said the police were sure to find Kurt pretty quickly, if he really ran away, and if he was guilty of something, so not to worry. But of course Fletcher *was* worried. "I'm taking Lydia out of the house," he said. "Maybe it's safe, but, well, it's got too many bad memories now. Chuck, maybe he'll stay and take care of Angelica, or maybe she'll go into a home. I don't know. It's her house, after all."

I wasn't really listening. I kept thinking of my conversation with Kurt, and how hard it was for me to think of him as a cold-blooded killer. Fletcher on the other hand was convinced—and he knew Kurt better than I did, after all.

But what Fletcher didn't know, and I didn't know, was that the end had come. The answer to all of our questions, and the solution to the whole tragic and messy affair, was in my hands at that very moment, wrapped in the familiar FedEx package.

23

I didn't open the package right away. No sooner had I hung up on Fletcher than I had another telephone call—an urgent one, from a client; it took the better part of an hour to handle his problem, at least for the time being. When *that* was done, I had to take care of three other calls that had piled up while I was talking to Fletcher and the client. I was vexed and consumed with curiosity; but I didn't allow myself to open the package until I had cleared all of this out of the way.

I was surprised to find two sealed envelopes inside the package, marked "Number One" and "Number Two." There was also a short letter, unsealed, on plain white paper. The letter simply said: "Dear Frank, Please open envelope number one first, and read it, then please open envelope number two. Thank you." It was signed John Gruber, and in parentheses: Kurt.

I followed the instructions. Inside the first envelope was a long letter, obviously typed on a computer and printed out. This letter too was signed John Gruber and in parentheses (Kurt). I began to read it.

"Dear Frank,

I feel I owe you some sort of explanation. As I said in the cover letter, I'd like you to read this letter first, before you read the letter in the second sealed envelope. When you finish reading both letters, please destroy this one, and the package it came in. You can do as you wish with the other letter. A version of it, I've been told, has already been sent to the police.

This letter is not an apology. It's not exactly a confession. It's simply a way of letting you know what actually happened. I'm writing this letter to tell you the truth, the complete, unvarnished truth. When you hear my story, I think you'll realize that every word of it is true. I can't tell you how good it feels to get this off my chest.

I did not in fact kill my wife, despite what everybody thinks. Not literally, anyway. I have done many things in my life that I regret, and, most of all, I feel directly responsible for Tracy's death, but I was not the person who actually pulled the trigger and ended her life.

Like many people in this world, I squandered many chances growing up. I won't bore you with biographical details. I was a rough, rebellious adolescent, and a brooding and troubled young man. I was a damn fool to marry Tracy. Maybe I'm not the marrying type. I know why I married her. She was a good woman, and she was in love with me. I didn't deserve her. I'm not sure I ever really loved her. I more or less drifted into marriage. She wanted to get married. I wanted to please her. I thought she would change my life. I should have known better.

The marriage wasn't completely miserable. Tracy tried very hard to make it work. But I was restless and unsatisfied. I was often rude to Tracy, sometimes even cruel. But I was never violent. The picture they painted of me at the trial was ridiculous. I'm not a monster. I would never physically harm anybody. Yes, I made her unhappy. I cursed, and I was moody, unfeeling at times. I hated myself for making her unhappy, but I couldn't help myself. Yet, still, we stayed together. We had our ups and downs, we were both dissatisfied, but so are millions of couples.

Then I met Crystal. Immediately, I felt this powerful attraction. Maybe because she was so obviously dangerous and disturbed. She was passionate, volatile, emotionally unstable. She was also beautiful, sexy, demanding, and ruthless. I was infatuated with her. We began a stormy affair. Tracy found out but kept quiet—at least to me. She vented her anger and dismay to her friends, but not with me. Meanwhile, I spent more and more time with Crystal. She kept after me to get a divorce and marry her. It would have been utter madness, but I wasn't thinking clearly. I never quite promised to leave Tracy, but I came close, and I guess Crystal thought she had a commitment. When I found out Tracy was pregnant, I was surprised, but also really excited. I realized I wanted a child, a son, a daughter, whichever—I had a hunger for a normal life. I thought and thought about my future. Our future. I knew I had been a miserable, irresponsible husband in so many ways, but now I wanted to make amends. I knew I had to choose. I knew I would never be ecstatically happy with Tracy, but I would have a decent life, and a family. I wanted a family. Crystal was so erratic. God knows what life with her would be like. And Tracy deserved something better than the way I had treated her. In the end I made up my mind to stay with my wife. I resolved to work things out, to turn over a new leaf. My conscience told me to do this. Tracy told me she knew about the affair. She confronted me and insisted I make a clean break with Crystal. At first I said no, and we got into a big argument. Tracy talked about divorce and even took some steps. But I realized this was not what I wanted. I went to Tracy and asked for forgiveness. I told her I would end my affair, and I'd be a decent husband and father.

I had to break the news to Crystal. I tried to do it in a diplomatic way, but she was furious. We had a tremendous argument. I lost my temper. I shouted that it was all over. I told her I couldn't leave my wife and child, I was sorry, but that was it. She screamed at me and started throwing things. She told me she hated me and that I'd live to regret it. I slammed the door and left.

A week later, Crystal came to my house, with a gun, and shot my wife to death. I was on my way to work at the time. She called me, hysterical, and I could hardly make out what she was saying. She was still in the house. She said I had to come, because she had done something terrible. I rushed home and found her standing over my wife's body, crying and moaning. She threw her arms around me and said, I know I did something awful, but it's because I love you and I can't live without you, and now there's nothing that can come between us. I thought she was insane. I was horrified by what she had done and at what I had done. I was the cause of it all. I was as guilty as if I had been the one who killed my wife and my unborn child. This was the wages of my sins.

I had to do something, and I had to handle Crystal. You can't imagine the scene in the house. Crystal's moods were incredibly changeable. First she was crowing and triumphant, then she was sobbing uncontrollably, and shrieking, what will they do to me, my life is ruined, I don't want to go to prison, and so on. I told her to calm down, I'd take care of it. We wrapped the body in a sheet, and in the dead of night, we buried her in the woods. I marked down carefully where it was, where it could be found. I told Crystal exactly what to do and how to behave. I told her to go home and stay there, and not to communicate with me in any way. I staged all that business with the boat and the duffle bag, I deliberately got the police on my trail. I wanted them to think the body was in the ocean where they would never find it.

I was pretty sure they would arrest me and put me on trial, always hoping to find the body. I knew there was a good chance I would be convicted, even if they never found the body. I knew I was facing a terrible ordeal. But in a way I was glad. It was my way of paying for my sins. I could have been sentenced to death as someone who killed a woman and her unborn child. Or I could have been sentenced to a lifetime rotting in prison. I was willing to take that chance. In my own mind, I was a murderer.

To be perfectly honest, I thought the trial, the horrible publicity, the public hatred and shame were punishment enough. Secretly, I hoped the jury would acquit me. It was a stroke of luck that Grapple took my case. I told him, I couldn't pay him much, but he was eager to represent me because the publicity was worth millions to him. As you know, he did a fantastic job. In the end I got the verdict I wanted. I walked out of the courtroom a free man. Well, not quite free. After all, everybody thought I was guilty. Everybody thought I was a monster. My life was ruined.

Crystal was heavily medicated at this time, and she managed to control herself. During the trial, she'd played her part well. She said she was the other woman, but a woman who was tricked into an affair by a married man. And I played my part silently. I never took the stand. But to the whole world, I was the criminal. I was the beast who snuffed out his wife's life and murdered his unborn child—all because of his selfish infatuation with a woman who claimed to not know he was married.

The irony was that Crystal could never have been faithful to me. She was too erratic, too volatile. And afterwards, at times, she was willing to throw me away, like an old rag. We stayed away from each other for the most part, for obvious reasons. We met when we could, but always in secret. Mostly she didn't even want to see me. For my part, I came to hate my attachment to her, but I also felt responsible for her. She was reckless and unbalanced. Sometimes she was almost hysterically happy, while at other times, she was sunk in a deep depression. None of her long succession of lovers stayed with her for more than a brief period. Finally, she seemed to be teetering on the edge of a total breakdown. Between each lover, she would come back to me. Sometimes she was just as passionate as the day she murdered Tracy and sometimes she was angry and despondent.

Then came this wretched earthquake. As luck would have it, it occurred just at the moment when Crystal was having sex with a guy named Vince who she had picked up in a bar. I forget his last name. She gave him a false name, so he would have no idea who she really was. They went to his apartment. When the whole structure collapsed around them, the experience drove her into a total panic. She was trapped in the wreckage, almost hysterical with fear and anguish. She felt God was punishing her for her crimes. She thought she was going to die. She began screaming and crying and told Vince the whole story. She never mentioned names, but she was shouting how she had killed a woman, and so on. Of course, she didn't die. She wasn't even badly hurt. A rescue team came an hour or so later and freed her and Vince. When she realized that she'd done something stupid, she made Vince swear he would never breathe a word of what she had said, to anybody, ever. He promised.

Vince kept his promise—for a while. Then he saw Andrew's ad, asking for stories about people who were having sex during the earthquake, and he thought he could make some money. Andrew did give him something, and promised him a lot more when the book would come out. Andrew was a lot smarter than Vince. Vince never really grasped how significant the story was, or how sensational. But Andrew could connect the dots. He realized who the woman was, and exactly what she was confessing. His first idea was to sell the story to the tabloids, but then he got bigger ideas. He thought it could serve as a kind of centerpiece for his book—he decided to save it for that purpose.

Then Andrew developed another use for the information. It gave him a hold over me. When he hatched this crazy scheme about murder in the house, he decided he had the perfect man for the job of the murderer. Andrew was no fool. He realized that if I would take the rap for Crystal, then I would do almost anything to prevent the truth from coming out. *I* couldn't be tried again for murder, but Crystal could. He told me that if I didn't play his game, he would tell the police what he knew. I didn't think it would work. Without the body, there wasn't any evidence to tie Crystal to the crime, but I couldn't take the chance. She was so vulnerable at times. If they arrested her, she would crack under the strain. I felt I had to protect her from that possibility, and from the ordeal of a trial. It was the least I could do.

Vince later died in an auto accident not long after he talked to Andrew. I can't prove anything, but I have my suspicions. I think somehow Crystal managed to kill him. She was capable of anything when she felt threatened. But I was still fascinated by her, and I imagined, sometimes, that if I could reach her, get through to her, then I could somehow turn her life around. I never really let go.

I used to go down to Los Angeles from time to time to see her. Sometimes she was loving and sorry about all the terrible things that had happened. Sometimes she was defiant and cursed me. Sometimes we made love, and sometimes we fought. She would flaunt her boyfriends, then turn around and tell me I was the only man she ever loved. At times, she was consumed with guilt and self-loathing; at other times she was proud. All the while, she was deteriorating, not eating much. She took drugs and drank herself half to death. I tried to help. I tried to get her to get therapy or go into some program, but it was no use.

The last time I saw her, she was in worse shape than ever. I was shocked at the way she looked. I told her she had to stop drinking and doing drugs. I told her to straighten herself out. But she refused. We had a terrible argument. She hated it when anybody tried to tell her what to do. Maybe I mishandled the situation. She screamed and went into hysterics. She was drunk when she ran out to her car, and she drove off before I could stop her. That's when the accident happened. I don't know if it really was an accident, or was some kind of crazy suicide. I got in my car and tried to follow her, but she was going maybe 90 miles an hour, and I couldn't catch up to her. I heard the noise when she crashed. She ran off the road and into a ravine. When I made my way down to the car, I found her dead. I got back in my car and drove to a gas station, where I called the police and told them what had happened, but not who I was. Then I drove back to my motel. I felt desolate.

When I came back up here, I told Andrew I was through. Crystal was dead, and I no longer needed to protect her. I told him I wasn't going to be part of his stupid scheme, and he couldn't persuade me. He said I had no choice—he said I wouldn't want to blacken Crystal's memory after all I went through. That didn't have any effect on me. I told him I wasn't concerned with her memory. Dead is dead. You can't hurt her anymore. Do what you want, I said, but count me out. This is the end, I told him. We had a terrible argument that I guess some people overheard. I held my ground. I refused to cooperate. I stormed out of there and found a payphone; I tipped off the police about Tracy's body, where it was buried. It was the least I could do to ease the pain of her family. They could get some sort of closure and give her a decent burial. You can imagine the kind of emotional roller-coaster I was on.

I'd like to clear up a couple of other matters. Yes, Andrew

really did have a scheme for pulling off his stunt—the on-camera murder. I think his original idea was simply to fool the network until it was too late, and also make it too hard for the police to find out who did it. The audience would see the murder, or think they did. They would see a figure in black, wearing gloves. They would watch this man strangle a sleeping figure. But they would never see the man's face. It would all be shadowy and dark. But Andrew soon realized that this wouldn't work, it was too risky. The police would find out the truth, and even if they didn't, they would make life miserable for everybody in the house.

So he hit on another plan. It was his ace in the hole. The audience and the police and everybody would think a murder had been committed. They would see somebody apparently strangling one of his housemates. But in reality, there would be no murder. The "victim" was already dead. The victim was Billy. This was the idea: Billy was practically a dead man. Why not hasten the job and get him to kill himself? Andrew made all sorts of promises to Billy. He would set up a trust for his daughter, that sort of thing. Billy would commit suicide by taking pills. By the time the autopsy report came out, the whole thing would have been a sensation. It would be worth millions in publicity and be a gold mine for everybody involved.

Was Billy willing to do this? I know Billy told you a slightly different story. The letter in the other envelope will give you the real story. Meanwhile, this letter is my way to say goodbye. I'm moving on. I don't want to be John Gruber any more, and I don't want to be Kurt Schmidt. I want to start a new life. I want to put all these horrible events behind me. There's no reason for me to stay around. Maybe I'll go to Australia, maybe I'll go to Canada. I need to go somewhere and start over one more time. Now that Crystal's dead and Tracy has had a decent burial, I hope my nightmare will be over. I'll never forgive myself, but I can try to lead a halfway useful life.

Yours,

Kurt
(John Gruber)"

* * *

    I read the letter once, I read it twice. It was astonishing—
and convincing. I understood now much of what had happened.
The letter answered a lot of questions and cleared up a lot of
the mystery. But it did not tell me, in itself, who killed Andrew
Wright and Garth Winter. For that, I had to read the other
letter, in the second sealed envelope. I tore it open eagerly, and
began reading.

24

"Dear Frank,

By the time you get this, I'll be dead. I've spoken to Kurt, and asked him to deliver this to you. I have also sent a document to the police. It doesn't have as much detail as this one, but it does cover the essential points.

I want to make it clear that killing myself was entirely my own decision. I want to end my life because there's no point going on. Nobody is helping me do this. Nobody talked me into this. I'm ready to go. But when I go, I want to leave a clean slate behind. I want to answer all the questions, and clear up all the mysteries. It bothers me a lot that I've brought suspicion, uncertainty and, unhappiness to a group of people I really care about. That's why I'm writing this letter. I confess to the crimes I have committed. I killed Andrew Wright and I killed Garth Winter.

Life is a funny thing. It's full of tricks. All my life, I've been a nerd. A quiet, unassuming guy. I guess in high school I would have been voted 'least likely to become a murderer,' if there was such a thing to be voted on. Yet, strangely enough, that's exactly what I have become at the end of my life: a murderer. Of course, it wouldn't have happened if I weren't a doomed man to begin with.

I'm not a brave person. When I found out I was going to die, I felt my whole world collapsed. I fell into a deep depression. This terrible news almost cost me my reason. It certainly cost me my marriage. It cost me a lot of my friends. But I gradually came out my depression. I resolved to go on living as long as I could. I realized I was beyond the reach of any human punishment. Not that I made up my mind then and there to kill somebody. But when the time came, and it seemed like the right thing to do, I did it.

I killed Andrew Wright because he was a worthless creature. He was a sociopath. The world is better off without him. Nobody misses him. He had no family and no attachments. All he was good for was making trouble. He was nothing but schemes, plans, and pain. You know about his project, the television murder, and you know that I was supposed to be the victim. I told you that. That part was true. But I also lied to you. I told you I had no idea who the killer was going to be, but I knew all along it was going to be Kurt.

That wasn't the only lie. I knew Andrew never gave you $50,000 to keep for me. Sure, he made me a promise and told me that he had done this. But a few days before I killed him, I had it out with him. The thing was, I needed some money, right away—my daughter needed braces on her teeth. So I asked Andrew to call you up, and authorize you to give me an advance. He said he couldn't do that. When I asked him why, he gave me some story about legal complications. Then the truth dawned on me. I looked him in the eyes and said, Andrew, you're lying. You don't have an advance. There is no money. You never gave anything to the lawyer. It's all one big damn lie. He laughed and said, OK, you caught me. But there *will* be money. This scheme is bound to work. It's worth millions, Billy. I stormed out of there. I was so mad! Then I decided, what the hell? This guy doesn't deserve to live.

But I hadn't yet decided to kill him. That came when I realized what he was doing to two people I really cared about, two people who were my friends. Kurt and Carmen. Kurt and I were close. Most people didn't understand Kurt, and when they found out who he really was, they tended to shun him. I don't think the people in the house, other than Andrew, recognized him. I did. But only after I got to know him. He was strange, moody, often depressed, but I liked him—maybe because I was moody and depressed too. Eventually he confided in me. Not only that he was John Gruber, but that he was innocent of the crime he was accused of. I found out he hadn't killed his wife. He told me the whole story. I think only the two of us—and Andrew—knew this fact, of all the people in the house.

I thought what Andrew was doing was totally despicable. The blackmail. Andrew knew about Crystal, and he was using that fact against Kurt. When Crystal died, and Kurt refused to go through with this terrible television murder, Andrew decided to use somebody else as his back-up. He chose Garth Winter, even though he was a worthless, violent man. Andrew was in contact with him, calling him on the phone, negotiating terms with him. Can you believe that? A man who'd battered Carmen, a man who was capable of killing her, and here was Andrew, trying to get him into his little scheme. Andrew was using Carmen as bait. Garth wanted Carmen back. He used the old line, oh, she's the only one I ever really loved, and so on, and I'm sorry for the pain I caused her. But of course, if Andrew betrayed her, it would be the same as always, the man was incorrigible, violent, untrustworthy, and Carmen might even end up dead. I decided I had to do something. I couldn't let this happen. But what could I do?

And then it came to me. I could get rid of Andrew, once and for all. Why not? I had nothing to lose. When I made the decision, when I resolved to put an end to his miserable life, I felt ecstatic. I felt tremendously alive—more alive than I'd ever felt in my life. I felt a real excitement, a thrill. Maybe that's sick, maybe it's disgusting. But that's how I felt. I could get away with it too. I was pretty sure of that. But even if they caught me, what could they do to me? I was a dying man.

Looking back, when I actually did it, I can't believe I had the nerve. It was right after dinner. I could only eat a mouthful, because I was so nervous. When the coast was clear, I went to Andrew's room. I had two purposes. I was going to take his files on the earthquake book, and then I'd kill him. I took the files, slipped out the side door, and stashed them in my car. I took them because they were nothing but misery. They had all kinds of stuff that would embarrass people. They had the story that Kurt had tried so hard to hide—and still wanted to hide. There was a lot of other stuff too. A lot of it was fake stuff that Andrew just made up. A lot of it was true, but that was even worse—embarrassing stories that would humiliate people. Andrew had no conscience. No empathy. No feeling for other human beings. But you know that.

Then I came back in the house. I was careful to see that nobody was looking, and I knocked on Andrew's door. He let me in. I told him, I had been there before. He demanded to know what I was doing. I told him I took your files on the earthquake stuff. He was surprised. He thought I was lying, but I said, just take a look. He went to the file cabinet. While his back was to me, I took a bunch of rocks that I had wrapped in a towel and smashed him on the head as hard as I could. He groaned, and dropped down to the floor, unconscious. I wrapped my hands in the towel so I wouldn't leave any fingerprints. I dragged him to the bed, and I smothered him with a pillow—that way I didn't have to look at his face. I was in a sort of trance, shaking and sweating, but still somehow exhilarated. I was on a high, believe it or not.

Of course, the high didn't last. Maybe 5, 10 minutes later, I fell to pieces. I started shaking all over, I became nauseated, and I had one of my attacks. It felt more violent than any of the others. I got in my car, and somehow I made it to the emergency room of the Stanford Hospital.

The next day I felt better. I was amazed, I had almost no guilt. And I had, for the first time in my life, a sense of power, a sense of accomplishment. I had gotten rid of him. He was scum, really scum. I took the files out of the trunk of my car and put them in a plastic bag. I drove to the Golden Gate Bridge. I parked, walked on the bridge, and when I got halfway across, I threw the whole thing into the ocean. Good riddance. I threw the towel and rocks in too. That was the end of that.

Then I made up my mind to get rid of Garth so Carmen could have a little peace and happiness. He was another one who didn't deserve to live. Another one the world is better off without. She's a wonderful woman, Carmen. She deserves better out of life. That psychopath would never let her go. Andrew had been willing to hand her over to the guy, just to satisfy his own stupid, crazy plans.

I wanted Carmen to have an alibi, and I planned my moves very carefully. But, Frank, as you know, the best-laid plans... Well, it all fell through. The alibi part. I knew she was going to see her sister and I thought, she'll be far away. She'll be in Los Angeles and nobody can connect her with this crime. It was stupid to kill him the same way I killed Andrew, but I'm not a professional. I don't own a gun. I couldn't imagine stabbing a guy to death, making a whole mess, blood all over the place. I just knew how to repeat what I had done once before. I went to Garth's house and I rang the bell. He let me in. He was alone. I was carrying a briefcase, with rocks inside. I got him to turn around on some pretext, and I hit him over the head as hard as I could. Then I smothered him. When I finished, this time too, I felt sick and nauseated. But I was glad he was dead. And like with the other stuff, I dumped the briefcase in the Bay.

I was worried about Carmen when I found out her trip was canceled and she had no alibi. I didn't want the police to harass her. The idea of Carmen killing anybody—even the police must have seen how ridiculous that was. But I couldn't be sure. I began to think about turning myself in.

I didn't have that much time left. The stress and strain had aggravated my condition. I went in for tests. The doctors agreed the end was near. I thought: maybe I shouldn't confess. Maybe I should try to do a few more things in the time left to me. I could be a one-man death squad. I could kill bad guys. I even thought I might go overseas. Maybe I could kill some dictator in Africa or some place, somebody truly evil. But I realized I just couldn't do it. The two killings had exhausted me. I was getting to be too weak to do much of anything. As time went on, the feeling of disgust came back, a kind of guilt. I was disgusted with myself. Even Andrew and Garth, I said to myself, were human beings. OK, they didn't deserve to live. Take Garth, he was worse than worthless. He was a minus. Now he can't rape or beat any more women. But there was still something there, maybe a spark of decency. Who knows? Unlike Andrew, he had family—an old mother, a sister, two nephews. Maybe they were suffering. I knew I couldn't do any more stuff. I'm not really a killer at heart. I don't have those instincts.

I abandoned my wild ideas, once and for all. No more kill-ing. Except one. Myself. I didn't want to go through the endstage of my illness. I knew the awful degeneration that lay ahead of me. I could feel it coming, and I choose not to inflict this on myself. I've confided in Kurt. I've put my affairs in order. I know everybody's been living under a cloud of worry, full of suspicions and fears. I know that Sheila's been unhappy, and Carmen has been fearful, depressed, and upset. That's the last thing I wanted.

So I decided to write all this down. I made two versions of this story. One is for you and a different version, less personal, is for the police. They've gotten it by now. Kurt saw to that. He also told me he was going to move on. I think it's the right thing to do. He can still make a life for himself. I want you to tell Sheila, Carmen, Chuck, Fletcher, and Lydia what actually hap-pened, so that they also can go on with their lives. Tell them the mystery is solved. There's nothing to fear any more. And tell them, I'm sorry."

* * *

That was the end of the letter. And the end of the affair. It was, all in all, a very sad business. I too felt sorry: for Billy, for Kurt, for Carmen, and even, believe it or not, for Andrew Wright. Life had never given him an honest break.

I called Sheila later that day and told her roughly what had happened. I knew she would let the others know.

And that was that. I went back to everyday life. Not with-out a twinge of regret. The very next day, as soon as I got to the office, I was up to my neck in the troubles of a client—a man with a chain of four car washes, an estranged wife demanding more and more money, a demented old mother, and all sorts of business entanglements. To be perfectly honest, I missed the excitement, the adrenalin rush, of the case of Andrew Wright. Murder is not my field, and it doesn't pay the bills; but Mr. Carwash and his wife and kids can get boring at an amazingly rapid pace.

Never wish for something. It might come true. Murder,

oddly enough, seemed to dog my footsteps. The very next year, in fact.... But that's another story.

About the author

Lawrence Friedman is a professor of law at Stanford University. He teaches courses in American legal history and law and society. He is the author of *A History of American Law*, *Crime and Punishment in American History*, *The Human Rights Culture*, and *Total Justice*, among other works.

In 2015 Friedman published *The Big Trial: Law as Public Spectacle*, which vividly recounts famous cases in history and their media coverage of the day. He asks, pertinent to the fictional "famous trial" in this novel as well: Are the "headline trials" of our period different from those of a century or two ago? And what do we learn from them, about the nature of our society, past and present? He also recently published *Dead Hands: A Social History of Wills, Trusts, and Inheritances*, a subject which is the backbone of Frank May's (fictional) practice.

Visit us at *www.qpbooks.com*.